Catastrophe's Children

Joseph Kopel

A note from the author:

This novel is fictional. While based on real historical events, the narrative is inaccurate because of alterations, regardless of scale, for storytelling.

This story's Interpol, its events and characters are entirely fictional and unrelated to the actual Interpol.

This story blends fantasy and reality, exploring strong mature themes such as objectionable political ideologies, non-explicit sexual content, substance abuse, tobacco use in minors, suicide, and graphic violence. Swear words appear frequently in the dialogues.

Contents

PART ONE   1

1. KARAOLOS   2

2. ADANA   11

3. ANKARA   17

4. BOSPHORUS   25

5. AYLA   32

6. BERETTA   39

7. ISTANBUL   46

8. MERZOST   52

9. GABRIEL   58

10. HONG KONG   65

11.	TIAN CHAO	74
12.	SCORPION	82
13.	BEAUTIFUL	91
14.	ARENA	96
15.	RING	105
16.	ATAKOBAT	112
17.	DOSSIER	119
18.	TRACE	126
19.	WANCHAI	133
20.	TIGER	140
21.	MEI LI	149
22.	KATASTROFA	157
23.	EVE	163
24.	CHRISTMAS	173
25.	SHEK KIP MEI	180
26.	BOXING DAY	186
PART TWO		191
27.	INTERPOL	192
28.	PALAZZO	198
29.	DONCELLI	205

30. ARRIVALS   217

31. FORZA   224

32. THE GENERAL   230

33. WHISTLE   238

34. KENDI MONGO   244

35. WOUNDS   249

36. DUBROVNIK   259

37. SARAJEVO   265

38. UPHEAVAL   276

39. BELGRADE   284

40. GRAVESTONE   298

PART ONE

Laura Doncelli

1
KARAOLOS

Si chiama Laura Doncelli e ha 10 anni.

The only thing identifying her was a charcoal writing on yellowed, crumpled paper pinned to her ripped blue dress, stained with sludge. Her attire was too small, and she had nothing else with her.

Her feet were raw and aching, caked in mud and dry blood.

Her presence was impressive at the modest post at the Karaolos refugee camp in Cyprus. In the late summer of 1946, the sun beat down on the official's place through a window as he received her. She was one of thousands who came with Jewish survivors who had the scars of German concentration camps, seeking refuge and a haven.

The officer, overwhelmed by the situation, stared at the girl seated before him. The silence was heavy. Despite using Italian, Yiddish and German translators, he got no response from her as his attempts at conversation proved fruitless. The only sounds were the frustrated sighs of the interpreters.

She focused her brown eyes, and her face was still. No word escaped her dry, cracked lips.

The British officer stared at the blank typewriter paper. The despair settled upon him. Once he adjusted his glasses, noted his observations. "The girl, presumably named Laura Doncelli, of ten years old, arrived on board of the frigate *Siniscalco* that departed from the port of Naples, which took in more refugees in Sicily. It is unclear whether she's from the Italian country or Sicilian, but allegedly, she is, because of the paper she carried attached to her clothes to identify her, which writings were in Italian. Although she also could be from Crete, where the frigate also moored. It is also unclear if she was Jewish, as well as the people that came with her, but she also could be from a family of gypsies."

Disappointed, the officer gestured to a uniformed woman, who led the girl into the camp and gave her bread, corned beef, and water.

With apprehension and despair, Laura escaped from the woman and looked for a place in the packed and broad camp to satisfy her hunger.

She wanted to be unseen.

Invisible.

Laura Doncelli had no childhood memories. It was as if her past and her mind had been wiped clean. Her only clear memory was of stepping onto the *Siniscalco* and traveling solo to Cyprus.

Unlike most war victims seeking new beginnings, Laura lacked any specific goal. Basic needs ruled her brief life—food, water, and survival—rather than rational thought.

Thousands of Jews came to Cyprus, aiming for Mandatory Palestine under British rule, fueled by the nationalist dream of a promised land.

Under different circumstances, Laura would have someone to care for her, but the war's aftermath has left people apathetic. The prisoners in German camps became desensitized to the daily executions.

Charities had no place in Karaolos. By themselves, the refugees sought survival, to regain lost time, and to restore their dignity.

The transfer of the Karaolos camp from a British command to another stricter one, unconcerned with the refugees, exacerbated the situation, resulting in food and water scarcity. Abandoned to their fate, refugees faced constant chaos and deceit, leading to a cigarette-based black market for food and supplies.

Laura's survival under the new administration depended on violence to get even a meager amount of food. She became a thief, sometimes resorting to violence—wounding victims—to steal food and cigarettes.

Confined and overseen by uncaring authorities, refugees in a large enclosed area created self-governing groups to survive.

Yet, no one cared for Laura, a mysterious stray girl of unknown heritage, who looked like a filthy beggar.

Hungry and despairing after days without food, Laura encountered a mature woman living alone in a nearby tent, who grew her own vegetables. She tried to attack the woman with a sharp piece of wood, but the woman overpowered her, pinning her down and holding a knife to her throat.

Murders were so common in that camp that the authorities ignored them. The woman could easily have killed her.

Death occurred daily, as if it were routine.

Results of the past war.

Defeated and frustrated, Laura curled up on the ground and cried, wishing for the first time in her life that she were dead. She remained in that position and eventually fell asleep from exhaustion until the following morning.

When she awoke and found a bowl of vegetable soup, she ate it in despair, only to realize her robbery victim sat nearby, looking at her.

"If you ever try to steal again from me, I won't hesitate to kill you." While toying with her knife, she said with a distinct, sharp accent. "I'll spare your life if you learn some manners from me. And you'll receive a daily meal in return."

Laura appeared to understand and nodded in agreement.

The girl learned the woman's name was Bertha and discovered she had a numbered tattooed left arm. The war saw her imprisoned in a German camp, like most people in Karaolos.

Laura had heard horror stories from the camps, yet she had no memory of them. She could not recall her past. There was no tattoo on her arm.

The girl has consistently followed Bertha ever since their argument and agreement, and Bertha didn't seem to mind her presence or persistent silence.

She assumed she was a mute girl, or someone with congenital impairment. However, she spoke to her in German, Italian, and English simply to have someone to chat with.

While squatting in her vegetable patch that day, Bertha discovered blood running down Laura's legs. Irritated, Bertha tossed her tools aside. "It has to be now!" The woman rambled, bothered. She shook, wiped the sweat from her forehead, and thought of a solution while sensing the sun's heat. "Stay here, and I'll be right back!"

Bertha entered her tent and took out half a pack of cigarettes. As a heavy smoker, she had to conserve her decreasing supply and didn't want to use it. She shifted to a corner, tossed aside her torn blankets, and uncovered a wooden compartment containing a hole in the ground.

From an elegant metal chocolate box, she uncovered almost a dozen cigarette packs and a small stack of assorted foreign currency.

Under the intensity of Laura's dark gaze, she quickly grabbed two packs, returned everything to its place, and left.

With purpose, Bertha hurried to a tent she knew well, where two men had piled up their loot. She used to trade mostly vegetables with them.

"May I assist you with something today?" A gaunt man with yellowed, decaying teeth in his smile asked. "You appear to be in a hurry."

"Get me a dress for a ten years old, Feivel! And. . . some fucking panties. . ." She demanded while extending the cigarettes to him. "I need them now!"

Feivel looked at Bertha in surprise, then turned to his companion—an older, stout man. "Zalman, do you have everything she requested?"

Seated on a small wooden stool, Zalman rummaged through the pile of clothes next to him. "A yellow dress arrived with panties from a girl who died of malaria."

He gave the clothes to Bertha, who tossed the cigarette packs to the traders.

Back at her tent, she found Laura still in the same spot.

Bertha filled a metal tub big enough to bathe the girl, whose months of accumulated grime on her clouded the clean water.

Although water was scarce, she got some by bribing a British soldier with a few pounds. A mysterious sponsor had given her a small sum, which she'd saved before coming to Cyprus.

As Bertha scrubbed Laura's back with a rough, used brush and a leftover bar of soap, she began her story in German. "I taught at the Hitler Youth Academy in Berlin, instructing boys and girls in both combat techniques and languages like Italian and English." While ensuring the girl's body was clean, she let out a sigh. "My Jewish grandmother, though deceased, was more than enough for the Gestapo to send me to a camp in Salerno."

Only after listening to the unfortunate story did Laura, previously silent, utter her first words—in German. "How did you escape?"

Stunned, Bertha answered. "The Americans freed us."

"Are you going back to Berlin?" she asked.

"Enough with the questions and answer me. Are you German? How did you know how to speak my language?"

"I don't know. I listen and I learn."

Bertha froze with a fixed look. "Tell me. What other languages do you know?"

"I speak Italian because you taught me. And as I go around the camp, I hear conversations in other languages and I learn."

Bertha realized the girl possessed unparalleled abilities.

Just by being in the camp and listening to the refugees, Laura also picked up Russian, Polish, and Yiddish.

Laura also learned French from Bertha.

The girl could seamlessly use multiple languages, comprehending intricate discussions, and spoke some languages fluently within the camp.

Laura, however, benefited from being multilingual. Her communication skills allowed her to trade, barter, and haggle successfully with diverse groups, including the most dangerous within the Black Market, acquiring ample goods and food for herself and her mentor. She learned Greek by befriending Cypriot guards working with the British outside the camp and gathering cigarettes at their posts and through the fences.

If she had enough cigarettes, she could trade them for books in various languages, which she could easily read.

Bertha, knowing Laura was in frequent peril while communicating with the camp's occupants, taught her self-defense. The girl learned it well and fast.

Laura encountered only a couple of problems during her entire time there. Empowered by Bertha's lessons, she successfully repelled bullies who tried to take advantage of her, humiliating them despite their age and size. Almost everyone respected her, and she unexpectedly emerged as a local celebrity.

People went to her for anything they needed. Laura didn't hesitate to help them. She received gifts for herself and Bertha, even though she hadn't asked for them.

However, her unusual influence and special treatment were short-lived, as the British mandate ordered the closure of the Karaolos camp and the expulsion of the refugees.

2
ADANA

Britain used chartered frigates to transport refugees to the newly formed nation of Israel in Palestine in 1949.

However, following their release from the Karaolos camp, Feivel and Zalman—the traders who had previously bartered cigarettes for Bertha's vegetables—envious of Laura's influence at the camp that caused losses in their business, rallied a group, primarily Ashkenazi, to investigate the woman's history.

Right where people waited for the ships, Feivel and Zalman's supporters began shouting and pointing at Bertha, calling her a traitor and a Nazi sympathizer, as planned. Dozens of accusations escalated to hundreds, then thousands.

The Jewish people picked up stones intending to throw at Bertha and Laura. They forgot the girl's kindness and popularity. Consumed by hatred, the people blamed both women for their suffering in the German camps.

The British guards' sudden intervention saved their lives. They separated and took them far away.

Much later, an official addressed Bertha, who sat beside Laura on a cot in the infirmary where a nurse treated them for mild injuries. Once he figured out the cause of the people's outburst, he spoke to the woman. "It is my obligation to send you back to Germany for prosecution."

"Just do it!" Bertha, irritated, pointed at Laura in response. "But let her go!"

A pensive puff of smoke escaped the official's pipe. "Instead, I'll send both of you to Turkey," he said. "Then you can go where you must."

"Why are you doing this?" Curious, Laura queried the aged official.

"I'm nearing retirement and eager to stay home after such a long absence. I want to avoid the complications of the paperwork and get my readies."

Bertha stared at him, stunned, then lit a cigarette.

"There's a boat waiting for you." He concluded.

British authorities thus welcomed a fishing boat that would transport both women.

They found themselves stranded on the coast of Turkey.

As Bertha settled onto the sand, let out a sigh and then, surprisingly, offered a cigarette to thirteen-year-old Laura after lighting one herself. "Come sit with me and have a smoke."

Although hesitant, Laura complied, sitting next to the woman and taking a smoke as offered.

Bertha ignited her cigarette. "Take your time. Or you will be choking." She cautioned while she was taking in the beauty of the Mediterranean Sea from her spot. "It will help to clear your shit."

Laura took a few quick puffs of her tobacco, initially grimacing, but soon she enjoyed it once the flavor of the tobacco snatched her. "What will we do from now on?"

Though robbed of their belongings in the commotion, the woman hid her money beneath her dress, inside her lingerie. "My remaining pounds and liras will easily cover a two-night stay at a local inn, with funds for meals and much-needed baths." A large plume of smoke escaped her lips as she paused. "You'll have no trouble mastering Turkish, I'm sure, and your languages will be an advantage in Ankara."

The girl nodded in agreement.

The stark reality, however, was that they were homeless foreigners, always watching over their shoulders for the corrupt Turkish authorities. Thanks to Laura's gift, learning the local language was easy, enabling smooth travel across the country for them.

Their promised stay at an inn never materialized, leading to great hardship. They were foreigners with no homeland on a strange land.

Authorities and the locals revealed antipathy toward the homeless, refugees, and war survivors.

Turkey remained neutral, benefiting from trading with both Allied and Axis powers, but entered the conflict only when a victor clearly emerged. Turkey's perceived isolation from the international stage resulted in the country reacting with antagonism to asylum seekers, in particular those coming from Greece. Yet, thousands of Jews still transited through Turkey to reach Palestine.

Adverse weather hampered the journey. Icy winds and winter's arrival, coupled with sudden downpours, impacted the woman's health. Persistent coughs ensued, but she dismissed them, expecting a swift improvement.

At first, in the Province of Adana, Laura learned Turkish quickly by eavesdropping on street conversations around the small towns. Her Italian look and new language, combined with Bertha's meager savings, provided new clothes and food that allowed her to blend with the locals in the city of Adana. During her time at the Karaolos camp, Bertha taught Laura poker, a skill that proved useful in local bars and hookah lounges on both sides of the Stone Bridge over the Seyhan River. Laura quickly displayed a natural talent, winning money in *Pokeri* games and astonishing the predominantly male players.

Complaints about Laura's constant wins triggered a cheating investigation thanks to the skeptical players, leading the police to search for a mysterious young girl and a blonde woman known to be traveling together. The unexpected turn of events prompted Bertha and Laura's immediate departure from Adana.

To evade the authorities, both women traveled north to the larger city of Ankara, sleeping in a small traveling tent along the way.

For some odd reason, Bertha felt obligated to go to Ankara despite her silent reluctance.

The trip became difficult as Bertha fell ill, and their fear of their arrest kept them from seeking a medic. She wished to be released from a life of constant disappointment and hindrances, finding a meaning to it only in Laura, a daughter she never had.

"*Danke!*" she said between pauses of harsh gasps. "*Gib nicht auf. . . Kämpfe weiter.*" Those were her last words, spoken in the crisp, sunny but chilly morning air, as Laura knelt beside her.

Laura lit a cigarette to honor Bertha as tears ran down her face. Even after her death, she still nodded in agreement with her request.

She made a small stone mound to mark her burial spot nestled between the forests and the mountains. Laura carved the initials *BS* instead of her full name, a decision influenced by her dark past and desire to distance herself from any judgment because of her connection to the Nazi regime.

Laura was fourteen, and from this moment on she had to look after herself. Circumstances forced her into adulthood.

She needed time to process her condition and consider her options, and stayed at the tent and burial site to decide. She lit cigarettes and ate barely anything while watching the mountains.

Finally, she removed her dress for more practical pants, shirt, and jacket—clothes she'd won at a *Pokeri* match. She packed what she needed, leaving only the tent by the gravesite, and left, heading north.

Her focus was on Ankara, where Bertha intended to go.

3
ANKARA

L aura had at last reached Ankara, in Anatolia. A bustling metropolis rose before her. Its avenues were swarming with tourists and locals, exploring the countless hotels, boutiques, museums and stores.

The city vibrated with the energy of the crowds as a sense of feeling blended with the smells of street food and exhaust.

In 1950, many sightseers visited Ankara, and other places like Istanbul that were well preserved and unaffected. As some European and Asian cities were still in process of reconstruction from the conflict's destruction, and their locals were still recovering from the war's wounds. Turkey's alliance with the U.S. enabled many Americans to either spend vacations or conduct business there.

No city she remembered was bigger than Ankara. Although she was fourteen and mature, she still had no memories of her early years.

During her journey north, she had spent most of Bertha's meager savings on food, a pair of packs of Americanized *Fatima* cigarettes, and some lodging. After the misfortune in Adana, she avoided gambling, even in Ankara's casinos and the hippodrome. However, she made enough money to rent a basic room on the rooftop in a poor and dangerous quarter of the city by selling her gently used pair of dresses to a vendor in the bazaar.

Laura's room was nothing but a squalid space filled with spiderwebs, cockroaches, and the stench of decay. A bucket served as her toilet as its contents having to be emptied into a nearby drain while she collected water from the same rooftop. She paid two months of rent in advance and used the rest of her money on a second-hand broom, mop, and blanket to sleep on the floor. Surprisingly, she kept her space clean, despite a complete lack of prior cleaning experience. From the street bazaar downstairs, she could only afford a small stack of pita bread, barely enough to last the week.

Although crime was rampant in her new suburb, Laura learned to stand by herself against thugs, thanks to Bertha's self-defense lessons. Despite several attempts, she beat and injured the thieves, forcing them to renounce their efforts to rob her. She became a local legend after subduing the robbers, earning the gratitude of the neighborhood and bazaar vendors. The robbers, deterred by her actions, never returned.

To show their gratitude, the vendors gifted her extra clothes, cigarettes and food each day, along with used furniture and a metal bathtub. They never found out her real name or age, but just figured she was a small young adult woman. They called her *Alpa*, referring to her exceptional courage and resolve.

Despite receiving gifts that improved her life a bit, she still needed liras for the rent. The owner, an old lady, had no empathy for her actions. "I don't care what you do! This room will not pay for itself!"

Despite the easy money from gambling, Laura, true to her priorities, explored other options. Her multilingual skills gave her a significant advantage in assisting tourists at the hippodrome, a popular spot for horse racing and sightseeing. She could get decent liras.

Her new outfit—pants, boots, a shirt, and her dark leather jacket—was like her previous style. But a new wavy perm on her black hair significantly improved her appearance. At fourteen, she looked much older because of her harsh attitude and cigarette habit, making people assume she was only short.

From the age of fifteen in 1951, for many months, she guided and translated for tourists from around the world—including China, Japan and India—, exchanging services for conversational lessons with some, widening her plethora of idioms.

A once-mute girl grew into a young polyglot, effortlessly speaking 11 languages and a few others with some challenge, revealing a brilliant and unique mind.

Having never attended school, she taught herself by buying secondhand books at the bazaar. One day, on her way home, she looked through many volumes from a vendor. Laura learned about the horrors of Nazi Germany and the Holocaust through a detailed book on World War II, including concentration camps and Hitler's operations.

After years of vague understanding of Nazism, she finally realized Bertha's torment, closing her eyes and nodding in empathy.

Her informal job gave her a consistent income from tourists, enabling a more comfortable life in her improved room, the same one she had rented. The fear of being discovered kept Laura from moving after she learned everyone believed she was a woman. Hiding her actual age was more important to her than having a proper bathroom, and she'd stay in her room with her bucket as long as she could get the privileges of an adult.

She was, however, constantly being watched.

Besides being a tourist attraction, the hippodrome served as a meeting place for illegal drug transactions, amphetamines and barbiturates, attracting locals, visitors, and foreigners alike. The public and police were aware of these activities, yet ignored them.

People around the place knew Laura's reputation as the *girl with a thousand tongues*. Her constant spotlight was the reason a man who seemed to be of Chinese descent but had clearer skin than typical Asians came to her.

It was an odd encounter.

Apparently, he had to hunt down a certain man in a clandestine spot.

His suspicious demeanor made her hesitate.

Although she initially refused, citing her exclusive service to tourists, she eventually agreed after extensive insistence and a generous offer in liras. To her surprise, a luxury black car driven by one of two Turkish men inside shortly appeared, inviting her to get in.

She spotted their holstered weapons and attempted to flee, but a third man, also of Chinese appearance, came behind her, with a gun drawn discreetly against her back.

It was in fact an abduction.

With a smile and a bow, the enigmatic Chinese man in a black suit touched the brim of his hat. "I heard what you have done to these thieves."

"Please. . . let me go!" She begged, afraid. Even with self-defense training, she was defenseless against them.

"We need to deal with that bastard, and I may require your services for my purposes!" He again bowed. "Accept my apologies for this unfortunate circumstance."

Laura sat in the back seat of the car next to one escort. The Chinese man sat opposite, and two other men were in the front, one driving. The car sped down across the overcrowded narrow streets.

The mysterious man opened a silver cigarette case. He offered one to Laura, who accepted with distrust. "Please accept my reiterated apologies, but your defensive skills made us take measures."

She took the man's lighter to have her first puff of tobacco, then she spoke calmly. "That's right, sir. I would have fought everyone of you. But a fucking gun pressed against my back stopped me from doing that!"

"Let me introduce myself," he stated. "I am Michael Yang, the Boss of the Jade Dragon Triad in Hong Kong."

"Drugs, I presume. . ." she nodded and studied him. "You look young to be a boss."

"Drugs, betting, sex business, fighting. There's something for everyone, Miss Laura Doncelli." Mentioning her name widened her eyes.

"How do you know my name?!" she exclaimed, distrustful and startled. "Can you tell who I am?"

"If you cooperate, I will get you everything you've ever wanted, including knowledge of your origins," Boss Yang said with a light smile. "For now, let's focus on our man."

As the sun dipped below the horizon, the black car crept into a crowded alley, parking before a building marked only by an opulent wooden door, but its purpose was a mystery. Laura noted the people and features of this Ankara section, realizing that it was a completely new place for her. To put it precisely, it was more decrepit and hazardous than her own home.

"Why did you bring me here?!"

"Listen to me, girl!" With a stern voice, Boss Yang silenced her. "You must obey my directions, interpret every word from that Turkish bastard, and tell me exactly what he said. Your part is also to be quiet and do nothing if we take action against him. Is that clear?" He said with a strange calmness.

Laura gave a shaky nod.

The men and Boss Yang quickly exited the car, gesturing for her to follow.

As the door swung inward from a forceful kick, a terrified woman emerged. She then allowed them entry.

A large clandestine casino surprised Laura when she entered. Excited shouts from the baccarat and roulette tables, with half-naked female escorts accompanying some already intoxicated customers with opium and alcohol, made their existence in the middle of a smoke haze. Rich, French-style red and gold walls, adorned with hanging chandeliers, added to a glum atmosphere rather than legitimate amusement.

The woman who opened the door stared fearfully at the men.

"Ask her where Ahmed is!" Boss Yang gave Laura a rigid order.

With trepidation, she obeyed him, addressing the woman in Turkish and receiving a reply. "His usual place, on the second floor."

With a nod, he and his people slipped between the gaming tables, unnoticed by the absorbed gamblers. They hurried to the rear, ascending the stairs by the restrooms.

Fearful, Laura didn't want to go with them, but the man who had previously held a gun to her back was right behind, making her escape impossible.

When they arrived at their destination, one person kicked the door open so frantically that it startled the man in his sumptuous office, prompting him to stand up from his desk. His face showed both surprise and fear. "Boss Yang!"

The Triad's leader spoke to Laura.

"Ask this cunt where in the fuck are the missing two billion liras and the documents!" His anger was clear, yet he maintained his composure.

Her own heart pounded in her chest as she watched Ahmed's dread in his tan skin pale face with widened brown eyes, as he backed against the wall, and translated the question. She got a shuddering reply in change. "He said he didn't know what you were talking about."

With a quick, piercing look from his small eyes at Ahmed, Boss Yang subtly nodded. A snap of his fingers got his men's attention. "*Ganba!*"

"*Hayır!*" Ahmed screamed in terror.

The boss's men cleared a path by discarding chairs, couches, and the desk before ambushing him.

Laura, with fear, retreated to a corner to witness the event unfolding.

From the floor, Boss Yang retrieved a chair, sat, and lit a cigarette as he oversaw his men's job. "Laura, give me a word-for-word translation of everything this bastard says." He said calmly.

4

BOSPHORUS

Two Turkish men dragged the bloodied and beaten, semi-conscious Ahmed through the hallways, past some horrified prostitutes standing outside their rooms. Ming, the third man, followed Laura and Boss Yang.

At the top of the stairs, they found themselves in another room. There, the men hurled Ahmed before a massive vault. His bruised face with blood and saliva oozing from a broken mouth, observed shaken the safe.

Boss Yang vigorously pulled Ahmed's hair. "What is the combination?!"

The wounded man said a phrase in Turkish.

Laura hesitated. A blend of fear and shock poured over her, but the pressure in her boss's sharp eyes pushed her to translate. "He said. . . go to the fucking hell. . . Kill me. . ."

"Ming. . ." Boss Yang's outstretched his hand and received a gun. Ahmed was struck in the face with the same weapon, knocking out some of his teeth.

"I will not kill you until you give me the combination!"

Laura translated.

With his head seized by the hair, Ahmed wept in despair, answering in Russian. "*Dva, pyatnadtsat', dvadtsat' odin, dvadtsat' sem'!*"

Ahmed's use of that language took her by surprise.

Boss Yang nodded at Ming, who then moved the vault's cylinder using the provided numbers, turned the handle, and unlocked it, revealing a room filled with various stacks of Turkish lira bills, along with American dollars, British pounds and Swiss francs. It included shelves stocked with many documents.

The boss threw Ahmed to the floor and shot him twice in the head. "When there is business to attend to, it's nothing personal," he said while returning the weapon to Ming, glancing at the corpse. "But when someone lies and steals from the Triad and me, it becomes personal."

Ming entered the vault as the other two men dragged the corpse away.

As he turned around, Boss Yang found Laura in a corner, visibly perturbed, with widened eyes. He pulled one chair from beneath the bare wall-table and sat down to talk to the girl. "I know you've seen death, but you've never seen an execution."

"Can . . . I go home?" a shaky question escaped her lips.

Boss Yang pulled out his cigarette case, lit one, and offered one to Laura, who surprisingly declined despite her habit.

"You shouldn't smoke at your age," he said with stillness. "You can fool everyone else, but not me."

With a steady stare, she fought back her fear and spoke. "Do you intend to kill me, too? Go ahead!"

A chuckle escaped him, followed by a puff of smoke. "You're one of a kind, Miss Doncelli," he said, with a nod. Boss Yang pulled a large wad of cash from his suit and unexpectedly tossed it to her. "Consider this your payment. Two hundred thousand liras should be enough for at least six months of rent."

Laura stared at the wad of bills in her hands, then slid down the wall until she sat on the floor. "I would rather repay this money and learn my origins. Where did you get all that information about me?"

"Keep that money, girl," he replied, gesturing with his cigarette in both fingers. "You'll learn about your past eventually, but until then, you'll work here at the casino to repay me."

"I'm not selling myself to any fucking repulsive pervert!"

"You have my word. No one will touch you. As a matter of fact, Ming will be here to look after you."

"What makes you believe I'll work for you?" She shook her head as she reached for one of her *Fatima* cigarettes.

"I know you will."

"What am I supposed to do?"

Boss Yang saw Ming leave the vault. "Is all the money there?"

"That's how it seems, boss," he replied with a nod. "Should I contact our Hong Kong accountants?"

"Please do it."

Ming left Laura and Yang alone when he exited the room.

"What do you know about me?" Laura, still seated in the corner, asked.

"A lot, enough to come myself and deal personally with Ahmed when I would have sent Ming just for you." He said with another nod. "I want your intellect for this place and the Triad."

"Do you think I'll be able to run a damn casino?" She said with a doubt. "I know nothing about managing it!"

"Besides Ming, I need an extra set of eyes to make sure the mistake that bastard made doesn't happen again. There is this Canadian, a friend of mine, who is going to fill in for Ahmed. I owe him my life, yet I find it difficult to trust him." He crushed his cigarette against the chair, then answered. "Remain with him at all times, monitor his actions, and alert me immediately if anything seems suspicious. These assets belong not only to me but also to the elders who own the Triad."

Laura observed the wad of bills she had in her hand and gave thoughts about his proposal. From the moment she saw Ahmed die, she knew things in her life would never be the same. However, she felt the boss intended to keep her alive for a strange reason. "I will do it, but I have certain conditions." A sigh escaped her lips, showing her modest mistrust. "I wish for a room, a salary, the ability to learn more languages, books, and the freedom to go out whenever I desire on a nice day."

"Fair enough. You'll receive everything you asked." Boss Yang stood and extended a hand to help her up. "Trust, loyalty, and secrecy—these are my requests in exchange."

Days following Ahmed's execution, Boss Yang and Laura awaited outside the *Bosphorus* casino that evening. From the elegant open doorway behind, light and music escaped into the sparsely populated alley. Everyone knew the Ankara casino's connection to the Chinese Jade Dragon Triad, even the local government and the police, but no one dared to mention it.

A taxi pulled up, and a passenger got out, attempting to enter the casino. However, a woman blocked his way and requested the password. "*Ankara'da boğaz,*" he replied, and she let him in.

"Bosphorus is in Istanbul, not in Ankara," Laura responded, almost with sarcasm after she listened to the customer.

A chuckle, accompanied by a whiff of smoke, came from Boss Yang. "Everyone knows it." He glanced again at the alley entrance before talking to her. "I'll head back to Hong Kong after my friend Gabriel Facteau gets here. But Ming will train you in all aspects, from martial arts to instructions, to guarantee your future in the Triad."

"So, when will you reveal my origin to me?"

"Once you've shown me the three things I requested," he replied.

An elegant black car driven by Ming abruptly cut short their conversation.

As the blond, blue-eyed man exited his car, removing his hat, Boss Yang welcomed him warmly with a hug and a smile. "Welcome home, my brother!"

In just three days with him, Laura had already seen two distinct sides to Boss Yang. She learned he was capable of brutal acts of violence in favor of the Triad, yet he also possessed a surprisingly gentle and kind nature.

"So good to see you again!" A handshake followed the Canadian's French-accented reply. He then glanced at Laura. "Who's this girl?"

"This is Laura Doncelli," he said. "The one I mentioned on the phone."

A brief nod was her silent greeting, followed by a shy question. "How did you two meet?"

"We fought the Japs in the war," Gabriel said. "They demolished Michael's city wall for airport expansion, but I helped him protect his home from destruction."

"They wanted to erase Kowloon from the map to enlarge the airport," Boss Yang stated.

"Enough, and show me the place!" With Laura behind them, Gabriel asked his friend to take him inside the casino.

5

AYLA

Laura extinguished her cigarette in a nearby glass ash-tray, next to her open calculus textbook. She stood at a podium, watching the staff come and go from the second floor. She wore a turquoise Turkish kaftan, a dress she detested, as it was part of her work attire.

Gabriel, the current *Bosphorus* administrator, appointed her as a hostess. Her promise to Boss Yang compelled her to obey his friend's requests.

By afternoon on a weekday, the casino had very few people. The bordello was so empty that the prostitutes played cards to ease their boredom.

To add sophistication and prevent any mix-up with the nearby seedy brothels, Gabriel, originating from the French region of Canada, named the second floor a *bor-*

dello. He desired a casino that exuded elegance and was exclusive to an upscale clientele.

While studying calculus, a complex subject that Laura found easy to understand, she yawned and occasionally looked from the casino to the stairs beside the hookah lounge.

It was 1952, and she was sixteen. Surprisingly, her height stayed about the same, despite turning into a woman. Concerned about her short stature, she consulted a doctor with her tutor and bodyguard Ming. The physician stated that her cigarette addiction from a very young age had interrupted her growth.

Even with the medical diagnosis, she persisted in smoking anyway.

Ming had become an important part of her life during her time working at the *Bosphorus*. He was her trainer and teacher. Laura had daily morning martial arts lessons with him at a nearby boxing gym, followed by weapons training at a shooting range on the periphery.

In Ming, she found a paternal figure she'd never known. Though she understood his actions were solely per Boss Yang's orders to assist Laura, including errands like buying her cigarettes, she felt a certain affection for him. When Gabriel first took over the casino, Ming, in his everyday black suit, projected a semblance of coldness and authority. Yet, his reserved presence softened, opening up only to her.

To her amazement, while eating kebab with him at a street establishment on an evening off she had, he confessed that he'd abandoned his farm in Hubei during both the Civil War and the conflict with Japan. He was a squatter in Shek Kip Mei, ultimately finding refuge and support—food, shelter, and education—with the Jade Dragon Triad in Kowloon. He couldn't return home because of his commitment to the Triad and the communists' ascension.

Laura also shared with him her younger years from a place she couldn't remember, and her presence in Karaolos. Although he never spoke, Ming's gestures suggested familiarity with her history. She preferred Boss Yang for answers and did not bring up questions of her origin.

Soon after extinguishing her cigarette, she lit another as she turned the pages of her book. While engrossed in a math problem, a disturbing scream from upstairs sent her racing to the upper floor.

Laura found a group of women outside a room in the bordello wing, with their faces revealing shock. "Ayla. . . " Her consternation accompanied the notion of her outcome.

The prostitutes, still shaken, allowed Laura to enter the room when they noticed her.

She found the girl lifeless, hanging from a golden chandelier, still in her travel clothes.

Ayla was only two years older than Laura.

For a short period, they were friends and confided in each other.

A family of fourteen children near Kirikkale was where Ayla came from. She was the fourth oldest of her siblings.

She worked as a cleaner at the *Boyette's* department store because of her limited education and resulting low wage that wouldn't be enough to cover all expenses and, besides, to pay for her place. Ayla considered finding a second job, maybe at a factory. That's when Gabriel Facteau, an avid shopper known for his weekly trips to the store, discovered her while she mopped the marble floor.

As an administrator of a casino and bordello, he always ensured that his female employees were beautiful and sexy enough to attract customers. He glimpsed Ayla's hidden beauty beneath her uniform, picturing her as a great fit for the *Bosphorus*. To earn her trust, he increased his visits to the store from weekly to daily, beginning with brief greetings that grew into casual conversations. She eventually opened up to him, revealing the difficulties she faced—a bedridden father, her brothers' education, and the financial burden it placed on her.

He took advantage of her situation and offered her a job as an escort and entertainer among the customers in the casino, nothing else. He also provided her free lodging on the *Bosphorus*.

Upon hearing that his offer was 50,000 liras per month, far exceeding Boyette's 5,000, she immediately accepted.

Gabriel introduced Laura to her at the casino and made sure Ayla looked presentable.

Two Turkish men, Ming, and some others, lowered Ayla from the chandelier, placing her on the bed and wrapping her in sheets. Silent and shaken, Laura observed everything with moist eyes and a cigarette, her arms folded across her chest.

Ayla had bruises on her arms and neck, unsure if the rope caused them.

"What are your thoughts about what occurred to her?" Laura asked Ming. "What crap was she in?"

As he finished with the wrapping, Ming turned to Laura, and his shoulders shrugged. "In truth, I don't know. It was all between Gabriel and her behind closed doors."

With a pensive look at the body, Laura tapped the fingers holding the tobacco against her arm. "There has to be something shitty that happened between them." She examined the room. Recently, Gabriel gave Ayla the place that served as a dwelling, and it was part of the bordello, which was strange.

She recalled conversations with her friend, finding some of her words regarding her job with no sense.

Ayla, who escorted gamblers and served drinks in the casino area only, mentioned a promotion. "Gabriel said I'll get a promotion and a pay rise!" she exclaimed with excitement. "This means I can support myself and send money to my family!" The conversation happened on a day when Ayla and Laura were together shopping at *Boyette's*. Ayla's transformation was so impressive that her former coworkers didn't recognize her. She was far more polished, changing her cleaning uniform for elegant dresses and makeup.

Laura went to the armoire, finding it locked, so she checked the nightstand drawer, hoping for a key, but found a pearl necklace case, a gift Ayla couldn't have afforded. In her mental review, she recalled Gabriel returning from an errand with an identical case about two days ago.

Laura had known Gabriel for only a year, and their relationship was rigid and formal, more professional than personal, largely because of Ming's constant presence. Gabriel feared Boss Yang. However, during her observation of his administrative duties, she noticed a pattern of extreme kindness towards customers, often promising them various favors. Sometimes, to satisfy unusual customer requests, he would lavish expensive gifts on prostitutes for special services.

She suspected Gabriel's involvement and spoke to Ming. "Do you have enough loose change with you?"

In his surprise, he responded. "Why do you want the change?"

"I must call Hong Kong using a public phone."

Ming nodded doubtfully. "Why don't you make a call here?"

"I believe is safer that way."

"Look, Miss Doncelli," Boss Yang said on the other end of the line. "I have known Gabriel since his time in Kowloon with the Canadian Army, where he was protecting my home, and I don't believe he is guilty."

While Ming waited outside on the street under the hot summer in his black suit, Laura listened inside the blue and white phone booth.

"But the evidence is all against him!" Laura shouted into the telephone.

The silence grew, leaving her breathless in anticipation of his response. "Gabriel is both a manipulator and a fucking womanizer. I don't deny it. But he lacks the balls to be a murderer." A sigh reached her ears. "He wouldn't shoot someone in cold blood!"

She gasped. "As you do," her tone was sharp.

Then another pause followed.

"I've got a better idea. Given the *Bosphorus's* nature, police intervention is, as you know, out of the question. Investigate the murder, get Ming's help, and report back to me."

"Why me?"

"Because your intuition is unique, and I trust you can handle it," Boss Yang cut off the call.

6

BERETTA

To find a well-recommended business, Ming sought suggestions from people in and around the *Bosphorus*. Once he got the information, collected Laura and a driver for a car trip to Atatürk Boulevard, which housed most Turkish government buildings. However, their true destination was a nearby alley containing a small, rundown, and inconspicuous shoe repair shop named *Ayakkabıcı Sokağı*.

As Laura examined the narrow alley—overflowed trash cans, dilapidated tires, children playing soccer amidst the grime, and a dubious storefront obscured by a tattered yellow and white curtain—she demanded an explanation.

"Boss Yang ordered it," Ming said, then quickly left the car.

She followed him into the shop.

A Turkish cobbler, an older man, sat at his work, applying glue and then nailing on the sole of a shoe. He paused his work to observe the two visitors as they came in. "Are you here to repair a shoe?"

"We're here to buy shoes," Ming said.

The man rose and gestured to his small, cluttered room crammed with carelessly stacked old shoes, materials, and tools. "Those shoes are all in for repair, but I do have some others available."

"I am looking for *these* shoes."

The cobbler eyed him and Laura suspiciously, but after a moment, he nodded. "Do you want a smaller one or a bigger one?"

"She already has some practice, so it's for her." Ming pointed to her.

Laura's eyes widened in surprise and nervousness.

The old man inspected her, then retrieved a small, rag-wrapped package from a drawer in a corner. He placed it on the table and unwrapped it, revealing a gun. "This is a new model, barely used."

Ming checked the weapon to be certain it was empty, weighed it, and then handed it to Laura. "I think this Beretta fits you."

With a surprised look, she turned to him. "Why did you give me a gun?"

"Boss Yang's orders. He believes you must be able to defend yourself if you're going to investigate Ayla's death."

As she examined the small gun, Laura felt a mix of amazement, awe, and ecstasy. "This thing is little."

"It is a Beretta 950, Italian-made," the cobbler said. "And I believe it fits you well."

"How much do you ask for it?" Ming asked.

"Sixty thousand is a good price."

Ming withdrew a thick wad of bills, about a hundred thousand liras, from his suit and gave it to the aged man. "Keep the change."

The cobbler, expressing his gratitude for the transaction, surprised Laura by taking the gun back, wrapping it, and placing it—along with bullets—in an empty shoebox. He handed her the closed box. "Thank you for purchasing my shoes."

Ming and Laura walked out of the shop.

"I noticed a few gun stores in the city. Why did we need to go to this hideous alley to get one?" As they returned to the car, Laura inquired.

"We needed a gun without registration to avoid the police," he concluded.

Before opening the door, Laura reluctantly glanced into the office. She found Gabriel relaxed in his chair with his feet up on the desk, speaking French into the phone and holding a cigar that emitted a large mist of smoke.

He invited her in with a wave, noting she carried something wrapped in cloth beneath her arm as she sat down. He still went on speaking in a heated conversation to the telephone, but for a moment he stood up and opened the window he had behind to let the smoke out.

Her fluency in many languages allowed her to understand him perfectly, and she almost interrupted. "*Bonjour à ta maman.*"

Pausing in surprise, Gabriel nodded, unsure if his gesture expressed appreciation or reminiscence of her unique talent. He ended the call with a goodbye. "My mother can be stubborn," he stated in French. "All that old bitch ever does is ask me for money!" In a sudden rage, he forcefully pressed his cigar into the ashtray, which was full of cigarette butts and surrounded by papers on his desk. He swiveled his office chair toward the window to relax.

Laura, ever calm, lit one of her *Fatima* cigarettes.

The click of her lighter made Gabriel swivel his chair around again. "You're here to interrogate me about Ayla. Right?" He nodded with no surprise. "Boss Yang gave me a stark warning."

"Where were you during the two days you were gone after we found Ayla's body?"

Gabriel smirked with a chuckle. "You'd be better off working for the police instead of at this crappy casino."

She blew out some smoke, then gave him a frightening stare that erased his smile. "Answer me!"

"I spent time at a shitty bar, passed out in a pool of vomit, and woke up to find that a fucking whore stole my wallet."

She was uncertain whether to trust him, so she unwrapped the package she had and tossed it onto the desk.

A red velvet case that held a necklace of pearls. "I know it was you, sir. She couldn't afford it."

With a chuckle, Gabriel, driven by curiosity, opened the case. "This is a fine gift for any woman who fancies pearls. Yes, I got her a present, but it wasn't this."

Laura's eyes grew wide when she heard him taking a break from smoking. "What do you mean?"

Opening a desk drawer, Gabriel put an identical velvet case onto the desk. "Same jewelry shop but different gifts, and different givers."

Inside, she found a golden necklace, which surprised her, and she stared at him.

"I had organized a date that included dinner and spending the night together. But when I got to the room I'd prepared for her, I found Ayla hanging from the chandelier. I went straight to the bar I told you about earlier." He replied, fighting back his tears with a shaking voice. "I'm a coward, I admit it. I saw her, shut the door, and ran."

"Was it a murder?" She said pensively. "Why? Who?"

"You better deal with that fucking problem! I can't get any peace until you resolve this issue, or Boss Yang will still be a pain in my fucking ass!" Like a child, he stood and wiped his tears with his sleeve. "I only wanted to help her get a place in the bordello. . ."

Laura stubbed out her cigarette, giving him a pointed, silent stare as his sobs continued. "I hope you rot in hell, Gabriel." With calm composure, she stood up and took the case with the pearl necklace. "Yes, you are a fucking coward and a despicable womanizer."

She exited the office and saw Ming waiting in the hall with his arms crossed. He was in his usual black suit. "What have you found out?"

"Seems that he didn't do it," she said, somewhat bothered. "Was it a murder? Was it a suicide by hanging? Why?"

Laura pulled the light cord in the storage room, illuminating the cleaning supplies as she searched. In a corner, amidst a jumble of buckets and cleaning supplies, she discovered a pack hidden under a pile of discarded new dresses that were removed from the armoire. "Ayla deserved better than that!" With disapproval and irritation, she removed the clothing, revealing a wooden crate. "Her hometown, not a cooler, is where she has to be buried!"

Ming, from behind, listened with a seemingly frigid expression. "We need to ensure this casino doesn't get caught by the authorities, Miss Doncelli. It is not just a place, but an important international asset of the Triad. We dispose of bodies for this reason."

"No matter what, we have to uncover the reason behind her death!" From the crate, she began removing Ayla's belongings. She unearthed a small black leather diary, hoping its entries would reveal something. To her surprise, pages belonging to the days before her death were entirely blank. While reviewing the blank sheets, she found a train ticket to Istanbul and a handwritten address on it. "Did not she go to Istanbul recently?"

"I recall her telling you about it," Ming stated.

"Yes, she seemed tense when she told me she planned to take the train, but she didn't say when she'd return," Laura said, in a thinking gesture.

"But returned."

"She returned just to meet her death," as she closed the diary, Laura concluded.

7

ISTANBUL

T wo phone calls and a map revealed the address written on the train ticket found inside Ayla's diary to be, astonishingly, the Soviet consulate on Istiklal Street.

By chance, Laura found herself on a train bound for Istanbul. It coasted along the Marmara Sea, past Izmit. She felt her destination was near.

For two years in the Turkish capital, Laura had no opportunity to travel outside of the city. She was an undocumented immigrant, unable to provide proof of identity or origin, not wanting to reveal herself. The war robbed her of her memory and her homeland.

As the darkness outside prevented her from seeing through the windows, she used the dim car light to reread the diary, piecing together clues while seated next to a snoring fat man with a fez on his head. While glancing casually, she noticed a mother giving the simit bread she had purchased outside the station in Ankara to her preteen daughter in the seat before her.

I must make this sacrifice. It's the only way to have a better life for my family, especially my father. Those were the last words Ayla wrote in her diary.

"What sacrifice?" As Laura lit a cigarette, she searched for answers in her mind. "Was her death a sacrifice, or was something else going on?"

The incessant clatter of the train brought back her memories of two days ago. She recalled Ming, usually so impassive, stunned to find that the address belonged to the Soviet consulate. He was insistent on accompanying her to Istanbul.

However, she persuaded him to watch the *Bosphorus*, particularly Gabriel, who remained as a suspect.

Convinced, Ming allowed her to go unaccompanied, providing useful safety advice and tips for a brief journey. Laura concealed her Beretta inside her clothes and got ready, following his guidance.

"Could Ayla have been a spy?" Laura reflected. "How could someone as sweet and naïve as Ayla become involved with the Soviets?" She glanced at the newspaper on the sleeping man's lap, noticing an article reporting a stalemate in the Korean War.

Further investigation revealed even more bizarre discoveries. Meanwhile, she tapped her cigarette ash into the armrest ashtray.

However, none of her observations resolved whether Ayla's death was a murder or a suicide. The motives remained unclear.

With no form of identification, Laura secured a room in a cheap hotel close to the train station—a place frequented by couples—to remain anonymous.

Aside from her Beretta, a supply of cigarettes, and a roll of cash from Ming, she was without luggage, so she opted to sleep in her lingerie rather than pajamas or a nightgown. However, the loud, rhythmic noises and screams from guests' acts prevented her from getting a restful night's sleep. Unable to relax, she kept herself awake, but she channeled her frustration into sketching explanations of the crime at the desk.

Even Ankara's bordello wasn't this loud.

Once the sunrise arrived, she wore back in her usual outfit—a white shirt, pants, leather jacket, and black boots. At just sixteen, she possessed the mature character of a woman.

Sunrise brought her outside, as a crisp Autumn path awaited. Many stray cats accompanied her on a walk of several blocks to the Soviet consulate. There she sat at an outdoor table across the street from the diplomatic mission in a recently opened, as-yet unfrequented cafe.

She carefully examined every detail of the beige structure. Guards in black monitored the gates from inside, with a scarlet flag raised on a pole on top of the major construction, and an inner garden that beautified the Italian-style architecture. With the consulate constantly in her view from the cafe, she carefully studied every movement inside and outside.

A waiter offered Laura service, and she ordered coffee and Menemen scrambled eggs. He proposed tea, citing the early hour, but she insisted on coffee, leaving him annoyed. Finding herself alone again, she lit another cigarette, as usual. That is when she spotted something.

A thin man in his forties, carrying a briefcase and wearing a gabardine, walked along the street. As he saw Laura, he startled her. He hesitated, trying to recall something, then shook his head and went into the consulate.

She noticed his odd behavior just as the waiter brought her breakfast and coffee. With the consulate in her sights, she suppressed her half-smoked cigarette and ate.

Less than half an hour later, the same man emerged from the consulate and locked his eyes on Laura by the gate. She felt uneasy and subtly turned away, reaching into her jacket for her Beretta, but not drawing the weapon. Driven by curiosity, she looked again, and he scared her by appearing right in front of her.

"Mind if I join you at this table, miss?" His request, delivered in heavily accented and reluctant Turkish, was difficult to understand.

With a hesitant nod and her hand still on her Beretta, she allowed him to be seated. Though she attempted to hide it, her fear was noticeable on her face. Her inexperience, coupled with Ming's absence for the first time, caused her anxiety.

With a calm disposition, he requested a cup of tea from the waiter, took out his blue and white pack of *Belo-morkanal* smokes from his gabardine coat, and lit a cigarette. "I thought I knew you from somewhere, but I only remembered after I recognized you." A puff of smoke left his lips as he nodded. "You are the hostess from the clandestine casino in Ankara."

As she saw his peaceful behavior, she lit yet another cigarette from her own. "I see so many faces daily that I don't recall yours." Her almost-perfect Russian response surprised him.

"Were you ever in the motherland before?" he responded in the same language.

"I picked up the language from refugees I met in Cyprus years ago, but I have not been to Russia," she said as she drank a sip of her coffee. "Who are you?"

The man expressed gratitude to the waiter for the tea on the table. "I'm Isaak Kovalev, and in my role as secretary of the Soviet Intelligence Services within the Foreign Affairs department, I serve the embassies and consulates in Turkey and Greece." He inhaled the tobacco and then drank some tea. "To put it another way, my shitty job with the MGB involves deciding who returns home—with their families or in *gulags*."

"Your work involves whistleblowers, and you punish them. Am I right?" Laura replied, in great distrust.

"Or reward them, whatever Comrade Stalin pleases," he sighed and continued. "We are afraid to confront the old, paranoid fucking bastard. Even after all I've been through, I'm still working for him—like a complete fool." He finished his tea. "I was in Stalingrad. You know? I had no choice but to fight the Germans. But what do I get in exchange? Stalin sent my wife and daughter to a *gulag* to die because he considered them a threat."

"What brought you to Turkey, and your visits to the *Bosphorus*?" Her question held a hint of both curiosity and suspicion.

"My best friend and I grew up together. Concerned about my safety after what my family went through, he found me a job in Turkey," he concluded.

"In truth, I don't care about your misfortunes. My focus is on seeking answers." A certain coldness marked Laura's answer. "Tell me, what were you up to at the *Bosphorus*?"

"Because of the rules against it, my comrades and I used to go to that hidden place for gambling and drugs. That prevented anyone from reporting us."

"Does Ayla sound familiar to you?"

A lengthy pause followed before Isaak, motionless and with his cigarette still in hand, responded. "The *Merzost*."

"What is that?" she asked in surprise.

He pulled some lira bills from his gabardine and put them on the table. "Your breakfast is on me."

"What exactly is *Merzost*?" she insisted.

"I'll see you at eight this evening at *Gar* restaurant in the *Sirkeci* Station," he said, getting up. "You'll receive the answers."

With Laura's strange expression, he returned to the consulate.

8
MERZOST

By eight o'clock, the man from the consulate was still a no-show. Despite being in the bustling train station, Laura waited patiently at a table on the restaurant's outdoor terrace.

Announcements of the Orient Express's upcoming departure reached her ears.

With a cigarette and a *Gazoz* soda, she informed the waiter that she was waiting for someone. She wondered whether there would be dinner after his arrival or if it was just a quick meeting.

Eagerly awaiting his arrival, she peered through the restaurant inner window, noticing tables filled with journalists from around the globe engaged in discussions and information sharing. Then Laura looked at the clock in the busy hallway. It was five past eight.

With a fresh pour of soda into her small glass, she spotted him from the crowd and headed to her table.

Though Isaak offered no apology, a somber expression showed on his face as he took his seat.

Sweat poured down his face, and Laura knew he'd been running, although she did not know why.

He pulled two sheets of paper from his gabardine and gave them to her. "I hope you're as good at reading Russian as you are at speaking it."

"Is everything all right?" She asked, having perceived a tremor in his voice.

He breathed out, filled with fear. "Without my family, nothing has sense." Isaak abruptly rose and glanced at her. "These papers have the information you need, so you must depart Istanbul at once for your safety."

With a simple nod, Laura watched him hurry into the crowd.

Laura didn't listen to him.

She ignored his suggestion to depart Istanbul. She followed him, driven by curiosity about his abrupt fear. Under the veil of darkness and the crowds near the station, she went unnoticed by Isaak. Except for stray cats, the streets became deserted and dark as they walked away.

The crescent moon in the clear night sky showed her their proximity to the *Hagia Sofia*, an iconic city mosque. Laura, however, saw him head the other way, disappearing down an alley behind a restaurant.

Her training under Ming prepared her for this—she crept through the longer-than-anticipated alley, using the trash cans as cover to stay hidden.

Concealed behind a large, rancid wooden crate that held discarded restaurant fish, Laura saw Isaak stop at the end. He appeared alone, waiting while he lit a smoke.

She looked everywhere, including the alley entrance, but saw no one. Only roaming cats. "What is he waiting for?" she asked herself. "Why the fear on his face?"

Laura again saw Isaak as a tall, thin figure materialized from the shadows, approaching him. She was in disbelief. It was like something from a dream or a nightmare.

The shadowy, faceless man appeared to give gestures, though he remained silent. Isaak whispered to him, but his words were unclear.

With a swift, violent thrust, the man pierced Isaak's chest, causing immediate death. He then removed what looked like heart and squeezed it. The body hit the ground with a heavy thud.

Laura gasped in stunned horror.

The creature turned around when she accidentally bumped a trash can.

He approached her with slow steps.

Panicked, she attempted to flee, but a muddy puddle caused her to fall. However, as he neared, she reacted by firing her Beretta until it was empty.

Though seemingly unfazed by the gun, the tall, shadowy figure appeared frozen in surprise. Laura used this opportunity to make a quick escape.

As she fled, the creature pursued her, running not only on the ground but also along the walls to gain an advantage. She had never witnessed such a supernatural being, leaving her awestruck yet terrified.

She ran faster, straining with all her might, with her empty Beretta clasped in her hand, to evade capture.

She made it out of the alley, crossed the street, and continued her race.

The creature aimed to pursue, closing the distance as fast as possible. The chase ended when a speeding grocery truck ran him over, sending the vehicle stumbling into a light pole with a deafening crash and a shower of sparks.

After the incident, Laura halted, turned and gasped for breath, then noticed his strange disappearance. It was as if the creature evaporated into nothing.

"I. . . I don't know what to do!" On the floor of the booth, a shaken Laura spoke into the phone as her fingers trembled while she held her cigarette. She already had Isaak's papers and was reviewing them on her lap. "You might think I'm losing it, but that fucking monster was chasing me!"

She could barely see outside the booth and realized that the crowd at Sirkeci Station had gotten smaller after ten at night.

"What was that monster's name again?" on the other end of the line, Boss Yang asked.

"They call it *Merzost*. It's a Russian word that means *abomination*." She inhaled deeply, catching her breath after smoking. "The text omits his identity and background, referring to him solely as Stalin's preferred secret weapon, besides the details I've already provided." She paused, inhaled another trembling puff of her cigarette, then continued. "If I hadn't seen him, I wouldn't have believed it."

Boss Yang responded after a moment of silence. "Odd things have been happening recently, especially since the end of the war."

Laura gasped, her eyes rolled as she tried to interpret his words. "Is it just me, or do you seem to know the answers?"

"You'll get answers eventually, but right now, you need to handle something," he said in a grave voice. "Though it grieves me, his removal is necessary, and you are to carry it out."

His request shocked her. "Why does it have to be me?! Why can't Ming do it?!"

"It's time you put your Beretta to good use. I believe you are the one to do it for me."

"But. . . ! I have never done it!"

"You need to take care of your own shit and follow my orders." Boss Yang replied in a strict voice. "Everything happens for the first time, and while regret is normal, you'll get through this bitch!" He paused, then went on.

"Truth, loyalty, and secrecy. Do you remember them? You owe your life both to me and to the elders of the Triad, who placed their confidence in you. So, what do you say?"

Silent tears streamed down Laura's face inside the smoky, fog-filled phone booth. Briefly, she considered abandoning her current life and starting anew, even knowing the perils she would face, but her longing for answers regarding her past and the truth about the *Merzost* prevented her from leaving. A sorrowful nod and a reply followed as she kept the phone in her ear. "I'll do it."

"Thanks, miss. The Triad will be forever grateful to you," he ended the call.

9
GABRIEL

M ing met Laura at the Ankara Railroad Station at sunrise, and hurried her to get in a black car, driven by a Turkish chauffeur, and sped through the city. Her quiet anguish didn't surprise him. Boss Yang had previously told him on a phone call.

She saw the city only from her car, recognizing most landmarks through the window, but after Istanbul, the world felt different.

"Once you finish your task, Boss Yang has other plans." Ming gave her the bullets from his black suit as he spoke. "Ayla's death and the Soviets' involvement make selling the *Bosphorus* the only necessary choice. The Triad's elders are no longer interested in this business. They want no more problems."

Laura held the heavy bullets, gripping them as she stared at Ming. "It makes sense. The Triad founded the *Bosphorus* to finance the Hong Kong resistance against the Japs. But it's no longer necessary now that the war is over." She shook her head. "Also, he's placing a precarious burden on a business he doesn't own."

His nod showed agreement, but he made no other expression. "Miss Laura, you've learned your lesson to perfection."

She pulled her Beretta from her jacket and loaded it. She gasped, struggling to relax her inner turmoil that revolved in her stomach. "Is Gabriel in the office?"

"If he is not fucking a slut, I am sure he is wanking himself," Ming answered, then glanced at his Omega wristwatch. "He's about to have breakfast in his office."

With a melancholic smile, she tucked her weapon back into her jacket. "You've done a fantastic job paying attention to every detail of his movements, even intimate ones." She grew serious again, peering out the window to spot a familiar neighborhood bustling with a bazaar despite the early morning. The place where she initially arrived and rented a nearby room evoked a nostalgic feeling. "Give those women some money and let them go. I doubt Boss Yang will reopen the casino once I'm done."

"I just popped my cherry!" In a moment of excitement, Ayla bit her lower lip. "I felt pain at first, but it was great!"

As she heard that, Laura froze. Her half-eaten street kebab got forgotten in her hand. She gazed at her friend, who was sipping her *Bixi Cola* from the table in the middle of the sidewalk. She immediately cleaned her hands with a napkin and abandoned her food. "When did it happen?"

"About two nights ago!" she said, then continued eating her kebab.

Laura had a bad feeling. Ayla was beautiful, but raised in a conservative rural family, she found the idea of giving herself to someone disturbing. "Did you sleep with Gabriel?"

"I can't tell you!" Her bossy reply led her to steal a *Fatima* cigarette from her friend, which she placed between her bright red lips.

Laura inspected her every move.

Disdain had replaced Ayla's modesty. Gabriel's promises of a raise and promotion, mixed with the corrupting influences of the casino and the bordello, changed her. The modest country girl was gone.

As she worked as a hostess for long, Laura was fond of Ming, but not Gabriel. She also wondered about the reason behind Boss Yang's protectiveness of her. The thought of being with a man for money didn't appeal to her. Her salary, books, and room fulfilled her. She desired nothing more.

Besides, Laura wasn't gorgeous like Ayla. Being short in stature and disliking dresses, she frequently distrusted others, yet she was determined and self-reliant, capable of standing by herself. These traits didn't attract anyone, and she had no interest in men.

"Is there something wrong?!" Ayla felt annoyed by Laura's intense stare. She rose from her seat, tossed away her smoke, and left, unable to bear her any longer.

Laura was sad and disappointed when she left.

Outside Gabriel's office, something reminded Laura of the time she ate street food with Ayla. That outing was their last time together as friends. After that day, despite finding themselves in the same place, a strained silence fell between them.

Ayla's last diary entries showed sorrow for betraying herself and the end of a short but valuable friendship. "*Will you forgive me, Laura?*" These were among the last words written before the blank pages. Laura assumed she had traveled to Istanbul when she stopped writing, only to meet her death upon her return.

"I forgive you. . ." Laura muttered to herself before knocking on the door. She found a serious, focused Ming to her left, positioned where two hallways converged.

"You may enter," a male voice said.

Laura walked into the office and saw the usual cigar mist hanging in the air, finding Gabriel smoking and eating breakfast from a tray on his desk at the same time.

With nothing on him but a dusky robe that revealed his chest, Gabriel placed his cigar in the ashtray and spread cheese on a slice of bread from a plate. He didn't look at Laura, but he knew she approached and took a seat in front of him. His hunger was more important, but he talked regardless. "Did you have a pleasant trip to Istanbul?"

The strong cigar smoke was unpleasant to Laura, so she lit a cigarette, giving him suspicious glances as she did so.

Her intense look made Gabriel interrupt his meal. He then resumed eating a piece of bread. "What?" With his mouth full, he asked.

"Remember Isaak Kovalev?"

With a surprised gasp, Gabriel choked on his food, spitting it into the trash can as his blue eyes widened.

"He frequented the *Bosphorus*, but to gamble and find whores on behalf of someone else," she nodded, as a plume of smoke escaped her lips. "How much did he pay for Ayla? A hundred forty thousand liras?"

Gabriel swallowed, then replied. "I have received no money from him."

"No, but that's how much the gold necklace you received costs. The Soviets can't carry large amounts of cash for covert payments." Her face held a serious expression. "That explains the necklace. Its value is almost enough to buy a small house."

"How dare to stick in my business?! You fucking bitch!"

With calm movements, Laura retrieved the Russian papers from her jacket and laid them on the desk. "It's all here. At first I thought Isaak's documents were from the consulate, but they were actually his typed confession." She paused for a smoke of her cigarette. "Stalin had ordered Isaak to monitor and please the *Merzost*, who was holidaying in Turkey following a covert Korean War operation. He revealed everything from the very beginning."

"All he said was that a comrade visiting Istanbul required a companion. He desired a fresh face from the bordello." Gabriel responded as he disposed of the cigar ash in the ashtray.

"This explains why you offered a *promotion* to Ayla. You, however, took her virginity before she could offer her services, just as you did with the other new girls. You are disgusting and despicable!"

"Yet I don't see why she died."

Laura blew out a puff of smoke and then answered before finishing her cigarette. "You fucking killed her!"

"How?!" He stood up, exasperated. "I found her fucking dead!"

She paused, breathing out. Despite her outward calm, she was in turmoil inside. "You subjected Ayla to something infinitely more terrifying than pushing her into a cage containing a rabid animal. The *Merzost* is something out of this world, and frightening. All for a hundred forty thousand liras!" A sigh escaped Laura's lips as her heart raced. "She entrusted herself to you and then ended up sacrificing her body to others because of you. She loved you!"

Despite his shock and paralysis, Gabriel remained remorseless. "You still haven't revealed why that whore died!" As he pushed his breakfast away, he exclaimed and pounded his fists on his desk. "You know nothing!"

"The *Merzost's* terror and a one-sided love resulted in her suicide. She realized you had exploited her by exposing her to that creature." Laura sighed again. "You may not have laid a hand on her, but your actions killed her."

"You don't even know what the fucking *Merzost* is!" Exasperated, Gabriel's face turned red as he screamed.

"I do," she responded, rising from her chair. "Istanbul is where I saw him. That thing is no man." Aware of Gabriel's gaze, she moved towards the door, then whispered a few words. "Boss Yang and I send you our regards."

"Eh?" he said, confused.

With a sudden spin, Laura drew her Beretta to take on Gabriel and opened fire.

After three shots to the naked chest, he fell dead behind the desk.

She watched his demise, gnashing her teeth with gleaming eyes, and with the weapon still in hand.

Though remorse arrived for Laura, anger and hate also invaded her.

And that was the first time sixteen-year-old Laura Doncelli killed.

10
HONG KONG

Laura never celebrated her birthday because the date of her birth was unknown. Yet, as 1953 arrived, she perceived herself as a seventeen-year-old young woman.

That same year, just before spring, she experienced her first ever flight—a feat she'd deemed impossible. With Ming beside her, she enjoyed a bird's-eye view from the window of their McDonnell Douglas DC-3.

She lit a cigarette, put the match in the seat's ashtray, and then examined the tobacco pack. Calcutta lacked her preferred *Fatima* smokes, but Ming found a satisfactory alternative for Laura.

"These are *Camels*, an American brand. It is Arab tobacco, much like the Turkish ones you're familiar with.

You'll have no trouble getting them in Hong Kong," Ming said as he bought them from a store at the airport.

As she returned her tobacco to her black leather purse—which also held her Beretta—Laura retrieved her passport. An exquisite forgery, provided by Boss Yang to allow her to travel, obliged her to assume the identity of Lillian Dover, a purported British Hong Kong citizen. She returned inside and set her purse down on the floor.

To avoid raising suspicion, she wore a champagne-colored dress, makeup, and her hair up. The pretense about her looks was displeasing to her.

She desired to continue being Laura, and not to be Lillian.

Laura stubbed out her cigarette and grabbed the timetable from the front seat. The last leg of her *Pan American Airways* flight from Istanbul to Hong Kong was a welcome relief after a four-day journey. Her trip with Ming required layovers in Tehran, Karachi, and Calcutta. She was just a few hours from her destination.

She attempted to sleep again, unsuccessfully. Haunted by the *Merzost* and the death of Gabriel, an execution she committed, she suffered from insomnia and rude awakenings caused by grim nightmares. In the past weeks, Ming gave her sleeping pills when insomnia became too much to bear.

Four months have passed since the events in Turkey. The vividness of Laura's nightmares made them seem like from recent days.

Following Gabriel's execution, Ming and his men took charge of his corpse, bribing a corrupt police officer to falsify a report of a robbery, and shipped him to Canada, to his mother, in a coffin.

Ming later took control of the *Bosphorus*, shutting it down and laying off employees. Unable to find a suitable buyer, they sold everything to secondhand shops and wired the money to the Bank of South Seas in Hong Kong. Boss Yang opened a new checking account in the name of Lillian Dover, a fictitious name given to Laura, to keep the Triad's involvement hidden. As she posed as the heir of a wealthy businessman who escaped the war, she alleged a return to Hong Kong after his death, and transferred seven hundred thousand sterling pounds—or eleven million Hong Kong dollars.

Laura saw Isaak as a tall, thin figure materialized from the shadows, approaching him.

The shadowy, faceless man appeared to give gestures, though he remained silent. Isaak whispered to him, but his words were unclear.

With a swift, violent thrust, the man pierced Isaak's chest, causing immediate death. He then removed what looked like heart and squeezed it. The body hit the ground with a heavy thud.

Laura gasped in stunned horror.

The creature turned around when she accidentally bumped a trash can.

He approached her with slow steps.

The light at the building entrance revealed his face. Gabriel's face.

"Miss Laura," Ming said, giving her shoulder a light push. "It is best for you to get prepared as we are about to land."

She woke with a gasp and her eyes wide, with heart pounding, realizing she was still on the plane, as the same nightmare kept clinging to her. Dazed but aware, she nodded, adjusted in her seat, noted the illuminated no-smoking sign, and buckled up.

Ming, with his usual seriousness, spoke. "Our landing might be rough because the airport is in a complex place. Regardless of what occurs, remain calm."

Though unintentional, his words caused her to worry. Looking out of her plane window after they broke through the clouds, Laura saw the Hong Kong harbor for the very first time. However, she observed a quick descent toward a mountain, followed by a sharp right turn, bringing the plane to an extremely low altitude, almost scraping the buildings. Her heart pounded again, especially when it was her first time flying.

"Oh, dammit!" she exclaimed to herself.

As the plane approached the airport, it swerved left, then righted itself, touching down on the runway and braking quickly to avoid the sea at the end.

"Welcome to Hong Kong. And to Kai Tak airport, a one-of-a-kind in the world." A slight smile played on Ming's lips as he loosened his belt.

With trembling hands, she unfastened her strap and stood up to exit.

April's warm spring air greeted Laura as she exited the plane. The humid tropical weather was a fresh experience for her. Although she had read extensively about diverse climates, she longed to experience them firsthand.

The sun shone brighter and more intensely than in Turkey.

As the airport transfer bus took Laura to the terminal, she was still in disbelief at the thought of living in a Far East Asian city, especially after her past as a refugee just a few years ago. Although she eventually made Turkey her home, Hong Kong was her best option.

But she felt fortunate that Ming, though stoic, never left her side. After all, being a seventeen-year-old orphan, he was the closest thing she had to family.

She noticed the vehicle carrying her and curious passengers speeding past grounded BOAC planes to reach the terminal.

As she got off the recently stopped bus, she paused before going into the terminal. Laura visually explored the bay and saw many junks—boats where people lived—with red sails. And low buildings on the land, but also new construction of taller ones.

"Let's go inside, Miss Dover." To remain inconspicuous, Ming called her that way while surrounded by people. "He's waiting for us, without a doubt."

With a feeling that things were about to be different, she nodded and followed him into the building.

As she arrived at the airport restaurant with Ming, Laura noted the few other patrons present. Lunch was over, and the afternoon was underway. The staff was preparing for the evening meal.

She searched the place, and she recognized someone. Even after all those years, he remained unchanged from when she first encountered him in Ankara.

Boss Yang still had the same black suit and had placed a lit cigarette on an ashtray.

He was alone.

He gazed intently at the runway through the panoramic glass, savoring the sight of a plane approaching, all while having just added hot mustard to his hamburger on a small square table covered with white and red cloths. He had a glass of water nearby.

"While you talk to him, I'll collect the luggage," Ming said, then left.

She comprehended and went to him.

Her appearance surprised Boss Yang as she stood before him. "I remember you wearing chap clothes, so seeing you in a dress and with a purse is a bit startling."

"You're the one who dressed me in these fucking clothes!" she complained.

As she swore, a waiter in a tuxedo walked by and shook his head in disapproval.

With a chuckle, Boss Yang stood and offered her a seat, which she accepted. "You have grown into a fine woman, Miss Laura. Or shall I call you Miss Dover?" He exhaled a puff of smoke before continuing. "Would you like something? Perhaps some food or a drink?"

"Just a cola, please." She watched him order a drink and then waited to ask. "If Gabriel used to be your best friend. Why did you order me to get rid of him?"

Without a word, Boss Yang continued smoking and stared out the glass on his left, leaving her question unanswered. After grinding his unsmoked cigarette into his uneaten hamburger, he finally responded. "Do you see the runaways?"

She gave a nod, dazzled by the answer.

"The Japs tore down the wall around our city in Kowloon to build two larger runways and expand the area for their planes. British and Canadian prisoners built it."

"So?"

"After escaping to Kowloon, Gabriel sought refuge and supported the Jade Dragon Triad to defend the city against the intended demolition of their homes. The elders remained grateful for his wartime help, overlooking his despicable actions. My indifference made me complicit."

"What did Gabriel do?"

"At the start, he used to fuck prostitutes, but as he became too drunken, he started raping women, including younger unmarried ones, causing pregnancies," a sigh escaped Boss Yang's lips as he lit another cigarette. "I wrongly defended him against accusations I later learned were true, hoping to gain the elders' trust. He was a local hero of sorts." He then shook his head. "Japanese brutality was another battle we faced during the war. It was him or them."

The conversation paused as the waiter filled the cola drink until it was half a glass.

"Excuses! You let him control the *Bosphorus*!" she frowned and slammed the table. "Do you have any idea how many women that bastard harmed?!"

Boss Yang's silence spoke volumes.

"You fucking knew! Right?" She bickered in annoyance. "You're just as guilty as he was because you also killed Ayla! You only used me to kill him after learning about his damn Soviet involvement!"

"I apology . . ." He barely said, with remorse in his eyes. "It's more than . . ."

"Sheesh! Get away from me and never try to contact me again!" Laura rose and shoved her chair back to leave. "I fucking hate this dress!"

"You've decided against learning more about yourself and where you come from. Is that right?" At last, Boss Yang spoke.

Upon hearing him, Laura hesitated, but ultimately chose not to abandon him, even though she showed her back. She brushed away the tears that were welling up in her eyes. She bowed her head, unable to speak. "Never do that again! I'm sick of being exploited and fucking disrespected!" Without glancing at him, she returned to her seat and lit one of her Camels cigarettes.

"I made a reservation for you at the *Four Generations Hotel* on Waterloo Road. I think you deserve a break after four tiring days of flights." He answered by exhaling more smoke. "I'll take you somewhere tomorrow and explain your nature and purpose in Hong Kong."

11

TIAN CHAO

She wasn't comfortable with the lavishness of the *Four Generations Hotel*. Yet Laura understood Boss Yang's motivation for posing as Lillian Dover. Moving HK$11 million from Turkey to a Hong Kong bank without raising suspicion was no small feat.

In a way, the Triad's trust in her was a blessing and a curse.

As a poor night's sleep plagued her, she tried to adjust to a new time zone, besides her insomnia and nightmares.

After a hot shower, she dressed in her favorite outfit—jacket, pants, and boots—and waited in the lobby, an hour early. The solitude in unfamiliar surrounding was unbearable, especially during her room service breakfast. Anxiety overcame her.

As was usual in her personality, she didn't stop studying her environment. The persistent scarlet, accented with gold, was inescapable to her. From her cushioned seat, amidst the smoke and ash of her cigarette, she observed the elegant room—dragon and Shih Tzu sculptures, floral carpets, and slightly damaged crane-patterned wallpaper. The agarwood incense made her feel like she was in an ancient Chinese palace, just as she'd imagined from books.

She'd been told by the receptionist the day before that the hotel had served as accommodation for Japanese officials during the war. Hence the damaged walls.

Laura sat in that chair quietly to overhear the businessmen's conversation and to familiarize herself with the language. Although she knew basic Cantonese, she wanted to improve her fluency because she'd be using it frequently, besides her English.

Out of the blue, a man's presence beside her startled her. Laura turned and looked up at Ming. "I didn't escape from my room with that money," a chuckle accompanied her sarcasm. "Actually. . . I'm wishing to get rid of this soon."

Ming, with his expression unchanged, suggested. "Or we could escape together with it."

Unsure if he was joking, Laura chuckled again.

"Let's wait outside. Boss Yang is on his way." Ming returned to his usual seriousness.

She consented, and subsequently they exited to find a uniformed porter opening the gates for them. In no time, they were waiting on the sidewalk of the Waterloo Road. This late morning, Laura at last enjoyed the lively street scene. Rickshaws pulled by runners with some carrying passengers, double-decker red buses, and a variety of cars and trucks.

Pedestrians were also present. Her observations included people from all socioeconomic backgrounds—wealthy Westerners in everyday clothes and impoverished barefoot Chinese wearing conical bamboo hats. Some, however, were Asians of middle and upper classes.

Naturally, since it was a popular Kowloon spot, she could easily detect tourists by their summer attire, despite being spring. Americans and British were the most noticeable.

What Laura saw mesmerized her, but then an elegant black Rolls Royce Silver Dawn astonished her upon its arrival. Ming walked to the vehicle to open the door and invite her in.

As she glanced in, she looked at Boss Yang, already seated in the back, gave a hat-tip greeting, and noticed his change into a stylish brown suit instead of the usual black one. With a nod, she entered.

Having closed the door, Ming went to the front and sat next to the chauffeur.

Although Boss Yang offered her a cigarette, Laura lit her own.

Curious, she watched the busy Hong Kong streets from the windows during their course.

"Hong Kong is a fucking mess." As smoke left his mouth, he spoke to her. "Seized because of opium, it fell under colonizers. But what is it? It's neither Chinese nor British in appearance. Those fucking Brits are belittling the Chinese!" He tapped his cigarette ash into the door's built-in ashtray. "Look at me. My mother was British, so I'm half Chinese. Just like this city."

His comments caused her to turn toward him. She finally understood why he had white skin despite his Asian features, thanks to his revelation.

"The war made the city confusing. Even that it ended some eight years ago, we're trying to rebuild it. Many displaced people live on the streets, in cheap wooden houses in makeshift suburbs, and on sampans." With a sigh, he continued. "Thousands of homeless people are currently fleeing the new China that was once ruled by emperors for thousands of years."

"What about me?" Laura asked, frowning. "You promised to reveal my nature."

Boss Yang watched the smoke curl from his cigarette as the vehicle ran on Waterloo Road, having just crossed Argyle Street. "You were definitely born in Italy. I assure you, it was Calabria."

Laura wasn't surprised—she'd suspected as much—but she still needed confirmation, since there was no proof of where she was born. "What else?"

"I will reveal the details in due time."

"After all this time and effort working for you, this is the lousy reward I get? That's bullshit!"

Ming heard her from the front seat beside the chauffeur, but he didn't react at all.

Boss Yang reacted with surprise, with wide eyes, but eventually nodded. He stubbed out his cigarette in the ashtray as the car drove onto busy Jordan Road. "We're going to Victoria Harbour, then taking a ferry to Aberdeen, which is where you need to be."

"What?!"

"Your place is in *Tian Chao*."

As Laura boarded the ferry, she remembered a similar route to Turkey from Cyprus with Bertha. Her memories from four years earlier were gone. Though it didn't feel like much time passed, the woman who cared for her returned with wistful memories, like a fleeting wave that soon vanished.

But there was no time for recollections.

She needed to concentrate on what Boss Yang wanted from her.

He'd already booked the ferry, so instead of its usual load of several dozen passengers, only six were aboard, besides the captain in his cabin.

As Laura watched the Hong Kong and Kowloon's distant skylines from the ferry, she spotted Ming and two men in black suits nearby engaged in an animated conversation in Cantonese difficult to understand. The many sampans and houseboats drifting on the water also caught her eye as a refreshing breeze cooled her face in the growing midday heat.

The boy watching the boat was the captain's son.

The ferry, navigating the waters between Green Island—easily spotted by its two lighthouses—and Kennedy Town, headed south.

Boss Yang approached with a paper bag and two bottles of *Green Spot* orange soda, chewing something in his mouth. Laura curiously accepted a drink and a bao-filled bread offered by him.

The snack filled her empty stomach, and the ground meat gave her a sweet taste in her mouth. She had her first taste of Chinese cuisine.

Leaning on the railing, he ate his food and drank his soda, tossing the empty bottle into the water afterwards. "The old Chinese Empire was called the Celestial Empire, or *Tian Chao*," he started the conversation. "But it is also reminiscent of ancient mythology featuring a powerful celestial emperor and his mighty warriors."

"What's this got to do with me or this city?" She asked between bites of her bao.

"There is a floating structure in Aberdeen known as *Tian* Chao. It is, surprisingly, a fighting arena, not a restaurant, as most think." He nodded. "Only wealthy people bet on the fighters, allowing the Triad to amass significant wealth and power. That's how the Jade Dragon makes most of its revenue."

"I suppose they're fucking karate fighters."

With a brief chuckle, he began, "Let me explain. During the First World War, German forces occasionally deployed unidentified chemical weapons that induced nervous collapses in soldiers. The extensive use of that chemical had a varied impact on the global population, primarily through atmospheric distribution. It's suspected, though unconfirmed, that it triggered the influenza pandemic. It passively affected many, passing down to their descendants. Until the end of the Second World War."

"What happened?"

Boss Yang gave Laura the paper bag with remaining baos to ease her hunger. Then he lit a cigarette. "The atomic bombings of Hiroshima and Nagasaki triggered some people to develop extraordinary, almost supernatural, physical and mental abilities. Only those whose blood contained the chemical were altered."

With a thoughtful look, Laura interrupted her meal, took a drink of her orange soda, then nodded in surprise. "That explains the *Merzost*!"

"Right. And you're one of them, too."

In a sudden reaction, Laura spilled her drink and dropped her buns, creating a mess on the wooden floor. "How?!" Her lips trembled as she asked.

"Don't you see how easy it is for you to learn and speak so many languages so fast? How does your intelligence surpass that of most others? Your brain makes you unique."

"What exactly is *Tian Chao*? Why do you need me there?"

"*Tian Chao* is actually an arena for overpowered fighters, not just martial artists, as you might have assumed," he let out a puff of smoke. "I'm counting on your exceptional intelligence to generate the highest profit from these bets."

Laura, startled and nervous, saw a large group of Tanka houseboats, sampans, and junks forming a floating village as she turned around. Off the Aberdeen coast, amidst a scattering of boats and a blend of mountains and buildings, a gigantic four-story wooden structure floated on the water.

The large red neon Chinese characters showed the name of *Tian Chao*, with a small English translation underneath.

The vast size amazed Laura, even though it stayed afloat. Its beauty was unconventional, even ugly in many respects, yet it was still impressive.

"This is your new home, and believe me, this is the most ambitious endeavor the Triad has ever done." As the ferry neared the boat, Boss Yang leaned on the rail. "Though it looks like a restaurant to tourists, only those with the password can enter the arena."

"What's the password?" She asked while still gazing at the jumbo boat.

"*Pukai*," he replied with a smile. "It means. . ."

"Go to hell," cutting off, she answered for him.

12
SCORPION

As the little ferry pulled into the massive *Tian Chao*, a figure awaited.

A woman in her late thirties, dressed in a red cheongsam with colorful flowers and with her black hair held up with sticks, eagerly awaited the visitors. She lit up with excitement as Boss Yang approached her after crossing the platform from the ferry to the jumbo boat. With no hesitation, he took hold of her, planting a kiss on her red lips, and also rubbed her rounded buttocks.

The sudden scene startled Laura, and she quickly whispered a question to Ming, who was in front of the other men. "Is she married to him?"

"No, Miss Laura," he whispered to her. "She is among the many women that Boss Yang maintains."

"How?"

Boss Yang, along with the woman in red, entered the ferry and interrupted Laura and Ming and pointed. "This is the girl I was telling you about."

"I see," she said, first in Cantonese, then continued in English, extending her hand and widening her eyes, but she didn't smile. "You're that Italian girl from Turkey!"

"This is Yanmu, Miss Laura," Boss Yang introduced her while placing his hand on her back. "She has our complete trust in managing this location."

"It is my pleasure," Laura responded, slightly nervous, while giving her the hand. "I suppose."

"Yanmu's been wanting an assistant for ages, and it seems like you're just the perfect fit," Boss Yang said with a nod.

"Come with me, Mui Mui!" Although they'd only just met, she grasped Laura's arm. "Let me show you your new home!"

A brief chuckle escaped Boss Yang, pleased with the manager's actions.

Laura's heart pounded, and she was reluctant to go to the *Tian Chao* at first, but Ming approached her. "Have no fear. You can count on her." A rare smile graced his lips. "I'm taking some holiday, but I'll be with you shortly."

Yanmu practically dragged Laura to the jumbo boat. After they boarded, the captain's son removed the platform, and the ferry departed with Boss Yang, Ming, and the others.

Yanmu led Laura into the floating structure.

Laura felt uneasy and disliked being in unfamiliar surroundings, especially in places like Hong Kong.

Stuck in an almost isolated, unfamiliar place, Laura could have easily swum to nearby Aberdeen, but she listened for the advice of her only confidante, Ming.

For many reasons, she had to face her uncertain future.

She was a person without a home or a place she considered her birthplace. Even that Boss Yang revealed she was from Calabria, a region she learned about from the books, though not much. However, despite her fluency in Italian—among many other languages—the Italian government wouldn't accept her, as she'd remain an outsider. Turkey's rejection stemmed from its strict policy against war refugees coupled with the widespread discrimination, so even though she lived there for years, it wouldn't be her definitive home.

The sudden adoption of the new identity—Lillian Dover, complete with a Hong Kong passport—provided a relief from her limbo, though it was for money laundering, the cited HK$11 million. It was a hidden blessing, even if it had illegal motives. Although risks were present, Ming's consistent training kept her prepared and strong.

The reality of her special abilities hadn't yet sunk in. Her remarkable aptitude for learning, especially languages and mathematics, suggested a hidden power. However, she didn't pay it any mind until he revealed her true nature.

Boss Yang stated that both the *Merzost* and she were consequences of the same chemical weapon he'd explained.

She pondered the existence of others like her, and the possibility of ever meeting them.

As Yanmu pulled her, Laura's attention shifted from the almost jarring exterior to the lavish interior. It was a luxurious restaurant featuring floral carpets, gold detailing against white walls and ceilings, sparkling crystal chandeliers, and large windows overlooking Aberdeen Harbour. Despite its size, which could accommodate a hundred round tables and chairs—though most lacked cloths, save for one—, Laura found the design oddly cramped for a boat of that scale.

The only set table Yanmu showed had sweet and sour pork, steamed fish, rice, and cups next to a ceramic teacup.

Though the table seated ten, the two women sat together, side-by-side.

"This is the restaurant everybody knows," Yanmu said as she poured tea for Laura. "Although the British authorities overlooked the ship's real purpose, certain influential and wealthy figures demanded bribes to maintain their silence." She then served her a spoonful of rice and pork from the bowls. "Hong Kong's prosperity is, in reality, fueled by a collaboration between the Jade Dragon Triad and some sectors of the colonial government."

Laura noticed the woman set out some sticks and a fork beside her plate, which she used to take her first bites. "I don't yet understand what my job is. Back in the *Bosphorus* I. . ."

"Shhh! Be quiet!" Yanmu placed her finger on Laura's lips. "No one ever brings up their past. What's done is done." Next, using chopsticks, she transferred two dumplings to her plate. "I made all this food myself, so please eat it. I used to help my mom out at her stall when I was younger."

With a mix of curiosity and nervousness, she tried the food, and a satisfied nod confirmed its deliciousness.

"I've heard all about you from Boss Yang," Yanmu continued. "I think we'll work well together."

Laura put down her fork on the half-eaten food, appearing thoughtful, then asked. "What's your relationship to Boss Yang?"

"He is my protégé and my mentor," she replied, tapping her fingers against the table and eyes glancing at the windows. "Around ten years back, those fucking Japs murdered my mother and raped me."

Laura's gasp showed surprise, yet her quietness spoke volumes of her curiosity.

"He rescued me and taught me how to fight back against those bastards. In the war's aftermath, we developed a close relationship, and he placed his trust in me."

"Is he your partner?"

"Don't misunderstand me, Mui Mui. Boss Yang's relationship is uncommitted. He uses intimacy to assess women's loyalty."

Laura was stunned to realize what kind of man Boss Yang was. She finally confirmed his immense power and influence, as she knew while in Turkey, but still couldn't explain the Triad elders' trust in him. It was appalling to see a man in his forties leading such a powerful Triad. Undoubtful, there was a reason.

"Do you know the password for that?" From across the restaurant, Yanmu drew attention to the impressive red doors, designed in the style of China's imperial past.

"*Pukai*," Laura replied with a nod.

Two women went through the entrance, down the hallway, and saw a red door at the other end with shih-tzu sculptures on each side. Despite minimal lighting, the place remained visible.

"That's where our special patrons go into the arena," Yanmu pointed, then went left, going to a nearly invisible small door that melded into the dark wall and opened it. "You'll see the arena soon. Meanwhile, we have to go in there."

Laura discovered a set of narrow stairs upwards and followed Yanmu in her climb. They stepped onto the next floor and into a narrow hallway that led to another entrance guarded by a warrior. His attire—ancient armor, a red cape, and sheathed swords—was unexpected given the assault rifle he carried, a detail that surprised her.

"We need to keep this place safe," Yanmu said, making a gesture to let them pass to the entrance. "We have our own small army, as we can't rule out the possibility of a mad fighter threatening everything." The next hallway was wider and more spacious, and she led Laura there, showing her the guards who were taking turns watching the many rusted metallic doors. "These are sleeping quarters where fighters can also eat and relax."

"Why do I feel like I'm inside a damn battleship?" Laura made an observation while studying her surroundings.

"The Japs intended to build it as an aircraft carrier, but construction halted with the war's end. So, it makes sense." She explained as she went to the next area. "The British government seized it, but Boss Yang persuaded the Triad to purchase and modify it."

They entered a spacious, well-equipped gym with an array of exercise equipment.

Laura noticed a lone man working out with a dumbbell seated on a bench. She noticed he was wearing gray sweatpants and a white shirt but was barefoot. A strange feeling stormed her as she touched her stomach, a pleasant feeling she couldn't explain. However, she found it a little unsettling.

The bald and slim man with serene blue eyes noticed two females standing beside him. As he noticed Laura, stopped exercising, wiped his sweaty face with a towel, then acknowledged her with a nod, rediscovering his large, crooked nose.

"He's one of our best fighters," Yanmu introduced. "James Trask comes from the Australian Outback."

"It's my pleasure, mate," a sweet and male voice escaped from his lips.

Overwhelmed by him, Laura could not reply.

Yanmu, noticing her silence, answered for her. "Let me introduce Laura Doncelli, my new assistant. She is originally from Turkey, but also from Italy."

James assumed a thoughtful posture before speaking. "An Italian from Turkey, or a Turk from Italy? Interesting."

"Whatever!" annoyed, Laura closed her eyes, shrugged off her irritation, pulled a cigarette from her leather jacket, and was about to light it when James snatched it away.

"Not in my presence, mate!"

Startled, Laura glared at him, with a hint of indignation in her eyes. "What do you fucking do as a fighter?!"

"They call him the *Australian Scorpion* in the arena," Yanmu said proudly. "Pain is his weapon against his opponents."

"Pain? How?" eager to smoke, Laura asked, tapping her fingers against her crossed arms.

Yanmu's gesture caused him to nod, stand from the bench, and reveal his steep stature.

James went to a nearby punching bag, stood still with closed eyes, breathed deeply, and then threw a quick blow. Astonishingly, a small luminous energy flowed from his extended hand, traversing the bag without contact, like a ghost. Seconds later, he removed his hand, leaving the bag undamaged.

"He inflicts unbearable pain without a trace, forcing opponents to surrender," Yanmu explained.

"Actually, what I did with this bag was minimal. I've learned to control the energy to avoid visible damage.

Worse yet, an uncontrolled power could wipe out this boat." While cleaning his hand with a towel, he said.

Laura disregarded him, lighting another cigarette to soothe her anxiety. "How did that happen to you?"

"It's vague, mate. I was flying near Shanghai when Hiroshima happened, and it changed my body." His eyes were sad as he let out a sigh. "I found myself on a beach after the crash, unsure of how I had survived." With his towel slung over a shoulder, James headed for the gym exit. "I'd prefer if you didn't smoke in my presence!" And then left.

13
BEAUTIFUL

Yanmu led Laura to a floor with a completely distinct style than the one before. The hallway, with windows on one side and red doors on the other, boasted an array of imperial Chinese decorations, including dragon and shih-tzu statues. "Only the most dangerous remain in this place."

"It seems like a shitting upscale location for the entitled," Laura stated, holding a cigarette in her hand. She continually scrutinized every aspect of the place. "I'm curious. Why are the most dangerous people kept in such a nice place?" She gazed through the windows at Aberdeen Harbour's vibrant sampan village, spotting two floating restaurants, insignificant next to the immense *Tian Chao*.

"To avoid arousing suspicion among our patrons, who frequently use this hallway to reach the restaurant or arena. We need to be discreet." As were both walking across the place, Yanmu replied, then halted at a double-guarded door. "Especially this one."

Laura's heart pounded inexplicably as she stared at the pointed door, as if a message was trying to reach her.

"You feel it. Right, Mui Mui?" Yanmu nodded with a smile. "Though only twelve, her psychic abilities are limitless. She is both telekinetic and telepath."

Laura stared at her in surprise, eager to learn more. "Tell me more." And she took a few more drags of her cigarette.

"We call her Mei Li, which means . . ."

"Beautiful."

"People know her as *Hallucination* within the fighting arena. The power of her mind alone crushes her opponents as her nightmarish visions paralyze them with fear."

Laura sensed her presence as a mental whisper while watching the door. She couldn't understand her, but she was talking to her. "How did she end up here?"

"When the locals found her, Boss Yang himself brought her," Yanmu replied with crossed arms. "They found her in a forest bordering Nepal, China, and India. Although many insist she's Bhutanese, her origin is unconfirmed." She then walked on after she said that. "You'll get to know our fighters with time." She waved her hand, inviting to continue. "Come, I'll show your place."

As Laura followed Yanmu, she heard whispers mentioning names of Boss Yang and the *Merzost* in her mind, arousing suspicion. Her gaze fixed on the woman ahead in her red floral cheongsam, but she said nothing.

The last floor, significantly smaller, boasted a different decorative style. While simple, the decorations maintained their Chinese aesthetic. It had no windows, just a hallway with half a dozen simple wooden doors.

Yanmu stopped, turned, and pointed. "This front room serves both as my office and sleeping quarters. It's also our business location, so any discussions should also happen there." She then gave steps to the adjacent door. "This is where you will sleep, read your books, and eat." Giving a brief nod and a few parting words, she excused herself and headed to her room. "Enjoy it, and I'll see you later, Mui Mui."

Just before entering her new room, Laura noticed the next door had a small white Japanese curtain—a noren—with an indecipherable symbol. Drawn by curiosity, she approached to admire it, but the door opened, revealing a motionless man whose eyes showed fear and distrust.

"Whatever you're planning, don't try," said the man in black robes, with a calm but strict voice. He spoke broken English. "Neighbor or not, peace is all I ask for."

"I apologize, sir. It wasn't my intention." Laura's reply reflected her feeling of being minimized before him. "I'm Laura Doncelli, and I'll be Yanmu's new assistant."

The man bowed and introduced himself. "I am Hanzo. Just another fighter, if that's what you're wondering."

"Tell me about your abilities."

"Have a good afternoon." Then he shut the door.

Laura was entering her place with dropped shoulders when Yanmu reappeared.

"He doesn't like people. However, I will answer on his behalf," she said, leaning against her door. "Unlike other fighters, he possesses no abilities but exceptional ninja and samurai skills."

"How did he come here?"

Exhausted from answering questions, Yanmu sighed with an eye roll. "To uphold his ancestors' honor, he hid himself from the Japanese Army in a South Asian jungle. Even after the war, a return to his homeland is impossible for him. Instead, he came here." Next, she folded her arms. "Do you have more questions?"

Laura watched the woman go back to her place after shaking her head.

Upon first seeing her room, Laura noted its pleasant features—a comfortable bed, desk, multilingual books, and a window with a breathtaking Aberdeen view. Yet, she focused more on the two names whispered in her mind by the unseen Mei Li.

Boss Yang and *Merzost*. What's her connection to them, and how are those two related? Laura had always considered the *Merzost* and Boss Yang to be unrelated, but a supernatural whisper sparked her suspicions.

In addition, she wondered how Boss Yang knew she was Italian.

Yet another question came to her mind.

Was his Ankara encounter with Laura planned? If so. How does she explain the sudden execution she witnessed at the *Bosphorus*?

More loose ends and heightened suspicions emerged than she initially believed.

A note from Ming awaited her at the desk. She saw her books were on the shelves and her clothes were already in the closet. Ming brought all her belongings from Turkey. She smiled.

She took her Beretta from her jacket, put it on the desk, lit a cigarette, and placed her pack of *Camels* there, too. She pulled the ceramic ashtray decorated with dragons and tigers closer.

Laura made a promise to herself. She committed to uncovering the truth, no matter the sacrifices, to pursue every lead, even if it meant deception.

14
ARENA

Every Friday, the arena hosted fights, and Laura, between trainings under her mentor and boss, Yanmu, spent the entire week preparing for her first time. Although six days had passed since her arrival in Hong Kong, she hadn't had a moment to herself, not even to adjust to the different sleeping times compared with Turkey.

Her rhythm had been hectic. With rushed meals and short, nightmare-filled sleeps, she was awake most nights, catching only daytime naps. Yanmu had altered her schedule because, she alleged, most of her work was at night. As she was on Turkish time, she felt no pressure about the exact hour.

The day after she arrived, the sheer scale of the floating complex amazed Laura as she saw the arena within the

Tian Chao for the first time. It resembled a miniature indoor stadium. Though small, the elegantly decorated space, with its Chinese elements, could easily hold over two hundred spectators, according to Yanmu. The oval fighting ring was deep enough to give everyone a clear view of the fights, with ample space for two fighters to move around freely. There was a gate underneath, typically closed, leading to a tunnel and a chamber beside the gym, and metal walls surrounded the ring.

Reserved for important figures—Boss Yang and his crew, Triad elders, and British colonial officials—was the section just above the aforementioned gate. While the other seats were open to the public, the audience was affluent as they could wager with considerable sums of money.

Laura's strenuous training revealed that guards in traditional uniforms and carrying automatic weapons escorted the fighters to the arena. Yanmu sometimes accompanied a few of them.

Laura had the chance to meet some other fighters who were in the massive floating building. However, some she couldn't meet personally and was told to wait for their turn in the arena.

She also observed a dozen men—Triad accountants—eating at the adjacent restaurant early Friday afternoon, before the fight. Next, at Yanmu's office, they'd set up a system to collect and organize the betting money. Then they would deliver the bulk to the Triad, keeping a minor cut for Yanmu and her people at the *Tian Chao*.

After dinner, the accountants went into the office while Laura waited outside. Boss Yang arrived and stopped before her.

"It's good seeing you again, Miss Laura," he said with an ominous smile that concerned her, and tipped his hat. "Yanmu tells me you're doing a great job!"

Laura nodded her thanks, and for the first time, she looked at him differently. Mei Li's whispers changed her impression of him from what it had been in Turkey. "About that money under the name of Lillian . . . ," she murmured.

"Not now!" he muttered back. "I'm afraid the money is on hold for a while. The Bank of South Seas is under investigation by the International Police and Scotland Yard," he replied with discretion. "I'm adding funds to your account to keep it active and discreet before we close and retrieve it."

Boss Yang cut off the conversation when Yanmu called him from her office.

Yanmu, aware of Laura's experience as a hostess in Turkey, employed her in the same role to welcome the special patrons.

Because of that, Laura had to put on another outfit that she disliked. She had a blue silk cheongsam, tailored by a city woman, adorned with flowers. She also struggled to pin her wavy and chaotic hair with sticks.

Boss Yang, with two elders deep in conversation about their bets and ignoring her, was the first to arrive at the special section without a word. They already knew their usual seats, so they didn't need her. She figured the elders belonged to the Triad because she saw their bodyguards nearby.

Laura suspected with her discreet yet constant gaze of Boss Yang because of the whispers and the ongoing bank investigation he'd mentioned, which she speculated meant he was in serious trouble.

Yanmu approached in an instant and spoke into her ear. "Please be kind to these gentlemen, but be watchful of their requests," she said, pointing to a group of British men just arriving.

Laura nodded in agreement with her suggestion.

The first man in a group of five, including an admiral, greeted her. "To whom do I got the pleasure of speaking?" He was a man in his sixties, of average build, whose black hair was turning gray.

"I'm just the hostess, taking you to your assigned seats," Laura said with kindness and uneasiness. She then called a waiter to take their order . "Serve whatever they want."

Boss Yang, seated in the next row from the British men, called for her. "Please make sure he is comfortable. He is the governor, Sir Daniel Whaley, and some of his cabinet," he murmured to her.

She nodded, realizing the significance of the Triad's ties to the British government.

Laura excused herself from Boss Yang to greet more guests. She saw that the reserved section was for entrepreneurs, entertainers, investors, and other influential people. While most were locals, there were a few foreigners, mainly from Britain and the United States.

A small band carrying their instruments headed to an open chamber on the upper level. Yanmu's rush startled her as she led them.

Laura observed the five musicians—all Britons—preparing their instruments in a hurry: a large drum, two clarinets, a trumpet, and cymbals.

Yanmu rushed them to prepare, eager to make a favorable impression, notably on the colonial government. "The band usually performs at the Jockey Club for British crowds only, but the governor made an exception, requesting their appearance at the *Tian Chao* for this single event." She said in an agitated voice.

"Why is this event so special?"

"Mui Mui, read that paper in your hand!" she replied in a rushed and irritated tone.

Laura inspected the mimeographed sheet she held, given to spectators by accountants as they collected initial bets. She noticed the schedule of fights in an upcoming tournament featuring supernatural combatants.

Yanmu had mentioned that the weekly arena battles rarely featured the most powerful fighters because of their unique, potent level. However, this week's event was exceptional, with both the named *Fireman* and Mei Li taking part.

The event, if not illicit, would be excellent local news. Ten years ago, amid the war, the existence of such powerful individuals was unknown. The Jade Dragon Triad elders and the British governor intentionally scheduled the special tournament for Labour Day.

As Boss Yang explained, Hiroshima appeared to have spurred the rise of these unique people, including Laura.

With a wave of his hand, the impatient Boss Yang directed Yanmu, who then commanded a musician. Then, a trumpet's blare silenced the crowd.

Scores of Chinese warriors, draped in ancient attire and armed with automatic weapons, surrounded the area with haste, particularly the ring, creating a tense and surprising moment. The spectators, however, received a warning about themselves.

In a black tuxedo, the announcer stepped into the ring's center, greeting the crowd with jokes before the introductions.

Yanmu whispered to Laura, "Go to the gate and wait there. Do what I said!"

Laura nodded, then hurried past the warriors and all the other sections to reach the gate.

"And now, introducing our first combatants!" the announcer shouted. "First, we welcome a master swordsman and knife maker from the Kingdom of Siam! Blades!"

On the opposite side of the ring from Laura, a half-naked slender man, attired only in a gold skirt, performed impressive sword maneuvers. Then he came to a stop and waited.

"His opponent hails from the land of volcanoes. Let's welcome the Fireman!"

A sudden rumble from deep within the tunnel startled Laura. Four guards wheeled a small, heavy steel and aluminum cube toward the ring, forcing her to step aside. As the public caught sight of it, the arena was once more still, punctuated by exclamations.

A warrior opened the heavy cube door and moved aside.

A gleaming red man, like molten metal, emerged naked to the audience's awed gasps.

Concerned, Boss Yang stood and leaned against the rail to call Laura, who remained in the ring. "Take the stairs and come with me!"

Though still awestruck by the Fireman's uncanny aura, she climbed the stairs as instructed. Laura trailed Boss Yang, but stood by the Triad elders to watch the first fight.

Dressed up in a Chinese-style outfit of a white shirt and black pants, the referee signaled the start.

The combat began with the impact of a gong.

Yet, the Fireman stood still, his face lowered, and stared at the ground.

The Siamese swordsman, craving the spotlight, performed his usual dazzling blade act, eager to begin the fight.

For a long time, the fiery figure stood still, giving Blades the opportunity to execute a dramatic sword maneuver aimed at intimidating him.

When Fireman saw his opponent approach, he fixed his opponent with a stare and grabbed his face with his flaming hand.

A pained scream escaped his lips as his weapons clattered to the ground, crouching. He covered his severely scarred face as the crowd noticed the fresh and irreparable wounds.

Laura, both impressed and horrified, saw Boss Yang subtly nod to the referee from his seat among the elders.

In response, the referee drew a gun, firing two shots into Blades' head, resulting in immediate death.

Back inside his cube, Fireman was locked in by a guard after closing the door.

Once the metallic cube reappeared from the tunnel, some servants collected and disposed of the dead Siamese.

Some of the crowd applauded as the accountants disbursed the winnings.

As though nothing had occurred, everyone went back to enjoy their drinks and chat.

While talking with an elder, Boss Yang had to excuse himself. He discovered Laura sitting pale on a step and went over to her. "What's wrong?"

She stared up at him with anger and disappointment. "So, this is the fucking reason you brought me here?!" She had wide, moist eyes when she yelled. "Is that how you treat the defeated—like fucking animals, ordering their damned executions?!"

He sat on the step beside her, shook his head, and offered a cigarette to soothe her nerves. She accepted and lit it from him. "We must execute only those with irreversible damage. You can be sure Blades will return home to his family with his honor restored."

Laura inhaled deeply, with the half-smoked cigarette shaking in her hands, closed her eyes, and then, more composed, looked into his eyes. "You are a darned asshole!" she stood up.

"Where are you fucking going?"

"I'm going down to the fucking gate!" she exclaimed. "Don't you want me to do this shitting job?!"

As she left in her blue-flowered cheongsam, he smiled and lit a cigarette.

15
RING

The second fight of the night was over. Pantera, an African from Spain, confronted Samurai, also known as Hanzo.

The Japanese swordsman defeated the powerfully built dark man. Following an intense duel involving swordplay and evasion, Pantera suffered a nerve-damaging cut to his left shoulder, leading to an immobile arm. The Spaniard knelt, recognizing his defeat.

Perched on the steps down to the ring, Laura awaited the referee's decision, terrified he might pull out his gun and execute the defeated. To her astonishment, a nurse and other servants aided the bloodied Pantera while leaving the ring.

Yanmu sat down next to her and wrapped her arms around her legs. "Mui Mui, I know how disappointed and scared you were after that first fight," she said calmly, avoiding eye contact. "Unlike Blades, Pantera will recover at a Kowloon clinic before returning to fighting."

Laura nodded at her mentor, accepting, despite her disapproval, the fighters' roles and the meaning of their tournament. "What is the winner's prize?"

"The winner gets some monetary compensation, and freedom to go anywhere for a day."

"The winners deserve better than this shit!"

"Remember, most of our fighters belong to the Triad. They have no rights of their own." Yanmu stated. "Let's get moving. Mei Li needs to get ready for the next fight, and a surprise is waiting for you."

Laura realized she needed to accompany Yanmu to the middle level, which boasted a sumptuous hallway with windows showing Aberdeen at night, and heavily featured Chinese decor. Only warriors could access that area as it was closed to visitors momentarily.

Laura saw a familiar figure in a black suit at Mei Li's doors. She recognized Ming and ran into his arms as he turned. His reaction was like a parent embracing his daughter.

He pushed her away gently, ending the emotional moment that had lasted only seconds.

Laura knew Ming wasn't the type to show affection.

"I've had a conversation with Boss Yang about not leaving your side, Miss Laura, and he's also instructed me to handle the security of *Tian Chao*," he announced.

Laura nodded with a smile she couldn't hide. Despite their sinister first encounter in Turkey, she felt an inexplicable connection to him from the start.

"Let's focus on Mei Li, ladies," he suggested as four warriors approached.

Merzost and Boss Yang's names resurfaced in her mind. Laura knew she was trying to tell her something again. Her persistence grew stronger every time she was in the hallway.

"Please look at her feet, avoid her eyes at all costs, and try to keep your thoughts empty," Yanmu warned everyone before unveiling a wall-sized golden and scarlet vault in the anteroom. From beneath her red clothing, she pulled an antique key, a signal for the warriors to prepare their automatic weapons and position themselves beside it. She unlocked and opened it, then glanced at the carpet as she took a few steps back.

As required, Laura, Ming, and the warriors glared downward. The first thing to catch her eye was her small feet, wrapped in black slippers, visible at the bottom of her dark pants. Her anxiety grew with each step Mei Li took.

Yanmu ended up following the warriors as they escorted her out of the room.

However, Mei Li halted directly in front of Laura.

Laura, afraid, kept her eyes glued to her feet. Though tempted to look up, she resisted.

"Be careful of them," Mei Li spoke to Laura through her mind, but no words exited from her mouth. "It is not what it seems." Then she proceeded down the hallway toward the ring.

The Triad's accountants, who handled the bets, gave out blindfolds to the arena audience with instructions to cover their eyes. They had already received a warning about Mei Li's dominant power.

Mei Li went down the tunnel, the same one Fireman had used earlier inside his metallic cube. Guards and others followed behind her.

Ming and Laura were also both trailing.

Though she shouldn't, Laura discreetly glanced at Mei Li from a distance. She saw a small, thin girl, remembering Yanmu had mentioned she was only twelve. Laura then looked down again.

Silence fell as everyone waited just before the ring.

"Let's welcome the Tiger from Malaysia!" the announcer informed the public.

The audience applauded.

"And over here, we have Hallucination!"

Silence.

Mei Li stepped into the ring, and the door closed behind her.

Startled, Laura stared at Yanmu behind her, wondering why everyone remained in the tunnel. "Why are we waiting here?"

"Believe me, Mui Mui. It is best that way."

Ming touched her shoulder and, pressing a finger to his lips and whispered. "Be quiet!"

Silence again. The gas lamps in the tunnel were mysteriously dimming, descending the tunnel into darkness.

A sense of fear gripped everyone inside, notably Laura, who was unfamiliar with such emotions in this special circumstance.

The fight seemed imminent, yet an eerie calm descended.

The rolling eyes and tense wait were a burden from the air, as a distinct tension broke with unspoken words.

A scream filled with raw terror came from the ring.

"It's over," Yanmu whispered with widened eyes. "With Tiger's defeat, Mei Li is returning to her quarters."

Everyone complied, looking down as the small girl walked back through the tunnel.

Laura noticed the vault secured with Yanmu's key. Then left, as the doors were closed behind her, and returned to the elegant hallway.

The four warriors resumed their duties.

"Mui Mui, you'll be handling the next match fighters." Yanmu mandated with a slight smile. "I know you can do it." With her departure, Laura and Ming found themselves alone.

Again, Mei Li talked in Laura's mind. "Boss Yang, *Merzost!*"

Laura's wide eyes darted between the closed doors and Ming, who instantly sensed something.

"What's troubling you?" Given his close work with Boss Yang and specialized training, Ming could easily detect if something was amiss from an expression alone. This was his job as an escort, and under specific conditions, executing people. Despite this, his expression remained unchanged as he studied her.

"Can I trust you?" she asked with shivering voice. "Please promise you'll keep our conversation between us."

As was his habit, Ming remained frozen and silent before speaking. "Tell me," he replied with a nod.

"Mei Li. . . Hallucination. She's warning me about Boss Yang and the *Merzost*. But I have my doubts."

Ming didn't seem surprised by her words and nodded again.

"It seems like you're hiding something," Laura stated in a serious tone. "Do you know anything about this?"

"It's uncertain whether Boss Yang knew about the *Merzost*. You shouldn't disregard the possibility, considering his biochemistry studies at Cambridge. Yes, he's a scientist who, even before the war, scouted the globe for people with potential extraordinary abilities."

Surprised, Laura lit a cigarette. "Were you aware that I am from Calabria, Italy?"

After a pause, Ming replied. "Yes."

With a rhythmic nod, she exhaled a plume of smoke. "What else do you know about me?"

"You were born on October 30, 1935. The afternoon you arrived in Monticelli was still hot, according to Boss Yang." A mask of impassivity covered his features, yet sweat betrayed his composure. "You'll soon be 18."

"In Turkey, with that shitting *Bosphorus*, I suspected you knew something but was hesitant to ask. I waited to hear it from Boss Yang." With another exhale of smoke, she went on. "As we were binding, I wish you'd told me then instead of keeping it to yourself."

"My apologies, Miss Laura. I was just following orders. . ."

"No. . ." She interrupted. "You are a bastard. Fuck you!" Laura tossed her cigarette on the floor and hurried off, leaving Ming by himself.

16
ATAKOBAT

L aura went to the gym at Yanmu's request, and there she found James Trask, relaxed and barefoot, seated on a bench, wearing only dazzling silver pants.

His blue eyes followed her as she came into the place. "I've seen you only three times since you arrived, and you look splendid in your Chinese garb rather than that bloke attire you had, mate." A subtle smile appeared.

"Knock it off with the damn flattery!" she replied, annoyed. His proximity made her uneasy during their only two encounters. "Time to fight! Don't make your opponent wait."

"My opponent is right there!" he pointed to a corner.

Laura spun around to see a very muscular man in a fake leopard-print outfit. His hairy chest and powerful muscles were visible as he lifted weights. He gave her a nod of greeting. "You're the Italian from Turkey."

"As you've seen, Bubba Carson is more an entertainer than a fighter," James explained. "Like me, the Hiroshima thingo also affected him. He was only a scrawny fellow from Liverpool, and by the next day he became strong as a Hercules."

"Why are you an entertainer?" Confused, Laura scratched her head.

As if they were feathers, Bubba put the heavy weights down and looked at her. "I joined the circus. But to earn extra money, I travel half the world for a match."

"Alright, guys." Laura impatiently exclaimed. "Don't keep Yanmu waiting."

Separated from the Triad's elders, Boss Yang sat well behind Governor Whaley's party, having reserved two seats—one for Yanmu, who sat to his left, and whom he touched affectionately despite her apathy. Much later, Laura took a seat on the other side. Then, unexpectedly, he touched her hand as if she were one of his women.

Despite wanting to withdraw her hand, Laura stayed put for reasons of her own.

Though many in the crowd remained stunned by Mei Li and the Tiger's previous fight, some stood eagerly awaiting the next match. Amidst drinks and cigarettes, spectators exchanged sadistic jokes about the fighters.

"Are they ready, Miss Laura?" Boss Yang asked in a whisper.

"Yes, they are," she replied, glancing away. Her hand remained in his.

The announcer entered the ring, and the crowd, quieting down, returned to their seats.

Yanmu's observation of Boss Yang interacting with Laura revealed a hint of jealousy. Determined to confront them, she was about to rise when a servant approached, causing to interrupt her intentions. "A gentleman is requesting a meeting with Boss Yang at the restaurant."

"Seriously? Who goes to a restaurant now, during all these fucking fights?" She replied, annoyed. "Tell him it's not the damn right time!"

"We informed him of that, but he persists."

"I will deal with that bastard myself!" Agitated, Yanmu rose and departed with the servant.

From where she was, Laura witnessed the exchange between Yanmu and the servant, noting Boss Yang's insensitivity as he waited for the announcer in the ring. She watched Yanmu pull a small, possibly silver, whistle from her pocket with no one noticing but her.

Yet, she felt uncomfortable with the way he touched her hand.

A loud, mysterious ringing, accompanied by fear, filled her head.

"We have on this side the Strongman from Liverpool! Bubba Carson!"

Despite her disgust at his touch and the inexplicable dread, Laura remained discreet.

"Next up from the Outback, the Australian Scorpion!" the announcer added.

The referee stepped into the ring to start the fight.

Out of nowhere, a booming sound and violent shaking came as the dust filled the arena, catching everyone off guard and resulting in a brief power outage. Panic quickly invaded everyone as the lights returned.

From her standing position, Laura spotted behind her a large, destructive hole from the restaurant. She found many injured and covered in blood people whose cries for help were in vain.

Boss Yang's reaction was to run to the place where the explosion occurred. The warriors and escorts trailed him.

Governor Whaley, rattled by the event's impact, hastily evacuated the arena, fleeing the *Tian Chao* with his entourage. The Triad's elders did the same.

Laura, who coughed from the dust, drew her Beretta from beneath her cheongsam and aimed it at an approaching man, believing she was under attack. To her astonishment, she recognized him.

"Are you all right, Miss Laura?" Ming asked.

Unsure whether to rebuke or express gratitude, she stared at him. "Let's go to the restaurant."

Amid the chaos of the arena, as panicked spectators scrambled for any boat—even water taxis—to escape the Tian Chao, Laura and Ming attempted to reach the restaurant. Despite their efforts, the warriors' attempts to control the people through force proved insufficient.

James Trask, the Australian Scorpion, caught Laura before she fell, saving her from an unexpected tumble. "I've got you, mate!"

Laura regained her balance, then noticed a woman's lifeless body below. The frenzied crowd, not the explosion, clearly caused her death.

Ming noticed that although the restaurant only had one narrow exit—making escape nearly impossible—most people got out through the hole blown in the wall. Still, it was impassable.

For a mere two seconds, Laura found safety in the Scorpion's embrace. But she prioritized finding out what caused the blast and separated from James.

She battled through the chaotic crowd, finding it impossible to pass with James and Ming behind her.

Bubba Carson, the Strongman, intervened and used his incredible strength to part the crowd, allowing them to cross.

Laura and her companions could finally reach the wrecked restaurant.

By the time Laura and her group reached their destination, the majority had fled. Both the explosion and the frenzied crowd devastated the restaurant. Broken chairs, battered tables and shattered windows.

With her Beretta in hand, Laura scanned while the warriors searched in the rubble and spotted Boss Yang at the kitchen entrance. She approached him, concerned.

Boss Yang's first reaction to the charred and wrecked kitchen was a silent assessment of the damaged appliances and distorted utensils. "It was he."

"Who?" Laura asked suspiciously. The four men behind also awaited the answer.

A creak from the spacious, dilapidated kitchen interrupted his reply, prompting Laura, Boss Yang, Ming, with their guns in their hands, to enter with caution. Inside, they saw charred body parts amidst the debris, but continued to search for the source of the noise.

James noticed a heavy section of the vent hood's metal moving and pointed it.

Bubba approached and lifted the piece with ease.

Yanmu was under. A pool of blood formed beneath her. She was shocked. Her face blackened, her red cheongsam torn, and her right arm missing. "I fucking tried!" she cried out, with widened eyes. "I tried to stop him, but he tore my arm and disconnected the damn gas pipe!"

In a rare act of compassion, Boss Yang made a tourniquet with his belt to staunch the bleeding from Yanmu's severed limb, gently lifting the almost unconscious and pale woman and carrying her out of the ravaged kitchen. "Don't worry. Everything will be fine."

Horribly surprised, James asked, shaking his head. "This kitchen is a dog's breakfast. Who made that mess?"

"The answer is there," Laura pointed to a blood-red hammer and sickle painted on an undamaged wall—the

Soviet emblem—as a mangled arm lay nearby on the floor.

"The *Merzost*."

17

DOSSIER

Governor Sir Daniel Whaley began his substantial breakfast with a piece of fried bacon, followed by beans, scrambled eggs, mushrooms, and browned tomatoes. As he took a sip of tea, his distrustful blue eyes flickered to the visitors seated opposite him at the round table.

Boss Yang and Laura sat in tense silence at the bare side of the table. No one offered them breakfast. Ming stood in a corner nearby in the same room.

The governor, setting down his teacup, remarked, "You must be wondering why I have summoned you, aren't you?"

"I believe it's about that incident from a month ago," with deep seriousness, Boss Yang responded.

"Exactly!" His tone was somewhere between sarcastic and annoyed. "That awful explosion nearly exposed me!"

Laura discreetly observed her surroundings while listening to him. The room was spacious, featuring attractive carpeting, white walls, garden views, and a framed portrait of the young queen behind Sir Whaley.

"I apologize for the inconvenience, sir. It. . . "

The governor slammed his fist on the table, interrupting Boss Yang and surprising everyone. "Bollocks!" Alerted by the commotion, his assistant entered and examined the room. The governor offered an excuse, claiming everything was fine. With the assistant gone again, Sir Whaley continued his lecture, maintaining his composure but not his tone. "You broke your promise of safety during the fights. You failed to protect us! How in the hell will I explain to the families of the dead Britons from that night?"

"I've got no words, sir," unseen by anyone but Laura, Boss Yang clenched his fists under the table as he responded. Caught between the Triad's elders and the Bank of South Seas investigation, he despised his subordinate position to a foreign man ruling his city. He had no choice but to obey to keep everything under control.

The governor retrieved a thick dossier from an empty chair and placed it on the table's bare side, directly in front of his uneasy visitors. "Though I shouldn't have, I asked for it after the queen and prime minister launched an investigation, and I consulted a friend at MI6."

"What is it?" Boss Yang inquired, clueless.

"The information about that. . . Soviet menace," he responded after taking a last sip of his tea. "I have to get ready for the Queen's Celebrations. I hope this helps you catch the bastard. But if you cannot keep my name clean, I will bloody expose everything and you will end up in prison, Michael Yang!" Sir Whaley quickly rose and departed.

Once the governor left, Boss Yang swiftly looked through the dossier's images and papers, then handed it to Laura. "I have a lot on my plate at the moment. You take Ming and that Scorpion to help with this." He got up from where he was sitting.

"It's not Scorpion. It's James!" she gave a strict correction.

"Whatever!" He opened the door. "I'll go see Yanmu and check on her," and left.

Ming took a seat in Boss Yang's chair.

Unconcerned about his nearness, Laura continued examining the dossier's contents. Ming's genuine concern after the blast, despite their unsettling conversation, strengthened her trust in him. "The *Tian Chao* explosion is officially being presented to the public as a kitchen accident. In that way, they can explain the deaths. Apart from MI6, the arena, the fights, and *Merzost* are not mentioned." She assumed a thoughtful pose. "It's like wanting to hide something or somebody."

"Miss Laura, where shall we begin?"

She looked him straight in the eye after closing the dossier. "I don't trust Boss Yang. Although he says he's going to Yanmu, watch him. I want to know what he's doing," she sighed. "His position in the Triad is in jeopardy, and his behavior has changed. I worry about the consequences of his actions."

Ming got up with a nod, leaving her alone.

Laura sighed, shrugged, lit a cigarette, and stared at the queen's portrait, lost in thought.

Laura walked out of Government House, crossed the gardens, and left the grounds under the watchful eyes of several guards. She tucked the dossier under her arm, opting for a light shirt instead of a jacket to beat the summer heat, but kept her pants and boots on.

She aimed to meet someone by Statue Square and wanted a taxi—or a rickshaw would do—but the flocks of people attending the queen's coronation celebrations, with many children carrying British and Hong Kong small paper flags, made it difficult. Laura had trouble finding transportation even after reaching Lower Albert Road.

She soon located a green taxi and got in, only to be warned by the driver that the fare would be three times the normal rate. Laura accepted the cost without complaint.

Even though it was only four long blocks, the vehicle had difficulty navigating the narrow, crowded streets. It stopped about a hundred feet from her destination because police in brown uniforms—shirts and shorts—were blocking the way as the British forces were preparing for a ceremony in the square.

Laura paid and continued walking. Within five minutes, she arrived at *The Roo*, an Australian pub in a secluded alley off the familiar Bank Road. Dozens of curious men stared at her as she entered the pub, making her feel somewhat uneasy. James waved to her from his high chair at the counter.

She made her way through the crowd of men and tables to sit next to him. Australian flags and icons heavily decorated the place, partly obscured by smoke, with music and chatter filling the air. Although it was early, the place was bustling. She assumed it was because of the festivities.

James gave a quick nod and took a sip of his *Toohey's* beer. "How about a coldie, mate?" as his blue eyes caught her putting the brown MI6 dossier on the counter, he asked, holding up his bottle.

Instead of answering, Laura asked the bartender for a non-alcoholic lemonade. "I thought you hated the smoke!"

"I wish I didn't have to, but I can't avoid places like this," he murmured, sipping his beer. "What is this thingo?" he asked as his fingers drummed the dossier.

Laura sipped her lemonade through a straw, and then she gave him the file. "Look, it's about the *Merzost*."

James opened it and reviewed every document, noting that although most were in English, several were in Russian and Turkish. He noticed one particular detail as he read the paper. "According to this, mate. A Cambridge scientist, who had spent years in Siberia, conducted extensive experiments on *Merzost*, whose birth name remains confidential."

"That's definitely Boss Yang," Laura said, sipping her drink. "Ming revealed he's a Cambridge biochemist."

"Bilmey!"

As Laura lit a cigarette, she asked. "How did you meet him?"

"I said, no smoking near me!"

"Yet you are in a place of smokers!" she slammed the counter, annoyed. "Stop being a damn dork and answer the fucking question!"

He stared at her with his blue eyes, drained his Tooheys, and then asked the bartender for another. "We Aussie pilots knew a legend about a Japanese fighter that would attack and then magically disappear into the clouds. We called him *Ghost*." He paid for his beer, took a sip, and then proceeded. "As morning broke, I was on a routine flight over New Guinea in my Mustang. Out of the blue, the same Ghost began pursuing me, forcing me to evade him as his Zero opened fire."

"Please keep going," Laura said with a lot of attentiveness.

"The chase continued for some time, but once we flew into a thick cloud bank, the Ghost vanished as mysteriously as it had mentioned in the legend," the deeper he got into his story, the more frequently he sipped his drink, as a certain anxiety increased. "Then, a fiery second sun flashed on the horizon. I didn't realize at the time it was the Hiroshima thingo. Moments later, a surge of energy emanated from my hands, causing my plane's engines to fail and sending it into a freefall. I ejected and landed by parachute on an Indonesian island, losing consciousness upon landing."

"But how did Boss Yang find you? I am still waiting for that damn answer."

"I was rescued by fishermen, yet my uncontrolled abilities caused harm, even killing an elder. They expelled me, leaving me to fend for myself in an unfamiliar place." He drank even more frequently. "I remember lying hairless on the beach, awaiting death as my internal fire had burned away my hair. Then, a stranger appeared. He introduced himself as Boss Yang and proposed a more promising future for me in Hong Kong." He sighed. "The condition was that I had to abandon my former life in the Outback, leaving behind my parents and siblings, and even my beloved fiancée who awaited my return." He concluded his story with a tap on the dossier. "I am a dead man now."

Laura's heart ached as she saw his humid blue eyes, prompting her to touch his left cheek in a gesture of sympathy.

A man rushed in with an announcement. "The festivities are about to start!"

Almost all the pub's patrons soon left.

A silent nod passed between James and Laura as they looked at each other. As she closed and took the dossier, they stepped outside to watch the festivities.

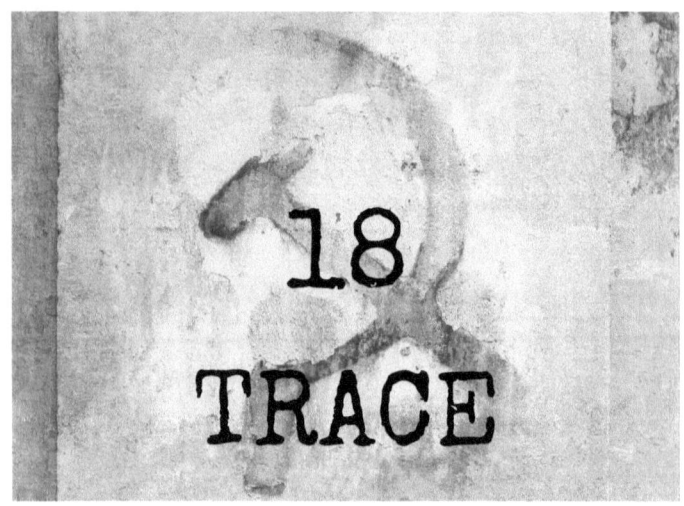

18
TRACE

I n meditation, she gazed out the window at Aberdeen bathed in the midday sun, a cigarette consumed in her hand while she crossed her arms. She pondered *Merzost's* motives. His recent trip from Istanbul to Hong Kong, and his decision to target the *Tian Chao*.

Laura turned and saw her unmade bed sprinkled with the MI6 dossier documents and photos Sir Whaley had given a month before. She nodded, grabbed a brown ballpoint pen, and scribbled some Turkish notes in her partially completed leather journal. She stopped for a moment, gathered her thoughts, placed her cigarette in the ashtray on her desk, and departed.

As Laura closed the door behind her, she looked at Yanmu's office and room. Over two months after the kitchen explosion, she was still in Kowloon.

While her arm's limb healed, Yanmu's most serious wounds were mental. The memory of her encounter with the *Merzost* still haunted her.

Despite taking charge of the *Tian Chao*, Boss Yang's frequent absences left Laura, Ming, and several trusted fighters in temporary control. His position as head of the Jade Dragon Triad was uncertain as the elders debated his continued leadership. The fate of the Triad would be determined by a council of worldwide elders later in the year.

Laura hurried through a small door and down a spiral staircase to the lowest level. The restaurant.

She arrived to find the place remodeled, with new carpets and decorations. In a corner were the new tables and chairs, stacked and covered with white sheets. The workers seamlessly replaced the wall separating the arena and restaurant. She entered the kitchen to find renovations still underway. The Japanese Hanzo, the mastermind of the new restaurant renovations, was overseeing the work, and James, with the help of the servants and Ming, was putting appliances together.

"How ya going, mate?" James said as he noticed her.

"Got it, James!" she replied to him with a voice filled with enthusiasm. "Please accompany me to Aberdeen. See you on the deck." And she was gone in an instant.

James scratched his bald head with a surprised expression on his face. "What's going on?"

"Women!" Hanzo responded, focusing on the blueprint in his hands.

With James and Laura on board, Ming expected his motorboat to reach the harbor soon.

"Explain to me why we are heading there," James asked, observing Laura's concentration on her journal. The breeze prompted him to assess their proximity to the harbour. He soon realized the half-empty docks were part of the recently opened fish market.

Laura shut her journal and looked at the floating village junks and sampans, but she was looking away from the destination. "I'm still baffled that the supposedly fucking intelligent MI6 agents overlooked this. Everything is in the dossier!"

"Whaddya mean?"

"The docks we're headed to," she said with a nod. "The fish market photos show differences, with a boat missing in the picture taken the day after the explosion, which was reported to the police."

"I getcha," James agreed with Laura's statement. "The *Merzost* stole a boat to reach the *Tian Chao*."

"Yes, we'll begin our investigation at the fish market, tracing his earlier locations. That way, we can determine his activities and predict his next moves."

"All that month for it? I expected you to be cleverer and figure it out earlier."

"If you mistreat her again, you'll face my damn rage!" Ming made threats while operating the boat.

"My apologies!" James exclaimed, raising his hands.

Laura, engrossed in her journal, spoke to Ming while reviewing her notes. "Don't listen to this baldy. He may be a tool, but had done a great job with the *Tian Chao*."

In disbelief, James abruptly returned to the topic of conversation. "What was the motive?"

With a glance at him, she closed her journal. "I feel he was carrying out a mission. To divert our attention from his real aim, he drew a hammer and sickle in the kitchen. But I doubt he fulfilled his purpose."

"I thought he might be a spy working for the Soviet Union."

"He was once Stalin's favorite secret weapon." Her eyes widened as she replied, glancing toward the fish market docks. "He's an abomination that keeps me awake at night."

Upon reaching the fish market, Laura instructed Ming to go back to the *Tian Chao* and look after Mei Li, who remained confined to her room. She also asked him not to wait for her and James.

Laura assured him they would return on their own.

They found the fish market nearly deserted when they arrived. Almost all vendors had departed, leaving only a few cleaners to clean up and dispose of trash in large bins before hosing the floors.

"What's here? I doubt we'll find anything, especially after a month."

"Sh! Be quiet," Laura urged. Glancing around, she paused, her gaze fixing on a point, then nodded. "That aged homeless man." Her finger gestured toward a low, wooden shack lacking a door almost outside the market, near the docks. An elderly Tanka man sat inside, eating what looked like rice and fish from a chipped bowl. "He knows!" She gave a HK$50 bill to the trembling elder as she approached him. Next, Laura's improved Cantonese, honed during two months in Hong Kong, was clear in her impressive speech.

Dazed, James looked on as Laura and the elder held a conversation he couldn't understand.

With a word of thanks, she turned away. As she left the fish market, she explained to James, who was right behind her. "He vividly recalls that night's *Merzost*. He described him as a dark figure who stole the boat. Although the elder explained it to the police several times, they wouldn't believe him."

"Did you find that out from the dossier?"

"The police report notes a witness deemed unreliable but omits his name." Laura replied as she rushed out of the market. "The photographs revealed a small wooden shack, which I recognized as the sole witness's dwelling." Though few, Laura looked among the trucks, cars, taxis, and rickshaws lined Praya Road by the market.

"What are you looking for?"

"Lei, a rickshaw puller," she kept scanning around. "The elder says the *Merzost* came by rickshaw earlier that night. Lei's rickshaw remains parked here until the evening, and he occasionally helps the elder with meals or refreshments."

The rickshaw pullers greeted James and Laura with distrust. When they approached the line of rickshaws, the drivers turned their backs. Laura's Cantonese surprised almost everyone she spoke to.

"I refuse to talk to anyone!" a puller in his forties replied in English. "We want nothing more to do with the bloody police!"

"Sir, we're not police officers," her voice was calm as she said it. "The fatalities are the sole reason James and I are focused on resolving this."

"What fatalities? Report it to the police! I am only a puller!"

Laura gave the man a thorough look and then nodded. "You are Lei."

"What do you want, miss? I am not in the position to answer your bloody questions!" he said, with the other pullers witnessing.

Laura used her arm to restrain James from using violence. "Is it possible to have a private conversation? The old man in the shack said you could help us."

Following a moment of hesitation, Lei nodded to both James and Laura. He guided them to an unpopulated small outdoor spot by the market, far from the people. He pulled a pack of Marlboro from his shirt pocket, took a cigarette, and offered them. Only Laura took one, and Lei lit both smokes.

"There is this man, whose accent is quite thick, used to give me jobs most days. I would meet Ilya at the Tiger Balm Garden. Eight in the morning, sharp." Lei whispered.

"Do you still see him?" after a puff of smoke, Laura inquired.

He replied with a shake of his head. "Not anymore."

"What sort of work did he offer you?" James asked pensively. "Were these illicit?"

"He'd always give me a list of wanted fish, plus money, for himself and his colleagues. To get everything on the list, I'd travel twenty kilometers a day in my rickshaw to the market and back." He breathed out a puff of tobacco. "When he asked me to bring that ominous man in black for that specific night, I stopped working for him the next day." His eyes widened as he shook his head. "The faceless, voiceless demon gave me a horrid dread."

"Faceless? Like an erased face?" James asked with skepticism.

"He always covered his face, sir. He wore a black gabardine."

"Is Ilya always at that location?" she asked.

"You'll find him near the tiger statue, but not always."

Laura thanked him, then left so quickly that James had to chase after her. She searched for a taxi. "We've got to find Ilya!"

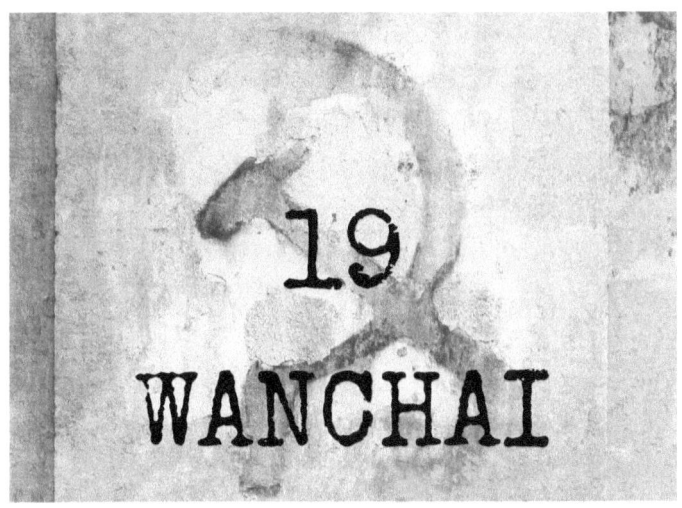

19

WANCHAI

"A room for two, please." At the hotel reception, Laura presented her counterfeit Hong Kong passport. "One night for Lillian Dover and her companion."

The male receptionist took the passport, examined it, nodded, and responded. "Two beds? A suite? What is your preference, Miss?"

"A suite will be just fine," she replied with a light smile.

"Allow me to see what I can do," the receptionist said as he headed into an office.

Laura nodded and studied her surroundings as she tapped the marble counter. In stark contrast to her first day's stay in an old Kowloon hotel, this newer hotel—only about two years old—featured extensive white marble and catered to a limited but affluent clientele. The place had more European than Asian features. The *Larson Aberdeen Hotel* in Wanchai.

She saw a sumptuous waiting area furnished with comfortable chairs and small tables, each with an ashtray arranged in a circle beneath a large chandelier. While reading a *Popular Mechanics* magazine seated on a chair, James remained calm and charming. His steady presence alone made her smile. Laura realized he could be foolish and irritating, yet she sensed an inexplicable appeal about him.

"We have an available suite, Miss Dover," the receptionist, dressed in a black formal outfit, returned and gave back her passport. He filled out part of a card, then handed it over to her, along with a pen. "How do you wish to pay for it? Cash? Bank check? Traveler's Check?"

"Cash," she confirmed the suite's price, then gave him a small wad of money she pulled from her leather jacket. She completed the remaining fields and signed the card.

"I'll call a bellboy," the man said, placing a key on the counter.

"It won't be necessary, sir," she said with a mischievous smile. "We can find it ourselves. Thank you!" Laura grabbed the key, sidestepped the receptionist's gaze, and stopped just short of James. "Let's go!"

James's blue eyes, serious, watched her as he returned the magazine to the table. "Was it needed? We could have waited at the *Tian Chao* and returned the next day."

Laura didn't answer, but urged him to follow her to the elevators, where an operator admitted them.

They spoke no words during their upward escalator ride. They reached their floor to find an almost empty, elegant hallway with scarlet carpets and white surfaces. A few Cantonese maids in western uniforms cleaned the room, and decorative tables displayed Roman-style vases, while some European Renaissance reproduction paintings hung on the walls.

Laura found the door with the number 914 and unlocked it.

Though impressed by the luxurious suite, Laura ignored its comforts and headed for the balcony, traversing the open bedroom and living area. She stepped outside and extended her hands to admire the sight. "To answer your question, James. Because of this!"

He followed her, scratching his head while admiring Victoria Harbour and Kowloon from Aberdeen, across the water. "I thought we were going after the *Merzost*, not playing tourists."

"Don't be a fucking tool! This!" she pointed to a sprawling, ten-story building a few blocks away from the hotel. "The Soviet Consulate."

"I get it, mate," he nodded in agreement. "Governor Whaley, I understand, had some difficulties with the Soviets. Was he the *Merzost's* target?"

"It's possible. The governor's authorization for American ships' use of Hong Kong's ports intensified the already delicate position caused by the Korean War." A lit cigarette followed Laura's statement, as she gestured towards the consulate's surroundings. "Do you notice the constant and discreet watch kept on the consulate by British soldiers from other buildings?"

James confirmed her words as he leaned against the balcony railing. "You're ripper, mate!"

"Time for a break from this!" Laura went back into the suite, placed her Beretta on the coffee table and her jacket on the nearby sofa. "Ring up the service and order supper! In the meantime, I'll take a shower." She went into the bathroom, closing the door behind her and taking her cigarette with her.

Amazed by Laura's remarkable intellect, James closed the balcony door behind him as he went inside.

After an abundant meal of British-style BBQ pork, tomato soup, and macaroni with James, Laura, in her white bathrobe, lounged on the sofa, with a cigarette in one hand and a grape juice cup in the other. The air conditioning cooled the room, leaving her refreshed after her shower. Deep in thought over the case's clues, she rested with her open journal on her lap.

Nightfall had just passed, and she had previously drawn the balcony curtains.

Backlit by a standing lamp, James, also cooler from a shower and only in a towel, read *Vogue* to kill time on his sofa. As he grew up in the hot Outback, he was used to being nearly naked.

Again, Laura's gaze shifted, lost in thought about him and his inevitable charm. He lacked the classic movie actor handsomeness, but she found him attractive. A strange feeling, which she couldn't describe and which sometimes made her stomach stir, overwhelmed her. Despite the relaxing environment, she yearned to break the silence. "Show me, James."

"What, mate?" His eyes remained glued to the magazine as he asked.

"This power of yours. I've spent most of my time with you, but your demonstration with the punching bag was the only time you really showed me."

He put down his Vogue and gave her a look from his blue eyes. "Believe me, I'd rather not use it."

"Just a little. Do it for me!" she insisted with a pointed gesture of her finger and thumb.

With a sigh and an eye roll, James relented. From his hand, a gentle, luminous energy emanated, passing harmlessly across the empty ale glass he held.

"Why do they call you the *Australian Scorpion*? Is it because of those Outback's *insects*?" Her question was sarcastic.

He sighed again and replied. "Although my name comes from the Outback scorpions, this is not why, mate." His tall, thin physique was visible as he stood, with his hands placed together over his head. "When I go in the blue during a match in the arena, I release a small amount of energy to overcome my opponent with enough pain to leave him paralyzed. Boss Yang calls it *The Scorpion Sting*." Back in his seat, he continued explaining. "But he warned me. If I unleashed my full power, I could destroy this very hotel, and I would die."

Following a silent pause and a glance at him, Laura replied to his explanation. "So you are a living bomb, then."

A silent, uncomfortable nod was his only response.

"Could you do the same with this glass for me?" She sat, put her journal on the coffee table, stubbed out her cigarette, and then offered him her hand.

Startled and slightly frightened, James stared at her. "I could hurt you."

"I'm okay with pain. Do it!"

In an unexpected gesture, he gently took her hand, and their fingers entwined with affection, before withdrawing his. "Sorry, I can't."

Disappointed, she collapsed onto the sofa with a sigh. "We have to wake up early to find that Ilya!" From the living room, she proceeded to the bed, threw a pillow at James, and got comfortable under the covers. "Good night."

James accepted the pillow without a visible reaction, positioning it under his head before sleeping on the sofa.

Laura's insomnia persisted, and as she lay in bed staring at the ceiling, the disturbing memories of the *Merzost* and Gabriel's execution receded, replaced by the stirring presence of James, just steps away. His proximity sent shivers of unexplainable excitement through her. "James?"

"Yes, mate?" his voice echoed across the suite.

"Why don't you join me? There's room for both of us." Laura waited for his reply. The time took longer, and she thought nothing would happen. Then, after a few minutes, she felt him beside her as the mattress shifted and the sheets settled around him. His nearness sent a tremor through her, accelerating her already racing heart.

Unable to contain herself any longer, she pounced on James as her lips devoured his. The comforting embrace of James' arms surrounded her as she took off her bathrobe.

Their moment concluded after a while, when they consumed their desires.

And a good night's sleep was finally possible for Laura after insomniac months.

Laura awoke near dawn. Her bedside clock showed five past six.

Laura's nakedness under the covers brought back the memory of the previous night. As she contemplated being initiated, she noted a difference between her experience and the stories from the *Bosphorus* girls in Ankara, including the late Ayla. Although in the beginning was difficult, she experienced no pain. James' gentle contact ignited a warmth within her, far exceeding anything she'd ever imagined.

She heard the toilet flush, then a door opened, revealing James, already dressed, as his blue eyes fixed on her. "Put your pants on! We need to meet Ilya."

20
TIGER

As smoke wobbled from her mouth, Laura kept her eyes attached to the Soviet Consulate. As of yesterday afternoon, the consulate remained under watch by soldiers in nearby buildings. She suspected Governor Whaley ordered the consulate's monitoring because of his belief that American vessels in Hong Kong, taking part in the Korean War against the Soviets, induced the *Merzost* attack on the *Tian Chao*. However, his objectives remained unclear.

She agreed with James that the governor could be the target.

As the sun touched her left side, Laura smoked her cigarette again. Her gaze drifted across the placid consulate from her balcony. The stillness of the early morning around seven o'clock was unique, but not unusual. James briefly distracted her by putting a cup of black coffee on the balcony railing. She gave a grateful nod as her gaze lingered on him, wondering about his reaction to their encounter from the night before.

It seemed as if nothing had happened.

"Meeting him at the Tiger Balm Garden would be easier, wouldn't it, mate?" His suggestion came as his blue eyes surveyed the consulate.

"Do you remember what that rickshaw puller said?" As she spoke, she took a sip of coffee. "You might not find Ilya. He could be there tomorrow or sometime next week."

"Are we going to wait till the cows come home?"

"We could stay at this hotel until he shows up, if needed," a bit disappointed, she sighed. James never mentioned the night before. "Do you know? I once watched the Soviet Consulate in Istanbul, where Isaak, an Intelligence officer who approached me, told me about the *Merzost*. He covered my breakfast." She tossed her cigarette butt from the balcony onto the street. "He made a wrong deal at the *Bosphorus* involving my late friend with Gabriel."

"What happened to him?"

"The fucking *Merzost* murdered him."

Speechless, James watched Laura survey the consulate before sighing and leaning on the railing to speak. "Mate, about last night. . ."

"Look!" Laura interrupted him. "The second window on the first floor. A man opened the curtains and is looking out at the street." She pointed at the building. "Could he be Ilya?"

"I see it, mate. It seems like he is aware of being watched."

Despite the distance from the consulate, she easily noticed him. He had a puffy face, graying hair, and the brown suit and red tie he wore suggested he was attending a special occasion. "He knows."

Ilya, presumably the man from the consulate, switched off the lights and closed the blinds.

"Get ready to follow him!" She rushed into the suite, donned her jacket, holstered her Beretta on her left side inside, and headed for the exit.

James followed her hurried.

They skipped the elevator and used the stairs, exiting through a nearby door.

Despite the flock of locals in simple Cantonese clothing and conical bamboo hats selling souvenirs to the first tourists of the day on the uphill Tai Hang Road, Laura and James maintained a discreet distance, following the Soviet officer.

Laura subtly glanced sideways and saw a black car with two British-looking men inside, who were watching him intently. However, the men didn't notice her.

"Who's catching up, mate?" James's blue eyes remained fixed on the man as he spoke. "Why is he so flashy?"

"I'm thinking he's meeting someone of importance, rather than a rickshaw puller. Or there's an important event scheduled to follow."

As he kept his eyes on the man, James saw a multilevel pagoda appear from the trees on a hill, surrounded by impoverished wooden shacks. James recognized the building as one of the major Tiger Balm Garden structures, and he noted his proximity to it. He'd visited there once during his recent arrival in Hong Kong years ago.

Pursuing their target, believed to be Ilya, they entered a no-car zone. Laura saw men parking a black car and waited rather than continue. Further along, she saw the entrance—a Chinese-style red and golden gate with the attraction's name in both English and Chinese. A mysterious, loud ringing abruptly filled her head. This feeling was identical to the one she had experienced before the *Tian Chao* explosion that night.

She realized her inner ringing was a newly found latent capability. The dread it caused led her to suspect an imminent threat.

As Laura passed through the gate, the sound inside her and the sight of bizarre, decorated artificial grottos depicting surreal Chinese mythology with grotesque sculptures frightened her even more, causing her to grasp James' hand.

Taken aback, he turned and looked at her. "We need to talk about last night."

"Not now!" As she pointed out Ilya's disappearance, they both began a visual search.

James found a tiger sculpture on a grassy ridge of concrete. "It shouldn't be hard. There's the damn tiger." He noticed Laura's tense, worried face as she shook his hand tightly. "What's wrong, mate?"

"Some hidden power has revealed itself to me, accompanied by a terrifying sound in my head that predicts something about to happen." Her gaze fell upon Ilya, absorbed by the tiger sculpture and lost in thought. "I must talk to him."

As James noticed his presence, he nodded and let Laura's hand go. "Have a chat with him, mate. I'll be observing from a distance. Don't worry."

Cautiously, she followed the man from the rear, sharing his contemplation of the sculpture. While she may have seemed unseen, he noticed her presence but showed no reaction.

"As you can see, Miss Doncelli, these bizarre sculptures in the grottos represent the Ten Courts of Hell as portrayed in Chinese Mythology," still, Ilya spoke. "Except for the tiger, it's just the image of the brand that comes with the balm."

Hearing him mention her name in Russian, a language she understood perfectly, astonished Laura.

James kept a close watch on them from afar, especially focusing on her safety.

"How do you know my name?!" she replied in his language.

Ilya presented himself in a well-tailored brown suit, a red tie, and a prominent red star pin featuring the Soviet emblem on his left lapel. "I was in Istanbul when Isaak met you, and I saw you follow him to his death in that alleyway. I was the best friend who got his job in the consulate."

"You know about the *Merzost*, then?"

"Of course, I gave him orders to execute Isaak. We won't stand for traitors who engage in gambling, bribery, prostitution, or, even worse, leak confidential information."

Though calmer after lighting a cigarette, Laura still felt the lingering effects of the ringing in her head, shaking her head. "Isaak was also responsible for Ayla's death. Right?"

"You are perfectly right, Miss Doncelli. Isaak's treacherous subordinate offered a young woman to the *Merzost* to appease his rage, but the girl's suffering was so intense that her screams resounded through the streets."

Tears emerged as Laura blew a plume of smoke. "It was a fucking rape! Unable to overcome her unforgettable trauma, she chose suicide. All for damn hundred forty thousand Turkish liras!" She nervously blew out smoke, again and again. "And what have you done to avoid that shit?!"

Ilya turned around to look at the tiger again, giving her the back. "Although I could have acted to avoid it, I had to obey Stalin's commands. It was about protecting something than just the money."

With a forceful stomp, Laura extinguished her cigarette, then wiped her eyes. "Why did the *Merzost* attack the *Tian Chao*? Was Governor Whaley the target?"

"Yes and no, he is part of something much bigger. Let's say it involves you and Hong Kong."

Though James fidgeted and watched from afar, the distance and language barrier prevented him from understanding the Russian conversation.

"What is it?"

"I'm not at liberty to share that information." With a sudden, surprising twist, Ilya whirled, aiming his Makarov pistol at her.

She evaded, then drew her Beretta from beneath her jacket and fired two shots, causing him to collapse.

Panicked, the small crowd around fled toward the exit at the sound of the gunshots.

She knelt before Ilya, assuring him that his weapon had fallen a distance away. "You bastard! Why did you try to kill me?!"

"The *Merzost* is here. . . " As blood poured from the Soviet man's mouth, he uttered his last words.

James had inexplicably disappeared when she turned to look for him. The persistent ringing in her mind confirmed he hadn't escaped.

The *Merzost* had captured him.

As if he were a lightweight rag doll, someone had effortlessly seized James by the neck and hauled him away. He struggled to break free because his captor was far too strong. He realized he was the *Merzost*, yet the dragging position prevented him from seeing his face.

He attempted to use his unique ability, but the *Merzost* absorbed it, leaving him vulnerable.

James remembered Laura and Ilya talking. The sight of shotguns prompted him to intervene, but before he could act, his captor grabbed him by the neck.

He tried again to fight back, but it was futile. Gasping for air, he could only watch as Merzost violently slammed him to the ground, pressing a heavy boot or shoe onto his bald head. He could hardly see the Laughing Buddha sculpture in front of him.

He was alone. Everyone fled after the shots rang out.

He sensed a hand on his back. He knew the *Merzost* was going to kill him.

The distraction of shots fired allowed James to use his returned power to attack the *Merzost*, causing a scream as he used his hand across the body.

In a flash, the dark creature jumped over the artificial grotto and vanished. His face remained unseen. It was like a shadow covering his inner being.

Laura hugged James after running to him, and she put her Beretta on the ground. She held him for a moment, then returned her weapon to its sheath before speaking. "We need to hurry before the police arrive!"

They agreed and raced, holding hands, out of the Tiger Balm Garden and onto Tai Hang Road. To avoid the police rushing to the crime scene, they darted into a food stall and discreetly ordered their meal in a hidden spot.

A silent look passed between Laura and James as the stall owner put down their rice and egg bowls on the bare, mistreated wooden table.

"Are you alright?" she asked seriously. "I thought I'd lost you."

"I am here, mate," he replied as he rested his hand on her cheek. "As that damn Yowie prepared to slay me, I feared I wouldn't experience another night with you."

A small smile touched Laura's lips as tears welled, then her gaze drifted to the street. "Ilya had that elegant suit because he knew his death was today."

As they stepped off the boat at *Tian Chao*, Laura and James found Hanzo and Ming already waiting at the restaurant entrance, much to their surprise.

"What's wrong?" A strange look accompanied Laura's question.

"The Triad reached a decision," Ming replied with a somber face. You are off the case. "You now belong to someone else."

With her pale face and a shaky voice, she inquired. "Who?"

"That would be me, Mui Mui." With a pretentious walk, Yanmu emerged from the restaurant. She wore her red cheongsam patterned with flowers, and a sinister smile played on her lips. She proudly and without hesitation showed her limb with the missing right arm. "You belong to me!"

21
MEI LI

Laura opened her eyes and saw James asleep next to her after a night together—just one of many since that first night at the hotel. She turned her head to the right and let out a breath, and looked at the familiar scene outside her bedroom window. Aberdeen Harbour in December 1953.

Contemplative and ignoring James's objections, she lit Camels, wishing it was her favorite Turkish tobacco, *Fatima*.

As she looked at the ring on her finger, the memory of her 18th anniversary dinner at *Tian Chao* on October 30th, her actual birthday, brought a smile to her face. To her surprise, James presented the simple dragon-engraved steel ring as a gift, a West Kowloon artisan's creation, brought to him by one of the few servants onboard.

Hanzo had cooked the dinner and, amusingly, Ming had served the table. For the first time in her young life, she had company to celebrate with. They had the remodeled restaurant all to themselves, since it could not open yet as Governor Whaley had ordered the Food and Environmental Hygiene Department to suspend the restaurant's license, and it prevented its reopening to calm the displeasure of his nationals inside the cabinet.

The Tiger Balm Garden incident infuriated the Jade Dragon Triad elders and the Britons, but strangely, the Soviets remained surprisingly unmoved. Laura, though acting in self-defense, had killed a diplomat in broad daylight with many witnesses present, and it angered them. Therefore, Yanmu, her new boss, confiscated everything *Merzost*-related from Laura as she followed orders. The dossier, her journal, and even her Beretta.

Reports from British agents stalking Ilya detailed everything they saw. Despite provoking the ire of colonial officers, the governor's intervention, however, protected the *Tian Chao's* hidden purpose: the arena. Even Governor Whaley, a passionate gambler, supported its continuation and promised it would be open by the same December.

Yanmu frequently bribed the governor's cabinet on behalf of the Triad, claiming she'd given the case to Boss Yang, who was serious about resolving it.

Laura and James couldn't leave *Tian Chao*. It was a command.

As she stubbed out her cigarette in the nearby ashtray, Laura noticed James waking and sitting up in bed.

"Smoking again? We've talked about this, mate!"

Laura nodded, a slight smile graced her face. "Stop!"

As he looked out at Aberdeen, he scratched his head. Unlike his small, windowless cabin in the *Tian Chao's* lower levels beside the gym, Laura's room, with its stunning view and unique design, was where he preferred to spend most nights with her. Next, he put on his wristwatch. "Time to hit the gym!" Just as he was about to get dressed, he paused, lost in thought, before even standing.

Laura sensed he was thinking of something. "What's wrong?"

James put on his pants, turned, and then replied. "I received a letter. Bubba bought a circus in Liverpool, and he'd like me to work there. Will you join me? We could escape that madness and begin again."

She nodded without hesitation, then the reality of her circumstances hit her. "It will be difficult to persuade the Triad and Yanmu to release us. We are, after all, merely their property."

James scratched his bald head again.

Laura threw back the covers and got dressed in the flowered blue cheongsam she had despised. "Let's talk about this later. In the meantime, I have to get back to my caretaking job."

In the end, she had accepted becoming a caretaker. Despite Yanmu's demotion, confining her to the Tian Chao, Laura welcomed the recess from the constant uncertainty and danger. Though her *Merzost* pursuit left her feeling that she had unfinished business, she left it behind.

As she stepped onto the middle floor of elegant hallway adorned with Chinese decorations, large windows, and statues, she encountered Hanzo, who was pushing a cart loaded with some food and a metal box under.

For a time, the Japanese managed the *Tian Chao's* food, serving everyone from warriors in traditional Chinese attire—some present on the same level—to the few maintenance servants.

"How did you go from being a samurai to a cook, Hanzo?"

With a disapproving look at Laura, he halted his cart before a seemingly wooden, red door. But actually it was as thick as a safe, made of steel and aluminum. "Fireman is next." He replied in his broken English.

With a nod, she struggled to carry the metallic box in her arms. Though athletic, her short stature hindered her, making even some tasks difficult, and carrying that heavy box, though small, was like a child struggling with something enormous. The close-fitting cheongsam also hindered her freedom of movement.

Hanzo opened a small compartment in the door, and Laura placed the box inside before closing it.

"That Fireman eats only molten plutonium," with hands on hips, Laura shook the head with a labored breath. "You are not cooking it. Right?"

With a glance at the door and some thought, Hanzo answered with mispronunciations. "They bring me from Kowloon, always in a box, every week." After a moment of quiet reflection, he stopped at the door. "Why is the Fireman that way?"

"Yanmu claims he was present during the atomic bombing of Nagasaki. His identity remains a mystery."

"Was he Japanese?" his voice cracked.

Laura's sympathetic nod showed her understanding. "I know that was unfair to them. The war was unjust to all."

To avoid further discussion, Hanzo pushed the cart through the next door.

With Laura entering Mei Li's anteroom, some warriors crept up behind her, readying their automatic weapons as a precaution. She used the key around her neck, entrusted to her by Yanmu, to open the vault. With everyone's heads bowed to avoid the eyes, Hanzo brought the food cart inside.

Laura almost shut the vault after Hanzo's quick exit, but paused in surprise, noticing everyone staring at her. She then addressed everyone. "I'll be with you in a moment. She's calling me."

"I would suggest not going." With a warning given, Hanzo turned to the warrior and made a request. "Call Ming."

An air of such determination marked her entrance into the dreaded room, instilling fear in all those who witnessed it.

Since Laura came to the *Tian Chao* a few months ago, she has not once stepped inside Mei Li's room. However, she did enter it.

She found a spacious, windowless area. Many square silk pillows and a mattress covered most of the floor in the elegant, chandelier-lit room. The sheer number of perfectly arranged books lining countless shelves amazed her as an avid reader.

Near the center, sitting on floor pillows, Laura saw Mei Li's back, adorned in a traditional red and gold dress—perhaps Bhutanese, Tibetan, or Indian. She couldn't be certain—with a long black braid hanging from her head. She looked at the twelve-year-old girl, noticing her slight, thin figure—she seemed more like ten. Laura kept wondering how such a small girl could be so strong.

A sweet voice emanated from her motionless body. "Have a seat in front of me, please," she requested in perfect Turkish.

"How do you know Turkish?!" Laura asked in surprise.

Mei Li responded by extending her hand and gesturing for her to sit.

Laura complied, and upon sitting down, she noticed the girl engrossed in a thick Chinese book on a low table, her dark eyes fixed on the text.

"Unlike you, Laura Doncelli. I don't speak many languages." A warm look filled her eyes as she gazed at her.

"You speak many languages, but your thoughts are in Turkish. Therefore, I've linked our minds."

"Are you as frightening as everyone says?" Laura remained calm as she asked.

"Some people called me Kali, while others knew me as Ekajati. In reality, I don't despise people themselves, but their tendency to overreact." A slight head movement accompanied Mei Li's explanation. "Contrarily, you've revealed a different side, and I've glimpsed your true nature."

"Why did you call me?"

"Perhaps I should ask you a question instead." The girl showed seriousness on her round, angelic face. "Do you plan to abandon your pursuit?"

"To be your caretaker and spend my life with James? I think it's all for the best." She kind of stuttered in her answer.

"Best for whom? You? Or them?"

A strange glimpse crossed Laura's face as she looked at Mei Li, a look that suggested she tried to understand but decided otherwise.

Her gaze fell upon her crossed legs, concealed by the texture of her dress. "I came here unwillingly, but I let Boss Yang bring me. I'd much prefer to be surrounded by books, take part in their games, rather than unleash fear on everyone." She glanced at Laura again. "But you have so much to give. You can move worlds and rattle lives."

"But. . ."

"It's natural for you to be afraid, Laura Doncelli. Perfection is unattainable. Sacrifice is inevitable."

A nod from Laura conceded Mei Li's truth, despite her desire to deny it. "What shall I do?"

"Begin with Yanmu. She is not what you think, and neither is Boss Yang, who has many secrets. Keep going. Don't stop. Learn about your forgotten past." And she returned to read the Chinese volume.

Laura got up and walked to the exit.

"The *Merzost* connects to you, Laura Doncelli."

She listened to her and then left the room.

22
KATASTROFA

Next to Ming, Laura observed James's search of Yanmu's messy office and bedroom. It had been months since she had last been there. The unclean accumulation was revolting. A contrast to her own clean, airy room.

James noticed how cluttered the office was. His time in *Tian Chao* under Boss Yang took years before he could finally enter. His status as a Triad fighter, a property rather than a person, meant he had no privileges, and one of them was to enter at Yanmu's place.

Hanzo stood guard outside the office. While Yanmu was with the Triad in Kowloon, and continued to address him as such, her surprise return to *Tian Chao* remained a concern.

The piles of paperwork, accounting books, unwashed teacups, empty alcohol bottles, and overflowing ashtrays—all discovered during James's thorough visual search—exposed the character of Yanmu and her male companions. The disheveled state of her combined office and bedroom, though she never openly displayed it, corroborated the rumors. Although she hosted various wealthy and influential suitors, in particular Britons, overnight, they were quite diverse.

Yanmu's suitors were many, and two notable examples were Boss Yang, who freely showed his fondness for her, and Governor Whaley, whose hurried departures—often leaving behind articles of clothing—showed his attempts at secrecy. James and Laura identified the white tropical gubernatorial uniform hanging in the office as one of the many pieces of evidence.

"That bush pig still had ways to seduce them!" James exclaimed as he rearranged the jumbled pile of things on the table.

Between the main bedrooms and the arena entrance, and thus lacking windows, the office was dimly lit only by some electric lanterns. Despite the unpleasant smell and the lack of anything useful in the hoard, they still insisted on finding something that could reveal a mystery. James and Ming trusted Laura and her encounter with Mei Li. They believed her when she said Yanmu differed from what people thought.

"Don't touch that pile, James," Ming, still with no gestures, suggested. "Secrets aren't out in the open for everyone to see."

James stopped and put his hands on his hips. "My understanding was that you worked for Boss Yang or the Triad, mate. Why are you still with us?"

Ming's first response was an eerie silence, motionless as a statue. Then he spoke. "My only boss is Miss Laura."

Touched by his words, Laura's eyes glistened and a small smile played on her lips, but she hid her emotions.

"Whatever," he said, a little jealous. "Where in the world am I to uncover these damned secrets?"

"The same place where you keep your valuables." Ming insisted.

James scratched his bald head, and his blue eyes scanned the area until he spotted something that brought a satisfied smile to his face.

Tucked between a messy bed and a cluttered table piled with dirty dishes, James discovered a small, black safe. "Do any of you know the combination of that thingo, mates?"

Laura replied. "Even while working alongside her, I never learned the combination."

Everyone inside jumped at the knock on the door. Then Hanzo's voice came from outside. "Everything alright?"

"Dammit! Don't scare us!" James said, fuming.

"We're good, Hanzo! We are still searching for this shit. Keep watching, please." Laura answered, then saw James deep in thought.

"I've figured out how to open it."

Laura and Ming, with questioning looks, attempted to understand his thoughts.

From James' hand, a small, glowing energy passed through the safe's thick metal. With a subtle maneuver, he invisibly melted the interior metallic components, opening it. Inside, he found documents in languages he didn't know, but spotted some Chinese. Then, he found more—typewritten Russian papers stamped with hammer and sickle emblems.

Laura also searched inside the safe and found a black box at the back, took it out, and opened it.

James' blue eyes grew wider. "What the fuck!"

A Makarov pistol was inside.

"It must be a fucking coincidence!" Laura exclaimed, pointing to the gun—the same model, or at least one like it, that the Soviet Ilya had used against her before she killed him in self-defense. She knelt, examining the Russian documents scattered on the floor after the bed, and arranged them in chronological order, starting from 1950. "These are orders from the Soviet MGB intelligence agency. Despite undergoing many changes after Stalin's death, it continues to operate under various names."

James and Ming, standing, listened to her. Their surprise could not have been greater.

"Just what the hell are these orders?" James asked with crossed arms. "Does it have to do with the cunt of Ilya and the *Merzost*?"

"Rather, the question is why Yanmu has these." Ming stated.

Laura scanned every paper at extraordinary reading speed. "The consistent mention of *Operatsiya Katastrofa* across all documents does not clarify its intended purpose. March 2nd is the date of the latest document." Later, she spotted a telegram among the documents. "This, from March 6th, says: *The Comrade has died. Abandon the operation*."

"Geez! They canceled everything for a buddy!" James shook and scratched his head.

A look of annoyance crossed Ming's face as he glanced at him.

Laura, meanwhile, rolled her eyes.

"That comrade is a reference to Stalin," she corrected, followed by an almost silent Turkish mutter to herself. "I don't know how I'm in love with such a moron!"

"Keep going, Miss Laura," Ming urged.

"Ilya's signature on most of these documents suggests he played a key role in *Operation Catastrophe*, but Stalin's death and the inevitable end of the Korean War seemed to ruin him." She assumed a thoughtful pose. "This explains why British agents found his gun unloaded after I killed him. He planned his death." She tapped her chin, lost in reflection. "Actually, the Korean War only paused, not ended, with the signing of an armistice. No winners or losers."

"But what about the *Merzost*?" James inquired.

"It's odd that these papers don't mention him at all." She stood, observing both men. "I'll be getting answers and a long-overdue promise from Boss Yang."

Ming, Hanzo, and especially James disagreed with her decision to meet Boss Yang following the discovery of Soviet intelligence documents. It took longer to persuade them. Ming and James agreed to wait nearby at the *Four Generations Hotel* in Kowloon, prepared to assist if needed, while Hanzo would manage the *Tian Chao* and its residents for the time being.

Laura saw James's despair and fear in his trembling hands as he hugged her. Though they'd spent countless nights together since July, this situation, embodying her similar feelings before meeting Ilya, made her doubt her relationship with James, even though he offered her to start anew.

Quite the opposite. She loved him, but that wasn't the reason. The war and her unconventional background instilled in Laura a deep sense of distrust, danger, and deception.

23

EVE

Ming, behind the wheel of the black Triad car, pointed with a nod.

From the back seat on the passenger side, Laura saw a building across the street in Kowloon. A profusion of overlapping posters and Chinese characters adorned the four-story building, the ground floor columns in particular, which framed the entrances to shops advertising American soft drinks. Laundry hung from long bamboo poles extending from many upper-story balconies, creating a cluttered look.

"It's on the top floor, Miss Laura. The one with no balconies is his home," Ming said. "I did as you said and followed him there."

From the car, Laura's surprise was obvious as she kept staring at the building. "I expected Boss Yang to live in a more elegant place."

"He's still a crucial part of the Triad." He then gestured towards the people in the shops. "Have you noticed that only men are present? It appears they're just standing around doing nothing. They're with the Triad that protects Boss Yang."

She continued her meticulous examination of the building, regardless of the fading light and minimal illumination. "I am ready."

"Are you sure, Miss Laura?" Ming's concern didn't stop. "I could wait here in the street. . ."

"Wait for my call at the hotel with James," she insisted.

"Use the narrow stairs to reach the top floor," he instructed. "The door will open after four knocks."

Laura's nod and sigh betrayed her sudden nervousness. As she left the car and approached the building, the Triad's men eyed her with a blend of suspicion and interest—a lone girl heading towards the stairs. As she predicted, some men boldly pursued her with obscene flattery.

When a man reeking of alcohol shoved Laura against the wall, she countered him with defensive moves, elbowing his stomach and kneeing his groin, forcing him and his accomplices to retreat some steps.

Ming watched her moves and chuckled, satisfied she had learned her defense lessons well. As told, he started the car and left the area.

As she ensured no one could approach, she fixed her leather jacket and located the concrete stairs between the shops. Laura observed a man purchasing whiskey, likely for Christmas Eve this same night, before ascending the stairs.

As Laura climbed the last flight of stairs, she encountered a man in dark clothing, his shirt somewhat undone, leaning against the wall, reading a Cantonese newspaper and smoking a Marlboro cigarette. He overlooked her, but pointed to the only door in a gesture.

A faint ringing echoed in her head as her eyes fell on the dragon-engraved steel ring—quieter than before—then she looked towards a dark wooden door. She took a deep breath to relax.

She knocked four times on the door and waited.

A long silence followed, but she insisted, knocking four more times.

Finally, Laura heard rushed steps approaching.

A young local woman, opening the door, appeared surprised by the appearance of Laura, a European, scrutinizing her from head to toe. Her assumption of being British led her to speak horrible English. "Me no speak well."

"I came to see Michael Yang, lady!" A hint of displeasure in Laura's Cantonese response caught the female unaware.

The woman vanished, leaving the door partly open. Laura closed it gently, only to find her naked and hurriedly putting on underwear while giving an angry look. "The last room down the hall, first right, then to the left, is where he is." She said as she finished getting dressed in her black dress and grabbed a pair of flip-flops. "He is a fucking junkie!"

Laura needed to make room after the woman's sudden and obnoxious departure. As she found herself alone in the reception room, she noticed its elegance despite its miserable surroundings in a Kowloon neighborhood. It was a hidden place.

Concerned about the woman's claims about Boss Yang's addiction, Laura took the first steps. She uncovered a surprising side of him but still needed verification. Advancing, she uncovered a collection of Chinese dragon statues on small tables against the walls, softly lit from above by circular lamps. As Ming previously mentioned, the Jade Dragon Triad owned this apartment, a fact confirmed by these sculptures.

Upon entering the circular foyer, she noted the kitchen to her left, but proceeded down the hall in the opposite direction. After the room of the dragons, a stark contrast appeared as an undecorated hall, lacking windows, featuring bare dirty beige walls marred by lipstick marks and softly illuminated.

Laura walked at a slow pace, cautious, especially without her Beretta.

She passed through a door and just kept going until she reached a corner that made her turn left. Her head started ringing louder, giving her sudden migraines and making her feel dizzy. She couldn't figure out why as she tried to catch her breath and look for fresh air, but it didn't help at all since there was no exit or window. The sudden feeling made her pause, leaning on the wall, but she looked the hall to an entrance beyond two doors.

The ringing was deafening. Much louder than the other times. Laura felt that a much greater danger was imminent.

Despite unbearable headaches, she continued to the last door, yearning for either water or air. She entered and to her left was a large, disordered bed in the spacious chamber. Though dizzy and in pain, she concentrated on her environment, observing the persistent lack of windows.

To her right, a sofa held a coffee table displaying drug paraphernalia. A spoon, a used half-candle, some aluminum foil, a crystal syringe, matches, and several vials. This confirmed her suspicions about Boss Yang's addiction, explaining his cold, direct manner, strict orders, and ruthless executions.

"That's an altered opioid I synthesized, Miss Laura. My formula," he said, gesturing to the table. "The base is the same opium that caused the bloody British to seize Hong Kong from China."

At the far end, she saw Boss Yang sitting at a desk piled with papers. In nothing but dark pajama pants, he smoked, placing the ashes in a crystal ashtray on the side of his desk. Laura saw a small metal fan on the desk. To ease her overwhelming nausea, she rushed to a chair, sat before it, and welcomed the cooling air as she moved it to her face.

She noticed the dossier, her journal, and her Beretta on the desk.

"You owe me fucking explanations!" Exasperated, sweaty, and breathless, Laura glared at him. "Were you aware that Yanmu was working for the Soviets?"

Boss Yang put a cigarette in front of her, and she lit it with his metal lighter. "Yanmu, Gabriel, Governor Whaley, and I were collaborating with the Soviets on this project. Sadly, the Second War, Stalin's death and the end of the Korean conflict killed it." He let out a sigh, then continued. "We're going forward without the Soviets, though."

The combination of the fan's air and cigarette smoke helped her ease her pain and dizziness, but still not enough. *"Project Catastrophe.* What the fuck is it about?"

"All you, miss," he replied with a grin. "You, James, Hanzo, Mei Li, the Fireman, and even Bubba Carson are all the project. We chose Hong Kong as the first. If it had succeeded, we could have brought it to more cities."

"For what?"

"Your extraordinary abilities can create pure devastation in Hong Kong, a catastrophe of immense proportions. With your help, we could reconstruct it and take Hong Kong from the British. An independent nation shielded by both China and the Soviet Union."

Laura was so surprised that she stopped smoking and stared at him in disbelief.

"Stalin envisioned an invincible squad to conquer lands to bring communism to the world—an exceptional army," he put out his cigarette in the ashtray. "But the war and his death ended it. The Soviet Union's internal divisions and disagreements led to the cancellation of many ambitious projects by the Supreme Soviet and the Politburo."

"What is the Triad's part in this project?"

"Power and money to fund this," Boss Yang nodded. "The elders are unaware of the *Tian Chao's* true purpose. A cleverly disguised fighting ring generated the Triad's profits. Some of these funds were diverted to this project."

"What made you do that?" Although her pain lessened, the ringing persisted, and could finish her cigarette. "I'm sure you also redirected the *Bosphorus* profits."

"Gabriel spilled the beans to Ayla, jeopardizing everything. That's why he sent her to the *Merzost* as a punishment, so I instructed you to get rid of him to keep his damn mouth quiet." He sighed. "We closed the *Bosphorus* afterwards to hide its true purpose from the Turkish authorities."

Laura paused thoughtfully, then asked a question. "Who is the *Merzost*?"

"Vasily Rostov," he replied with a nod.

Laura attempted to find some logic.

"Who is he?"

"Here's a proposal, Miss Laura," he said with a sinister grin. "If you offer me your body for my purposes, I will reveal everything to you. I know you're desperate for all the information." He nodded. "You've waited years for this! So, I wanted to share my formula with you."

Her face remained still, revealing no emotion as she looked at him. Though the pain lessened, a loud ringing returned to her head, as a growing prediction of danger. A barely perceptible nod followed.

"Head to the bathroom there," he said, pointing to the opposite side of the bedroom. "Cleanse yourself, take off your clothes, and put on the robe placed there. By the time you are out, I'll be ready."

Laura stood and walked to the bathroom, closing and locking the door without hesitation. She flipped on the lights when she went inside, then leaned against the green tile wall, as anxiety breached inside her. Unable to wait any longer, she rushed to the toilet to relieve herself.

Finishing up, she went to the lavatory to wash her hands. As she looked at her reflection in the mirror, the dragon ring James had given her slipped from her finger and disappeared down the drain. She sighed deeply, anticipating the lost ring was an ominous sign.

Laura looked in the mirror, then reached into her jacket pocket and placed something inside the dark blue robe hanging nearby. She then removed her clothes.

As she left the bathroom, Laura discovered Boss Yang seated at the coffee table, using a spoon and candle to heat a substance. He checked its readiness, then filled a syringe with it.

"I found success in managing my formula by combining it with heroin, an opioid," he spoke as he saw Laura coming and taking a seat next to him. Gently, he took her arm and secured it with a rubber band. "I tried it myself, and all I got was a nasty personality and a fucking addiction."

"How can you make sure it works?" She seemed calm, but her heart was racing and her mind was still ringing.

Boss Yang injected his formula into her arm. The initial sting made her gasp. "The *Merzost* was the first, resulting in his improvement into a near-omnipotent being." He took the syringe from her and put it on the table. "My years of research reveal that you possess unique aspects distinct from the average person like me. All you are perpetually evolving after a nuclear trigger, each of you manifests powers unique to your personality."

"How does personality influence our capabilities?" As dizziness returned, Laura inquired, but an unfamiliar calmness washed over her, silencing the ringing. Still, she was conscious.

"Based on my research, your bodies are always in constant transformation, making impossible to bear children, but I haven't figured out how your personalities affect your powers." He checked Laura's pulse by holding her wrist. "Everyone rejected my thesis, even fucking Cambridge."

Despite feeling sleepy, she persisted in asking. "How did your involvement with the *Merzost* and the Soviet Union begin?"

"To maintain my research projects, I presented my thesis to several governments and institutions to get funds. Only Stalin offered support and interest." He noticed Laura was drowsy and wobbly, so he stayed near to catch her if she fell. "My search for children affected by the chemical, through their parents, led me to Vasily. So, I took him to work on him."

She faintly questioned, "Was. . . he part of the operation?"

"He was like many others." Boss Yang lifted her onto the bed and visually examined her. "Stalin, aware of your presence in Calabria, sent an agent to watch you, believing your abilities could match Vasily's and the rest of the future squad. That agent was the Turk Ahmed."

Extreme drowsiness and blurry vision overcame Laura, making impossible for her to continue speaking. However, she could still hear Boss Yang and looked at him lowering his pants, understanding his intentions. He had used his manipulative nature to exploit her.

"Naturally, Ahmed didn't recognize you because you'd grown. Money wasn't my motive for executing him. It was my research files he stole from the war." He exposed Laura's body when he opened her robe while she was partially unconscious. "German resistance against Americans destroyed Monticelli. Ahmed discovered this but found you after the war." His fingers brushed against her right cheek. "He bribed some British officials in Karaolos to allow you to travel to Turkey. Coincidence drove you to Ankara . . . and to me."

Because of her extreme weakness and dormant state, Laura could not move, as she felt Boss Yang laying on her. She lacked the strength to fight him.

24
CHRISTMAS

L aura heard Yanmu's voice during a heated conversation with Boss Yang.

Asleep, yet part of her mind was still alert.

She heard footsteps in the distance. Then the door closed.

Laura opened her eyes to see Boss Yang in his pajama pants, sitting at his desk and sorting through a pile of papers. She remembered the repetitiveness of his abuse. The persisting effects were obvious in her body. But serene, she rose, secured her robe, and walked toward him.

She recalled all the revelations she had longed to hear. The long awaited ones. The truth was out.

"You slept almost a day, Miss Laura," he said, never looking away from his task but to check his wristwatch.

"What time is it?" Laura asked with a slight smile. She neared the desk, where her Beretta rested atop the journal and dossier. She picked up the gun, carefully checking its contents.

"It's almost 9 PM on December 25th," Boss Yang replied and observed her. "The gun's empty—I removed the bullets myself—you can have it back."

A ringing in Laura's head appeared as she looked toward the hallway from inside the room, but disappeared when she looked away. She realized that she now could control it.

Boss Yang guessed her reaction and grinned. "This is why I've injected my formula into you. It will enhance and refine your abilities."

"So, were you also meant to help by fucking me?" she asked with a nod.

He snickered and replied. "You were my special Christmas surprise."

Laura aimed the Beretta at him. "Here are some more gifts for you."

A serious look replaced Boss Yang's chuckle as suspicion arose.

She didn't hesitate. Five bullets, two to the head, three to the chest—her revenge for his five violations.

He fell to the floor with a thud, dead.

"Rot in hell, you fucking asshole!" She looked again in the same direction. The ringing confirmed her suspicions—the threat, almost certain that the *Merzost* was in the next room. From the robe pocket, she loaded the remaining bullets into the gun's magazine.

She had no time to cry over her disgrace.

In her haste, she gathered her clothes from the bathroom and got dressed. Her plan was to meet the *Merzost* as she believed he was in the same residence, but she also gave Ming and James instructions to come after 24 hours if she didn't appear at the hotel, even if that meant facing the Triad.

With her Beretta, she carefully left the bedroom and proceeded down the hall. She knew the danger was around the corner, but her ringing suggested a second threat in a slow approach.

Just as Laura turned right, Yanmu appeared, yelling and forcing Laura to the ground with a saber at her throat with only a hand. Laura fought back after accidentally dropping her gun.

"It had to be you, bitch!" Yanmu screamed while trying to slay her in despair. "I used to be her favorite until you showed up, you fucking whore!"

Despite Yanmu's missing arm, her unusual strength made her impossible for Laura to overcome.

Three shots rang out, and Yanmu's body fell onto Laura, forcing her to move it.

Ming was standing with a gun in his hand. "She was the whore." He delivered his words with his usual coldness.

Laura gave a brief nod of thanks, then picked up her dropped Beretta. As she turned, she saw James hurrying towards her. His worried expression was obvious as he tried to embrace her. However, a sudden, spontaneous feeling of revulsion drove her to push him back, marking the moment she understood the previous night had transformed her. "Not now! The *Merzost* is here!"

A dreaded surprise overcame James and Ming.

Laura went to the first door beyond the foyer, the one she'd seen the previous night. She recognized it because of one of the dragon statues. With her Beretta aimed, she targeted it. "I sense his presence inside."

Ming, with his MAC 50 drawn, was followed by James, whose hands crackled with energy.

Laura's opening of the door filled everyone with trepidation.

The discovery of an equipped, softly lit laboratory surprised them. However, they found another door at the far end.

Rows of tables laden with messy microscopes, syringes, colorful bottles, and other lab equipment stretched before Laura as she walked. She recognized the metallic spoons, the unlit torches and substances containing heroin. In a corner, she spotted a bookshelf overflowing with horizontally stacked papers and files, instantly recognizing them. "The most valuable and detailed information is there." A unique ringing, only she could hear, drowned out her whisper as her eyes focused on the door, growing ever more intense. "The *Merzost* is inside." Laura pointed at the door.

With speed and care, Ming opened the door and aimed his weapon inside.

Laura gave a little nudge so that Ming could see better.

A lone figure, dressed in black, sat on a bed in the pitch-black, almost bare room.

Ignoring the silent objections from James and Ming, Laura concealed her Beretta and advanced towards the man, stopping at a short distance. Despite her racing heart, she spoke to him in a soft voice. "I know you are Vasily."

Surprise and confusion overcame her companions.

Immobile as a statue, the *Merzost* sat. His silence was heavy and brutal.

"They treated you unfairly. Let me help you."

"What?!" James gasped, but Ming, startled, covered his mouth.

The darkness of the room hid the *Merzost's* face, though he finally reacted by turning his head in her direction. He walked over to stand before Laura, gave her a long look, and offered a silent, curious nod.

Laura smiled and offered her hand, hoping he'd understand.

He spent nearly a minute gazing at her hand as the *Merzost* lowered his head. He lifted her off the floor and against the wall with a speed barely perceptible, seizing her neck and making her gasp for breath.

To rescue Laura, James charged, raking his radiant hands across the man's body, expecting to cause pain. However, the *Merzost* used his other arm to shove James against the wall, knocking him unconscious.

Ming shot at him, emptying the gun's clip, but still failed to injure him.

Laura, gasping for air and fighting back, was still being choked by *Merzost*. She was helpless. Her body moved like an uncontrolled puppet.

A deafening crash announced a hole blown through the roof. A glowing man tumbled in, triggering partial collapse and some widespread fires.

The Fireman's grip around the *Merzost's* body forced a scream, freeing Laura from his grasp. With the fire spreading to the residence and even threatening the building, the man of fire leaped incredibly high, taking *Merzost* with him, and landing some distance away.

As Ming realized the rapidly escalating fire, he quickly woke James and helped him make a speedy escape after Laura, and they immediately ran down the stairs and exited with haste, to witness from across the nocturnal street the building consumed by an ever-growing inferno. They further noted that the building's occupants had all departed, almost certainly escaping, especially those employed by the Triad.

While catching their breath, Ming glanced towards where he thought the Fireman and the *Merzost* had landed. "Damn it!"

"What's wrong?" James, out of breath, inquired, with his hands resting on his waist.

With a blackened face and a painful neck, Laura gasped for air, then looked at him, waiting for an answer.

"They landed in Shek Kip Mei!" Ming's reply showed alarm. "That place is a shantytown of squatters!"

F ive-year-old Laan didn't mind the chilly night as he played in the dirty, makeshift streets barefoot. His joy came from jumping over the filthy puddles, likely wastewater from the squatters, which left a strong, unpleasant odor throughout the sprawling shantytown of wood and aluminum houses.

It was the night of Christmas. Celebrations in Aberdeen, Hong Kong Island, and even Kowloon continued through Boxing Day on Monday. However, in Shek Kip Mei, it was just another ordinary night.

The boy, ceasing his puddle play, gathered small rocks, hurling some to the ground and striking them with others. He stayed in the game by squatting often. The dark streets didn't bother him. The huts' soft glow did not affect his vision.

A man came up to him with a small satchel on his back. Laan stood up, smiling innocently, and allowed him to stroke his head. "You going to work?" He asked in his very basic Cantonese.

"Umbrellas don't wait." His reply lacked a smile. He gave the boy a coin from his pocket.

Laan looked at the HK$5 coin his father gave him, noting the queen's engraved image on the other side.

"Merry Christmas, son." He stroked his head once more and departed.

It was impossible for the boy to mask his joy. He pocketed his gift and ran home, but stopped, mesmerized by the starry night and the approaching fireball from the sky.

The Fireman and the *Merzost* clashed. Propelled from Boss Yang's Kowloon residence, they smashed into Shek Kip Mei, crushing huts and causing a massive blaze that would expand.

The supernatural battle raged fiercely, but the *Merzost*, though consumed by flames and stripped bare, appeared unharmed. The fire revealed his dark body.

The fire spread rapidly, impacting dozens of houses, a number that quickly climbed into the hundreds.

Because they couldn't drive up the hill to the shantytown, Laura, James, and Ming arrived running. Following a distant, bright blaze, they pushed through a flee-ing, panicked crowd of squatters. They arrived to find a fight taking place within the burning debris.

Instead of punches, the Fireman and the *Merzost* were engaged in a wrestling struggle.

With sparking energy in his hands, James, the Aus-tralian Scorpion, was ready for combat, but Laura pre-vented him, shaking her head.

"You'll die if you go near them!" Laura warned, stop-ping him by the chest. "They are too strong for you!"

Instead of staying to watch the fight, Ming aided the inhabitants in their evacuation, a decision that Laura and James subsequently followed, joining him in his efforts to assist the residents.

While clearing debris from wrecked huts near the fire, hoping to find survivors, Ming found several peo-ple already dead and charred. Even though death was familiar to him, it still impressed him.

Many in the panicked crowd, including many aged people and children, fell down, requiring Laura's help to get back on their feet. She saw Laan sitting under a fiery beam by a fallen wall, ran and immediately lifted him into her arms. As the fight intensified and the destruction worsened, she took the boy to a safe place.

When the vehicles couldn't make it up the hill, Gov-ernor Whaley arrived with soldiers and local police. His eyes widened at the sight of the Fireman and the *Merzost* wrestling. He commanded his men to ready their rifles and open fire.

The *Merzost* was unaffected by the bullets, but the Fireman grew larger as they hit him.

Ming, with his face smudged with lines of ashes, confronted the governor after exiting the hut's rubble. "Stop the damn shooting and get your men to help the squatters!"

Governor Whaley took out his gun and whacked Ming in the face, knocking him out. "Go away, you bloody Chinese!" He persisted in ordering his men to shoot.

Laura could not see Ming because she was getting Laan to a safe place. But at a glance, she saw the Fireman engulfed in a giant ball of fire that absorbed all the *Merzost*.

With a surprise punch to the chin, James knocked down Governor Whaley. The energy radiating from his hands stopped the soldiers and police from firing as they looked at him. "Put down your damn weapons, or there will be consequences!" As he looked at the heart of the fight, he realized things were dangerous. "Help the people evacuate and run for your lives!"

While Laura carried Laan to safety, James assisted Ming's escape.

As suggested, police and soldiers helped most of the population evacuate to the neighboring Un Chao.

A colossal, glowing sphere emerged from the rubble, its incandescent explosion spreading flames far and wide to engulf the area in an enormous, all-consuming firestorm.

A roaring inferno, marked by massive flames and the constant crackling of burning structures, completely consumed the shantytown, leaving only ashes and debris in its wake.

Although the firefighters arrived, it was too late to save anything.

Shek Kip Mei was gone. All erased.

The blaze continued late into the night, ending the following morning.

Only ashes remained of the shantytown.

Thousands of homeless people waited, aware that they had lost their homes.

Many died.

The *Merzost* and the Fireman were nowhere to be seen. Only a barren crater marked the epicenter. Ming examined the scene and confirmed that both were dead.

"It was for the best." With the first light of morning, Laura displayed her face, stained black. "Both lived in perpetual torment."

Ming nodded as the dry blood crusted on his right temple. "I agree, Miss Laura." From afar, he saw Governor Whaley, in handcuffs, being taken away by his own troops. He spat on the ground in disgust. He glanced down and discovered Laura holding the boy's hand. "What are your plans for him?"

"I suppose we should bring him to the *Tian Chao*." Distantly, Laura discovered James' still form staring at the crater, comprehending that she had, deliberately or not, submitted to Boss Yang. Her behavior since last night made her question whether he suspected anything.

If justified, her determined pursuit of the truth demanded a significant and painful sacrifice. Laura knew beforehand that she had lost him.

Dressed in black, a highly respected elder made his way to the crater, examining it in front of the onlookers, and finally turning his attention to speak with Laura. "The Jade Dragon Triad wishes to speak with you."

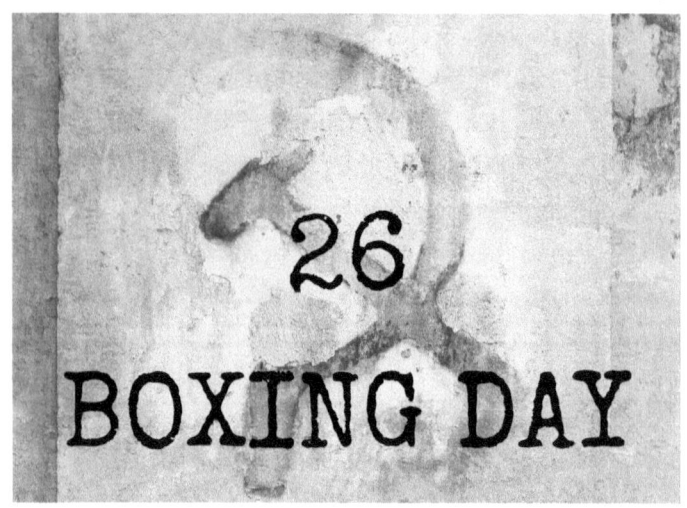

26
BOXING DAY

I t was Boxing Day night at the *Four Generations Hotel* in Kowloon.

Ming got off the elevator with Laura, who was wearing her usual leather jacket, pants, and boots. A hotel hairdresser had styled her long, wavy black hair. Men in black were to escort them to the hotel's restaurant, while British agents monitored them from the entrance, immobile.

Laura spotted James sitting on one of the elegant chairs with coffee tables. He flipped through *Charm* magazine while waiting.

Actually, James waited all weekend until Monday to see her—ever since the Shek Kip Mei fire.

Sad-looking Laura addressed the head-bandaged Ming and the surrounding men. "Please let me have a moment to talk with him."

Ming and the men nodded in agreement.

At a slow pace, Laura approached James, settled into a cushioned chair across the small table from him, lit a Camels cigarette, and exhaled. Though engrossed in his magazine and disregarding her, he said nothing. Her heart pounded, and she was speechless.

"I initially thought I'd racked you off away, mate. I've wondered for the past few days why Ming has repeatedly separated us." James lowered the magazine and gazed at her. "Then, one conclusion kept coming to my mind. You fucked Boss Yang. Isn't?"

Laura remained impassive, disposing of her cigarette residue in the ashtray while avoiding his eyes. "Instead, he fucked me multiple times."

"All for what, mate?" Moist eyes accompanied James's reply. "To get the secrets you have waited for years? Was sacrificing our love for those damned secrets worth it?"

Laura's eyes welled up without her looking at him. "There's no way to answer or apologize."

He looked at her, gave a nod of understanding, and rose to his feet. "Even though you're mature for your age, I forget you're still young. You might have an exceptional intellect and unique abilities, but you struggle with your emotions."

His striking height, familiar yet noticeable, made her finally look up from her chair, noting his new blue shirt, long brown pants, and black shoes. "What will you do now?" Then she took another drag of her cigarette.

His tone softened. "I'll be working at the circus in Liverpool with Bubba. I am done with this charade of fights and spy games."

"I wish you well, James." Though she longed to hold his hand one last time, she lacked the courage.

He gave a nod of thanks.

Laura saw James walk through most of the reception before leaving past the British agents who were watching her. Unable to contain herself any longer, she dropped her cigarette and covered her face, sobbing.

Ming and the other men accompanied Laura into the luxurious hotel restaurant. A captain greeted her, and after a brief exchange, led her to a private dining room at the back, reserved for special occasions.

Ming, accompanied by the men, chose a table in the public area, settling down to wait.

Laura paused, breathing deeply to steady her nerves as she gazed at the sliding doors flanked by golden statues of imperial Chinese maids. She knocked, and a man's voice granted her entry.

Five elders greeted Laura at a round table overflowing with vibrant Cantonese dishes. The aroma of sandalwood scented, mixed with the food's smell, loaded the air as one elder poured her a fragrant cup of tea as she took a seat.

Two of the men were familiar. She'd seen them with Boss Yang during the *Tian Chao* arena fights. Yet, her gaze swept over them, noting their unremarkable appearance and how easily they could melt into a crowd. The youngest was in his sixties, whereas the eldest, the one with the long beard, appeared closer to eighty.

Five ordinary elderly people owned the Jade Dragon Triad.

"We failed our people and you by entrusting the Triad to Michael Yang. We mistakenly believed his wartime defense of Kowloon qualified him for this responsibility." The oldest spoke Cantonese with a humble head bow. "We continue to express our gratitude for your rescue of the Triad and our people from the insanity of Yang and his Soviet collaborators."

"I did it for reasons other than saving you. I was simply trying to understand the truth behind all that chaos and the nature of the *Merzost*." With a curious glance, she lit a cigarette. "Michael Yang was far more evil than you could ever know."

The elders looked at her, wanting more answers. The oldest suggested. "Please continue, Miss Doncelli."

She let out her smoke, paying no attention to the food on the table. "He experimented on Vasily from infancy, inflicting unimaginable tortures that created a monster. After the fire at Yang's apartment, I discovered an undamaged safe holding all his biochemistry records from his early years. Also, a journal documenting his human experimentation while in the Soviet Union." She continually blew smoke out. "His plans for the *Tian Chao* fighters, aiming for chaos to give Hong Kong to the Soviets, were inconceivable."

"We are aware of it," the elder said.

The youngest of the elders intervened with a question. "What are you going to do from now on?"

"To be honest, I don't know." She extinguished her cigarette in the ashtray with a shake of her head. "It seems I'm headed back to Turkey."

"Governor Cecil and the British government advised against keeping you and the others in Hong Kong," the same elder revealed. "Michael Yang has deposited millions of dollars into your Lillian Dover account for his own purposes, despite being under investigation by the Scotland Yard. We're avoiding it to prevent issues with the authorities. Start a new life with that money. You're still young."

A surprised Laura nodded, taking a moment to fully realize what she'd heard. She glanced around, then at the elders. The opulent Chinese imperial decor evoked memories of a specific restaurant for her. With a nod, she posed a question. "May I purchase the *Tian Chao* and bring it with me?"

"No, you can't," the oldest replied. "Take it, including the people, as far away from Hong Kong as you can. We don't want more problems with that boat. Consider it as a compensation gift for you."

A light smile touched Laura's lips as she gestured towards the elders with her teacup.

PART TWO

Forza Catastrofe

27
INTERPOL

A nnoyed by the chaotic move to the new head-quarters, Henri Garnier hastily tucked the thick dossier under his arm. The thin man in a gray suit and dark tie in his early thirties had to navigate a maze of obstacles—boxes awaiting placement, workers putting the finishing touches on their tasks, and scattered tools and materials—in the hallway. "*Merde!*" he exclaimed to himself, frustrated by the obstacles and the relentless summer heat—the air conditioner wasn't working yet.

In June 1966, less than a week, all staff moved from their old Paris building to a new headquarters at *22 Rue Armengaud*, in a wealthy western suburb named *Saint-Cloud*.

"*Merde!*" Henri cursed upon entering the main office reception, finding two female secretaries frantically filing countless files into the new cabinets.

A secretary paused her work to answer the ringing phone. As she noticed Henri, she gestured for him to enter the president's office.

Henri entered after noticing the stylish door bore a new and brilliantly inscribed nameplate—Monsieur Alain Durant.

As he entered, the thin man saw the president gazing out the large window, lost in thought. "*Excuzes-moi?*"

Durant, a man in his late fifties wearing a black suit, turned and saw him. "Is that the dossier I asked for?"

"Yes, sir. Locating it in the right place was difficult amidst all the moving." He set the file down on the vast desk amidst stacks of folders.

Durant walked over, sat in the chair at his desk, in his new office, as the agency's emblem was visible on the wall behind him. He opened the file, leafed through some pages, and then looked up at Henri, his assistant. "Though Interpol includes almost 100 countries, I received a request from an unexpected non-member nation." He sighed with a nod. "The Soviet Union and its KGB are struggling with a problem of the past and have discreetly sought this organization's help."

"Perhaps an intelligence agency should handle this? MI6? CIA?"

"That's what I thought too, and even suggested, until I saw the pictures from the incident in Yakutsk. Trust me, I've never seen a crime this grueling."

"What is it about?"

Durant relaxed in his chair, retrieved a cigar, bit off the end, spat, and lit it with obvious enjoyment. "They call it the *Merzost*. Believed dead in Hong Kong, 1953, but it seems he's still around, slaughtering people recklessly." A large puff of smoke from his mouth filled his spacious office. "He's one of the altered people from the atomic bombs at the end of the Second World War."

"Do you mean those freaks who appear in the circus, monsieur?"

"Is that famous Liverpool circus that performed in Paris you're thinking of?" as Durant closed the dossier, he said. "Surely, the owners had connections to that year's events in Hong Kong."

Driven by curiosity, Henri fetched a chair and sat, ready to listen. "Tell me everything."

"The fire of Shek Kip Mei, a shantytown of Hong Kong. The British government officially attributed the fire to a bucket of hot charcoal that fell." He blew out another plume of cigar smoke. "In truth, it resulted from a fierce battle between *Merzost* and a powerful being known as the Fireman."

A knock interrupted their conversation. A secretary then entered, putting two airplane tickets on Durant's desk.

"*Merci, Diane!*" He revised the tickets and spoke to Henri once they were both alone again. "Go home now, pack your clothes, and be sure to bring your passport."

"I beg your pardon?" Henri said, surprised.

"We're flying to Rome this afternoon!" Durant replied with a chuckle. "We're meeting someone in Calabria."

"This case surpasses Interpol's capabilities, especially with a supernatural criminal involved." On the airplane seat next to Henri, Durant sipped his cognac and stated. "We're seeing Laura Doncelli because she's way more experienced with these things. She'd know what to do with this case."

Henri, holding his drink, listened and then answered. "Isn't she also a criminal?"

Durant placed his leather briefcase on the airplane's tray table. Choosing one from many dossiers, he opened it to find a red cover sheet, photos, and information. "I've secured and hidden it from the organization. I was told by the British MI6 to stand down. She seems valuable to them. Yes, she'd done some pretty criminal things." He sipped his cognac, observing his companion light up a *Gauloises* cigarette. "Her links to a Hong Kong Triad and several murders have brought her to the attention of the authorities. But the nature of her stance among the supernatural people makes her untouchable."

"What's your plan, monsieur?" The slim Henri asked.

"Given his experience at Scotland Yard and MI6, Mr. Bart, my predecessor, designed a plan. This is a White Notice, Interpol's only confidential file that we cannot acknowledge." Durant placed a white dossier, clearly marked

CLASSIFIED, on top. "The *Doncelli Directive*, named after her. It is also called *Interpol's Supernatural Special Operations Group*."

"From what I understand, you plan to create a special supernatural task force to tackle these crimes."

"*Exactement*!" Durant returned the dossiers to his brief-case, closed it, and placed it under the seat. His excitement was obvious as he received the small tray with *Calabrese Salad* and *Arancini* from the stewardess. With a smile, he rubbed his hands.

That evening, with few people around, Henri anxiously checked his wristwatch, seated on his large bag while watching Durant enjoy his cigar. He witnessed many vehicles, including taxis and *Vespas*, arriving and departing to collect relatives, friends and significant others.

Despite the evening, the persistent summer heat continued in Rome. This led Henri to remove his suit and lay it on his lap on the *Rome Fiumicino Airport* sidewalk. "Perhaps the train would have been a better choice? Or perhaps contacting someone at the local Interpol?"

While not frequent, the noise from late-arriving planes persisted.

"Remember, this is a White Notice job. We can't expose ourselves to the secrecy of the mission." Durant said, exhaling his cigar smoke. "That's why I asked Nico to pick us up."

"Who's Nico?"

"We both fought within the Resistance during the war. He was in France." A large puff of smoke came from him. "Like me, he was once a police officer. He's now with Interpol in Italy."

As if by chance, a tiny white *Fiat* pulled up right before them, prompting Henri to get up from his perch on the luggage. A sturdy man with a big mustache, dressed in a plaid short-sleeved shirt and shorts, came out and warmly hugged Durant.

Henri's curious eyes followed the delight of the two mature men.

"We've got a long journey ahead of us!" Nico loaded the bags into the back of his *Fiat* and gestured for them to get in. "I got some *panini* for you."

28
PALAZZO

As dawn broke that morning, the white *Fiat* left *Trebisacce*, heading south along the E-90 coastal route, beside the *Ionian Sea*.

Uncomfortable in the cramped back seat, Henri, tired and sleep deprived, lit a cigarette. His eyes almost closed as he watched the sun emerge from the horizon over the sea. "*Merde!*" He longed for a bed in his home of Paris, even as he wished to reach his destination. In contrast, he noticed Durant had repositioned his seat and was sound asleep, leaning against it. Henri remembered his boss and friend's long, boring war stories, particularly in that *Naples* 24 hours diner last night.

Nico drove in silence, enjoying the trip as if it were a vacation, not a mission. "Wake up, Alain!" he yelled and pushed his friend, never letting go of the wheel. "This is *Monticelli*."

As Durant opened his eyes, he saw the ruined remains of a small coastal town, abandoned, as they'd veered off course.

Henri's curious gaze, reflected in the mirror, prompted Nico to explain. "The Germans seized this place and massacred its people, resisting the Americans' recapture efforts."

The amazement was unavoidable as they traversed the ghost town.

To avoid hitting debris, Nico carefully maneuvered the *Fiat* downhill as Durant and Henri observed the dilapidated condition of houses and buildings, marked by bomb and bullet damage.

Despite the town's robust rock construction, the war left a lasting, silent testimony to its brutality.

Henri was astonished to find houses with second floors ravaged, and some weather-worn dolls left on the street.

To Nico and Durant it was too familiar, as they had experienced the war in blood and flesh. Henri, however, was only four at the time and has no memory of it, just fragmented flashbacks of German soldiers in his village.

The *Fiat* pulled up next to a ruined church. Its tower, with its bell, was still standing.

As Nico got out of the car and leaned against it, Durant also exited the vehicle and looked where his friend was pointing. "This is the place where it happened."

Curious, Henri got off and discovered a small, overgrown square with weeds pushing through cracked stone tiles.

Durant gave his assistant an explanation. "The Germans, for reasons unknown, massacred the town's population with automatic weapons after seizing it." He nodded. "We can assume that Doncelli's parents and relatives were among the casualties."

Once more, Henri looked around the decaying town, finding no people. "Who's in charge of this place?"

"Laura Doncelli herself," Nico intervened and answered. "She bought everything here."

With hands on his hips, Henri's face reflected pure astonishment as Durant tossed a dossier on top of the *Fiat*.

The three men observed a magnificent Italian-style mansion between the sea and the land on the coast, an attractive structure with verdant gardens, all enclosed within a fence. They were only one hundred meters away from the place they admired.

"They call it the *Palazzo*. That ten-year-old place came from Hong Kong, but back then it was the *Tian Chao*, a secret fighting ring pretending to be a floating restaurant." Durant read from the dossier and commented. "Laura Doncelli remodeled most of it, making it a permanent place, although some parts stayed the same."

"What's the reason behind that impressive palace being below the ghost town of Monticelli?" Henri noticed. "In complete seclusion and distanced from people?"

"What do you expect?" Beside his friend, Nico drummed his fingers on the *Fiat*. "If everyone rejects the altered people, where would they go?"

"Interesting," Durant kept reading the file. "She also owns property in Monte Carlo, Monaco, including two casinos. And one more in Ankara, Turkey."

"How was she able to purchase them?" Henri asked.

"The funds came from the Jade Dragon Triad. Apparently, a substantial sum of money belonging to their previous boss, Michael Yang, was deposited into a bank account in the name of Lillian Dover, which is Laura Doncelli's alias." Durant closed the dossier and looked toward the *Palazzo*. "What are we waiting for? Let's visit her!"

As Durant and Henri leaned on their *Fiat*, Nico tugged the fancy metal fence's string, making a bell sound.

They awaited. The mansion showed no signs of activity.

Nico pulled the bell a second time.

The three men waited once more.

"Perhaps we should try again later or tomorrow," Henri said nervously.

Despite the sea breeze, the sun's relentless heat beat down on them, marked by their despair and sweat.

Just as Nico headed back to the car, an old woman limping out of the building's main door caught his attention. She descended the stairs, slowly crossed the garden, and reached the gate. The men, finally seeing her clearly as she drew near, were terrified by her striking face—round, weird eyes and a mouth full of uneven teeth that created a monstrous look. "*Buongiorno signori. Posso aiutarvi?*" Her voice was hoarse as she asked from behind the gate.

Nico's response was hesitant. "*Buongiorno signora. Dobbiamo vedere Laura Doncelli.*"

"*Chi sei?*"

"Interpol."

She nodded, opened the gate, and invited them to follow.

"*Merde!*" Henri muttered, unsure about going in. In the end, he trailed the woman, behind the other two.

As the three men walked, they admired the gardens, whose beauty and variety rivaled even Versailles, though on a smaller scale. On the *Palazzo* stairs, a nearly imperceptible fault line between the sea and land caught their eye, revealing the gardens' beachside origin and prompting them to visualize the sand's replacement with soil.

Durant confirmed that the *Palazzo* was actually a boat, not a conventional building.

Upon entering, they were awestruck by the grandeur of the hall, complete with elegant furniture and a central chandelier. A luxurious staircase climbed towards the upper floors, flanked by closed side doors on the bottom floor.

As she slowly limped upstairs, the aged woman asked them to wait.

Durant placed his briefcase on the floor when he saw she'd gone to whisper to his other two companions. "I have a feeling that woman is one of the altered."

"I don't know, but she gives me shivers!" Henri replied with widened eyes.

Nico explored the hall, drawn in by the many paintings and art pieces. "Look at that! She owns *The Old Guitarist* from Picasso!"

"That's right. I got it at an auction in Paris."

The three men gazing up the stairs spotted a woman in a dark, flowered silk robe that nearly covered her body. She was identifiable by her long, wavy black hair and round eyes.

"Miss Laura Doncelli," Durant named her with a nod and a smile. "We didn't expect such a hasty reception."

Barefoot, she descended the stairs. Her small stature surprised the visitors as she approached without a word. Such a small woman with great power. She studied each of the men. However, she fixed her gaze on Henri longer than the other two. "You're a very nice-looking and pleasant gentleman."

Henri was speechless, captivated by her eyes.

"Why are three Interpol men here?" Laura directed her question to Durant.

"Did your maid tell you about us?" He showed the upstairs with a pointed finger as his response.

"What maid?"

"An old, limping lady opened the gate and greeted us."

Laura assumed a thoughtful pose and then nodded in understanding with a smile. "Mei Li, one of my residents, created that illusion to play a prank on you. She can be quite a joker."

Her response stunned the men, leaving them speechless and staring at each other.

Henri's eyes widened as he cried out, "*Merde!*"

"There's nothing to be afraid of," said Laura, gesturing towards the next room. "Let's discuss things in my office, shall we?"

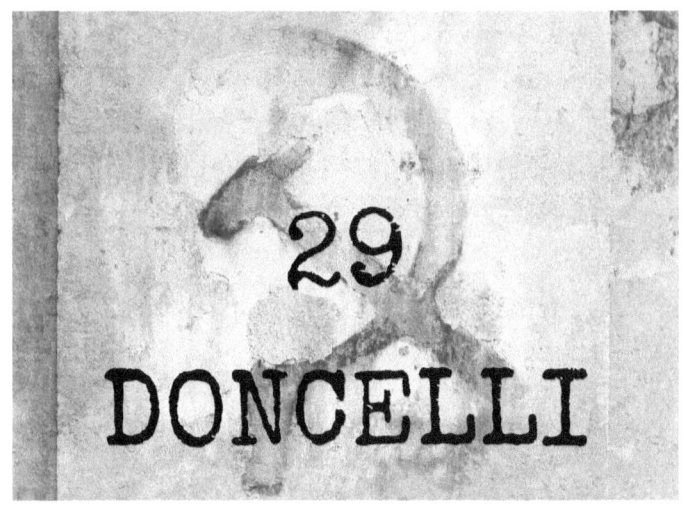

29
DONCELLI

L aura, behind her desk of wood and gold, ignited a
Fatima cigarette in its long black holder. She relaxed
in her chair. The large windows in the back offered a view
of an internal garden, complementing the one outside.
She saw her guests were curious about the large, Louis
XIV-style room. "My office decor projects an image of
wealth and authority."

"It's quite intimidating, miss," as he lit the remains of
his cigar, Durant replied.

"This used to be a restaurant in Hong Kong, did you
know that?" she stated with a nod. "Behind me lies the
garden where the hidden arena once stood."

"I am aware of this, Miss Doncelli," he said while placing
three of his dossiers from his briefcase on the desk. Next,

he retrieved a notepad, opened it, gave over some pages, and wrote some quick notes.

"Can we get to the point?" As she settled her cigarette down in the ashtray, Laura inquired, noticing the files and the behavior of Durant. "You came all the way from Paris to see me. What's the urgent matter?"

"Except for me, *signorina*!" Nico clarified. "I am from Rome!"

"The matter is quite delicate, Miss Doncelli. With your permission, I'd like to ask some questions to clear up a few things. May I?"

Henri Garnier lit his *Gauloises* cigarette with a nervous hand.

"I am usually reserved and avoid answering questions. But since you came such a long way, I'll overlook it this time."

"MI6 files allege a conspiracy to transfer Hong Kong to the Soviet Union. The extent of the Soviet Union's involvement with people like Michael Yang and former Governor Whaley, among others, is still unclear. Who were they? Spies?"

Laura took another drag of her cigarette, retrieving it from the ashtray. "They weren't spies. They advocated for Hong Kong's separation from Britain by using a defunct Soviet operation. Stalin made a deal with Yang to form an army."

"If Governor Whaley was indeed part of the conspiracy. What would make him support the American ships in Hong Kong, being a communist?" Durant wrote in his notepad with the answers he heard.

"He was not a communist. It was a diversion to mask the conspiracy. Anything else, monsieur?" She clearly wanted the meeting to end. "I don't believe your purpose here is just to ask pointless questions."

"How about one last question?" Durant's pen tapped against the notepad as his two companions watched the interview. "Who was the *Merzost*?"

Laura hesitated, took a moment to gather herself, and after another puff of tobacco, gave her answer. "Only three people knew who he was—me and two others who are now dead. And I don't plan to reveal it."

With silent nods of approval from his companions, Durant presented Laura with a plain dossier. "The KGB contacted Interpol for help. The *Merzost* is back at it again."

Laura fixed her gaze on Durant as her eyes widened, before shifting to the dossier. "I saw him die in Shek Kip Mei!"

"Everyone assumed the same, miss." A serious look accompanied Durant's reply. "There was a massacre in Yakutsk. The *Merzost* seems to be more chaotic and murderous now than it was before. It's all in that dossier given to me by the KGB."

Laura's hand hovered over the file, but she couldn't bring herself to open it. A tremor in her chin accompanied her glare at it before she turned to her visitors. "What do you want from me?"

"Your help. That menace is beyond the capabilities of both the KGB and Interpol. We trust your people are best equipped to handle this," Durant, smoking his cigar after placing his notepad on the desk, said. "Naturally, we will compensate you."

"Are you aware of all the shit we faced because of him and that fucking conspiracy?" With a slam of her fist on the desk, she surprised her visitors and rose. "I experienced exploitation and abuse, and this fucking cruel world denied my people their existence!"

"And so?" Durant's calm indifference took Henri aback, unlike Nico, who was familiar with his nature. "Are you going to help us?"

"I'd rather not!" In a state of agitation, she rapidly smoked cigarette after cigarette.

"Very well. . ." As he circled his cigar in the air, Durant opened the Red Notice file and read. "Your Beretta 950 was used to perpetrate murders in Ankara, Hong Kong, Bombay, Tehran, Cairo, Italy, France, and Monaco. Shall I go on with the victims' details?"

"Why the fuck are you telling me that?!"

"This Red Notice means we can extradite you to Switzerland to face charges for your crimes, Miss Doncelli," he gestured with a nod. "We might do it if you don't cooperate with us. Even that MI6 requested you remain untouched, we could change it."

With a furious scoff and gasp, she stormed out, leaving the three men alone.

"Did that need to happen?" Henri asked as he finished his cigarette. "Was blackmailing necessary to make her work for us?"

As Durant was about to respond, closing the Red Notice file, a tall, graying Chinese man in a black suit walked into the office.

"Gentlemen," Ming said. "Your rooms are this way. Please remain as our guests at the *Palazzo* until Miss Doncelli reaches a decision."

"Are you real or just another illusion?" Nico asked, unsure.

Laura smoked and meditated while lying on the bed.

Despite her apparent serenity, apprehension raged within her.

After placing the cigarette butt in the ashtray on her messy bed, with her black cat resting close, she turned her head, re-experiencing the Ionian Sea's familiar sight, which conjured a multitude of memories. She invoked a mental image of Aberdeen Harbour, Hong Kong, in 1953.

Laura put the ashtray on the nightstand next to the bed and sat down to appreciate her large room. After that the *Tian Chao* anchored off Monticelli, and secured an agreement with the Province of Cosenza to purchase the town, the Italian-born Laura, along with Hanzo and Ming, undertook a major redesign of the vessel.

To enlarge Laura's bedroom, Hanzo gave her his room, which included a small library, a modest bar, and a combined TV and LP record player. It also had its own restroom with a bathtub.

Just like the room, Laura had transformed in thirteen years. Driven by nostalgia about her past, scarred by killings, experienced good and bad sides of sex, and manipulated under Boss Yang, she was no longer the eighteen-year-old who lost her innocence much younger.

She was thirty and wielded considerable power. With the funds she inherited from Boss Yang—money the Triad rejected—she invested in real estate, profiting from two casinos in Monte Carlo and one in Ankara that specialized in baccarat and roulette. She also undertook hidden operations for clients and victims, targeting individuals involved in drug trafficking and sexual exploitation. Despite being a contract killer, her motivations were less about money and more about personal matters.

Although Laura had power and owned luxurious properties, she preferred the comfort of the *Palazzo* as her primary residence.

She adjusted her robe—her only garment—before settling onto the desk. Among the cluttered papers sat a framed picture of Francesco, her adopted son, whom she'd cared for after the Shek Kip Mei fire. She reviewed the letters her son wrote from his San Francisco private school, placing them in envelopes.

Laura, still deep in thought, opened an old accounting book from one of her casinos, letting out a sigh.

Interpol's sudden arrival was a game changer, particularly given Durant's blackmail. The resurgence of the *Merzost*, presumed dead, mainly threatened her life as she knew it.

Should she assist Interpol? Should she live clandestinely?

Laura had to consult her confidante, the only person who knew her fully.

Laura recognized the large, windowless space—a section she left untouched, preserving its original *Tian Chao* design—including the Chinese-decorated hallways.

Mei Li's room.

The elegant, chandelier-lit space still contained many square silk pillows and a floor-covering mattress. Countless shelves overflowed with perfectly arranged books, and Laura's gift of hundreds of LPs completed the impressive collection.

Near the center, sitting on floor pillows, Laura saw Mei Li's back. A plain pink dress, more in line with Western fashion, had replaced her traditional attire. At twenty-five, she'd grown into a young woman, despite retaining her slender, girlish figure.

While listening to the *Beatles* on a nearby portable record player, Mei Li read a large, complex book written in ancient Chinese. Laura's presence in the room caused her to lift the headshell, stopping the turntable. "I know why you are here."

Laura smirked subtly and chuckled, anticipating Mei Li's familiar phrase. "Don't joke around with the visitors."

As she sat facing her, she commented on her pink dress. "I brought it to you from Monte Carlo."

"Laura," she smiled, "you're still wearing that robe, and nothing else. Don't you care about being like that in front of men?"

"I've been with so many that I don't care anymore, you know." A common disdain colored her reply.

"After five years of near seclusion to recover from the trauma of Boss Yang's drug abuse and sexual assault, you have found intimacy again. I helped you get over it." Mei Li's expression became serious. "A fortunate encounter with Monsieur Laurent's son led to your purchase of his deceased father's property."

"Once more, I'll be forever grateful to you. I couldn't have done it without you." She let out a sigh and rolled her eyes. "My brief relationship with Jules began with a simple sunbath on the exclusive beach of a Trebisacce hotel."

"But through his father, you avoided his casino's near collapse, leading you to purchase it. That's how you gained power, wealth, and influence." Mei Li nodded.

"And eliminate men just as comparable as, or even worse than, Boss Yang," Laura spoke in a low voice.

Mei Li offered no response to what she said. Instead, she gave a stare that bothered Laura.

"What is it?"

"You won't find inner peace by murdering drug dealers and rapists. Though you've accomplished much more than you ever thought possible, your wounds still need proper healing. Your hatred of Boss Yang is obvious in the murders you've committed." With a shake of her head,

Mei Li looked down. "You'll receive healing and find your destined path with these men who arrived here."

"How?" To Laura's surprise, Mei Li appeared to have solutions to her predicament.

"You belong to Interpol." With a look at her, she softly restarted the record player, deliberately selecting *Here, There and Everywhere* after her reply. She then displayed the *Beatles' Revolver* album cover. "They are from Liverpool. Right? There is someone from there who can help you with the closure you deserve."

Laura nodded in understanding, but hesitated. "I can't bring him back, not after what happened back then in Hong Kong."

"You must bring him if you are to confront the *Merzost*," Mei Li said firmly. "He is crucial."

"This is exquisite!" Durant voiced his contentment at his breakfast. Toasted bread topped with eggs seasoned with herbs and olive oil, served alongside fresh fruit, a glass of orange juice, and a cup of black coffee—a Calabrian breakfast. "But where is that woman?"

Nico and Henri, perched beside him, shrugged, clueless. In the dining room, the three men occupied a long, rustic table for twelve, which was decorated with fresh parsley plants in pots.

Beside the chimney, gray-haired Ming, in a simple white shirt and brown pants, stood motionless as his eyes scanned the visitors.

"I am here, gentlemen!" Laura entered the room with a changed appearance compared to the previous day. Her white, flowered dress, though barefoot and fresh from a bath, surprised the men. She sat at the head of the table, lighting a *Fatima* cigarette.

Hanzo, a bit more overweight than he was thirteen years ago, came over to give her just a cup of coffee. "*Ijōdesu ka, okusama?*"

"*Arigatō*," followed her reply to the three Interpol men, whose mouths hung open. As she watched Durant reach for his cigar, her eyes met his. She offered her metal ashtray. "I will help resolve the *Merzost* case, as you requested."

"Let's get started then!" Durant exclaimed with satisfaction.

"There are conditions," she said, before drinking her coffee. "The freedom to work independently and to select my team."

A massive plume of smoke, nearly fogging the room, billowed from Durant's cigar. "Tell me, Miss Doncelli. Who do you have in mind?"

Laura, following his lead, blew smoke from her cigarette through the holder. "No one knows the *Merzost* better than I and my people, so I plan to take them to the mission." She gestured toward the chimney. "Ming, who's been my constant companion since my Turkey days, is like the father I never knew. Gentle but stoic, he's an expert in martial arts, weapons, and other things you can't imagine."

As the Japanese refilled his coffee, appreciative Nico ate his breakfast while also listening to her.

"This is Hanzo, who prepared this enjoyable breakfast. He is a remarkable ninja and samurai who aided me in my personal missions targeting these men."

"The same ones you have executed." Durant stated as he relaxed in his chair. "I have to admit, you did us a favor by getting rid of them. They were despicable criminals."

"I'm considering others for my team," she nodded.

"I also have conditions, Miss Doncelli." From his briefcase on the floor, he removed a White Notice, setting his untouched breakfast aside before placing it on the table. "I want Henri on your team."

Henri Garnier almost choked on his coffee, needing a napkin to clean his mouth. "*Merde!*"

"You must also adhere to the instructions in this confidential notice." Durant's hand tapped the white dossier. "Mr. Bart, my predecessor, designed this project with you in mind. The *Interpol's Supernatural Special Operations Group*, or ISSOG."

Laura made a curious gesture while listening, as she held the cigarette between her fingers. "Pardon me. What the fuck did you say?"

A look of astonishment overcame Durant as he stared at her, perplexed. "I said that you must . . ."

"Not this shit. The other thing."

"The ISSOG?"

"This is bullshit!" Laura took the white file and snatched a pen from Durant's shirt pocket. "I got to know my team thanks to the Soviet *Operation Catastrophe*." Below the CLASSIFIED title, she scribbled on the dossier cover in large letters. "I want this name!"

Durant repositioned the file for a clearer view of the cover. He read it aloud. "*Forza Catastrofe.*"

30
ARRIVALS

Laura pressed for the choice of the *Palazzo* as the *Forza Catastrofe* headquarters, refusing other locations, even the nearest Salerno. This was an additional condition to join Interpol.

Hence, they brought a computer, the same model as the one in the new Saint-Cloud building in Paris, over from Britain.

After one week, Laura observed the transformation of her Louis XIV-style office into a space mostly filled by the machine. Henri typed at a desk with a keyboard and screen, while intermittent lights flickered on a large mainframe and tall devices with large, rotating tapes. The computer's immense size and intricate complexity filled her with wonder as she studied it.

"This computer is an ICM 7991 model." Henri, noticing her presence, settled back in his rolling chair and lit a cigarette. "Aside from Interpol, the CIA and MI6 are the only other entities possessing this specific model."

She raised her eyebrows and extracted a cigarette from the pack of *Gauloises* on the desk. "I feel honored to have it in my home." She stumbled upon some thin dossiers, and without thinking, opened one. "Are these Cristal and Juliette's files?"

Henri noticed that Laura, departing from her attire of dresses and robes, had instead opted for a more refined ensemble comprising pants, a shirt, and sturdy boots. He thought she'd changed her appearance for the members' expected arrival this day and lit her cigarette with his metal lighter. "*Oui*."

"Why Cristal?" Her question came as she examined the dossier. "She's just sixteen years old!"

With his elbows resting on his legs and his smoke in hand, he replied. "That Cali girl got caught between the guerrillas, so we had to get her out of Colombia and away from her family. We hid her in Switzerland, hoping Interpol could use her, although we didn't expect it to happen so quickly."

Laura reviewed the computer-printed file, leaning against her desk. "What does she do?"

"In stressful situations such as fear, anxiety, or panic, a damaging invisible shield forms around her, deflecting any potential threat."

"So, you're essentially exploiting her emotions." With a disapproving sigh, she looked at the other file. "Is the reason you picked Juliette Bernard simply because she's French?"

"She's been through so much," Henri said with a sad gesture. "War, rejection, and her abilities led to a 21-year prison sentence."

"And what abilities might those be?"

"Her hands produce natural acid." He said with a nod. "For protection, she must always wear metallic gloves, even she cannot touch her own body."

"Oh, fuck!" she exclaimed in surprise.

Ming's sudden entrance distracted Laura and Henri as they turned to look at him. "Miss Laura," he said, "they've just arrived."

"Are you ready for it, partner?" Bearded Bubba Carson checked out the *Palazzo's* fancy entrance, racking his brain to figure out why it looked so familiar. He was behind the wheel of his blue-white Triumph Herald, which drove for nine days from Liverpool to Italy. "If you prefer, we can return home and enjoy the *Jules Rimet* tournament on the telly during the holidays."

"Fair enough, mate." Anxious, bald James Trask observed the building from his left-hand passenger seat. He inspected the building with his blue eyes, trying to recognize it. "I can't believe that bloody thingo used to be the *Tian Chao*!"

As Laura left the building, she met a joyous Bubba, dressed up in a black, short-sleeved shirt, who, after seeing his old friend after a considerable time, quickly went to hug her. His muscular arms enveloped Laura, making her feel small and fragile, like a kitten in a gentle giant's grasp.

"I appreciate your coming all this way, even if you weren't obligated." Laura, showing a rare smile, tenderly pushed him away. "You are growing older!"

Despite her small stature, Bubba looked at her with surprised pride, noticing the changes of her transition into adulthood as a glamorous and sophisticated woman. "Look at that!"

Laura's smile faded as a serious, mature James, in a jersey, jeans, and leather boots, slowly approached, with his tense face.

Bubba grasped the situation and left them alone. He greeted Ming at the door, and they entered the *Palazzo* together.

"Hello, mate," James said with a nod, but no expression showed. "Got your telegram."

"I had to call you. There was no alternative."

"So, you are working for the good fellows now." He remained standing in the same spot. "I thought *Merzost* died with the Fireman that night."

"Interpol contacted me with the news. I couldn't believe it myself." She came down the stairs to be near him.

The sight of her lighting a cigarette finally brought a smile to his face. "Some things just don't change! Like your smoking habit!"

James noticed several stone sculptures—Buddhas, dragons, and Shih Tzu dogs—during his walk along the paths of the *Palazzo's* central garden. He remembered the Tiger Balm Gardens in Hong Kong, where the shooting and his encounter with the *Merzost* took place. He swept the area with his gaze, and the surrounding four-story Italian-style palace amazed him. James looked up and saw that the original roof was gone, replaced by a view of the bright blue sky. "Crazy to think I fought here so many times!"

"Even after everything, I still considered the *Tian Chao* my home." On a garden bench, Laura fixed her boot. "The Triad gave it to me, wanting it removed from Hong Kong. But I've always disliked arena fighting."

"You did an amazing job, mate." He observed Laura from the same bench he sat on as she readjusted her somewhat worn outfit. "I read about you in the news. You are cashed up now. Men are after you, mate," James said, getting a bit choked up.

Laura glanced at him, seeing that he was trying to hide his feelings. She didn't react, just stood there. "How's the Scorpion in that circus?"

"I enjoy showing off my powers to people. Kids always want my autograph." He nodded. "Bubba is both my best friend and an admirable partner."

"Any woman with you?"

"I had a few, but nothing serious." He showed his emotions quietly. "None of them were like that girl I met ages ago when she was eighteen."

Laura looked down and lit her *Fatima* cigarette. "She's not around anymore, James. I am sorry." She hurried to walk away from him.

James saw her leave the garden before she disappeared through one of the many doors around.

Shortly after James' reunion, a black Mercedes-Benz Pullman arrived at the *Palazzo*. This time, Laura and her two companions, Henri and Ming, waited outside.

She spotted the Zurich license plates, realizing their thirteen-hour journey from Switzerland to Monticelli was a long one. Henri told her that their Naples stop had been relaxing, and the car was comfortable enough for the new members who had just arrived.

As Laura neared the car, she saw a woman in her forties, with blond hair, wearing steel gloves to the elbows and an olive green sundress. She opened the Pullman door and assisted the somewhat tense woman in exiting. "*Bienvenue Juliette. Je suis Laura Doncelli.*"

With a nod, the French woman struggled against the weight of her gloves before letting her hands drop.

Laura gently directed Ming, with both sympathy and tact, to escort her indoors using her Cantonese. As she observed a shy Colombian girl with long black hair getting out of the car on the opposite side. Fearful, she stared at the *Palazzo*. Her almond eyes reflected her terror.

"*No te preocupes. Estás en buenas manos.*"

"*Merde!*" Henri exclaimed in surprise at Laura's fluency in various languages.

As if Cristal were a child, she gently carried her inside by the hand.

31
FORZA

Mei Li stared at Laura, whose surprised and disbelieving expression filled the space between them. "I can't believe you'd ask me that!"

"Please forgive me, but I believe your help would be invaluable." A placid expression masked Laura's inner turmoil and uncertainty about how she would react.

For thirteen years, Mei Li avoided using her fearsome abilities, even though the former Hong Kong arena fights had made her known as *Hallucination*. Despite her ability to predict Laura's thoughts, the invitation to join *Forza Catastrofe* still surprised her. "This room is my only home, and you're the only person I've seen in all these years!"

A profound fear gripped Laura, yet she stood prepared for what Mei Li's powers might bring. "Like you did for me, you can help the new ones."

The girl looked up at the chandelier, sensing something. "Cristal is terrified, and Juliette is in complete sadness."

"More reason to help them."

Laura was the target of Mei Li's terrifying blank stare, which inspired fear. The square room underwent a rapid transformation, becoming a dark tunnel where spiders were swarming, while the sounds of a giant arachnid's footsteps echoed, growing nearer. At that moment, Laura's first hallucination began, and fear stayed. She gazed around, seeing how real everything was and how easily the terror could break her mind.

Ming did a great job teaching her how to face her fears, no matter how difficult the situations were. She remembered an exercise akin to yoga, which involved exhaling continuously. Then, with eyes wide, in complete control, she screamed to Mei Li in the dark. "Stop it!"

In an instant, the women were back in the room.

"Go away!" Mei Li begged with tears running from her eyes. "Don't come back!"

Laura nodded, got up, and left her alone.

Laura, surprised, saw Henri put dossiers on the long, rustic table with parsley plants, and asked while toying with her lit cigarette. "What are those files?"

"The computer files with information about each member." He responded with a *Gauloises* cigarette between his lips.

As she sipped her coffee, she observed Ming and Hanzo arrive first and sit on the right. Soon after, James and Bubba appeared and sat together on the same side, settling into the rearmost seats. The newcomers, Juliette and Cristal, sat beside Henri on the left.

Hanzo had prepared the breakfast in advance and laid it out on platters and jars next to the parsley pots, so anyone could serve themselves on plates and cups from a small table nearby. But just Laura and Henri had coffee. Everyone else declined anything, which highlighted the tense atmosphere.

Laura saw the fear and tension in everyone's eyes and, realizing the gravity of the situation, lit a *Fatima* cigarette. "I think we are all complete."

"You are not complete!" All eyes turned toward the last person who came in and sat in the chair opposite Laura. Surprisingly, Mei Li, wearing a simple yet bright white dress, attended, even though she had previously declined to join. She had sacrificed her confinement to be seen in public. "You may begin."

A slight smile accompanied Laura's nod. "Mei Li, welcome." But deep down, she was worried that she might lose control and affect the ones in the room.

James had never met her in person, which surprised him.

Henri was surprised to encounter the person who used an illusion of an old monstrous woman to trick him, Durant, and Nico.

Bubba recalled the moment he battled her in the arena, and she defeated him. "I remember a hallucination where you attempted to drown me in a compact car filled with water." He observed her growth with a smile showing his uneven teeth. "You're no longer a small girl!"

Mei Li listened, yet she offered no response. However, she turned her head and saw the two females observing Juliette's thick, metal gloves covering her hands on the table, sensing her sadness, and noticing the fear in Cristal's eyes as she remained still and quiet. "I'm here to help."

Laura examined the stack of files, chose the top one, and set it down in front of her. It was a KGB copy. After that, she moved the remaining files and shoved them against Henri's coffee cup. She showed everyone some pictures.

The photographs, in black and white, displayed striking visuals of a small town, with human remains scattered throughout the streets, in buildings, and on the outskirts. Unsurprisingly, some felt grossed out and shocked.

"It happened in Yakutsk, Soviet Union, last spring. The Red Army uncovered proof that the *Merzost* had slaughtered a population of two hundred."

James raised his hand and got everyone's attention. "How'd they know it was the *Merzost*?"

After going through the pictures, Laura picked one to present to him. "Do you recognize it?"

The picture displayed the Soviet emblem, the red hammer and sickle, painted on a nameless wall that was partly destroyed.

"Yah, the kitchen at the *Tian Chao*," he replied with a nod.

"He doesn't look like the *Merzost* we used to know, Miss Laura," Ming stated.

"I had the same opinion when I read this dossier. Even the Soviet scientists are puzzled, but there's evidence of him, and he appears to be heading west."

"And what do you want from us, Miss Doncelli?" Juliette, with a French accent, referred also to Cristal. She raised her heavy gloves to reveal her hidden hands. "I can't eat with these hands! I feel worthless. My life has been stolen. Yet, you bring us here against my will to be among you like a fucking freak circus!"

All eyes followed Laura, expecting her reaction.

"I've read your dossier, and I have a few things to mention. Would you prefer a private discussion?" Laura responded with unexpected calmness.

"Why not embarrass me in front of everyone now that you've exposed my shame?! Let's have a discussion right now!" She slammed the table with her heavy gloves, making it shake and knocking over some jars, which spilled their contents. Her actions left everyone stunned.

Henri, as he was told and ready, was going to pull out a gun hidden beneath his clothes, but Laura halted him with a hand on his arm and a headshake.

"Do you want the discussion now? Sounds good, let's do it." She responded and then lit another cigarette. "Despite the German invasion when you were fourteen, which disrupted your happy childhood, you still went on with your life. At sixteen, you and your best friend got married, and he rapidly had to become an adult to support you both, while you were also trying to conceive a child of your own."

"Stop it, bitch!" Juliette stood and slammed the table again.

"In August 1945, the police charged you with murder as your hands burned and killed your husband with acid, and they decided on a life sentence." Laura went on, remaining unaffected. "Interpol's involvement freed you from prison, allowing you to join my team."

Juliette's gloved hands rested on the table as she gritted her teeth, and tears ran down her face.

Laura put out her cigarette in the ashtray, got up, and calmly hugged her. "I sympathize. I've been there." Looking over her shoulder, she saw Mei Li's tear-streaked face, realizing that she had linked minds with Juliette. She mouthed a *thank you* to her.

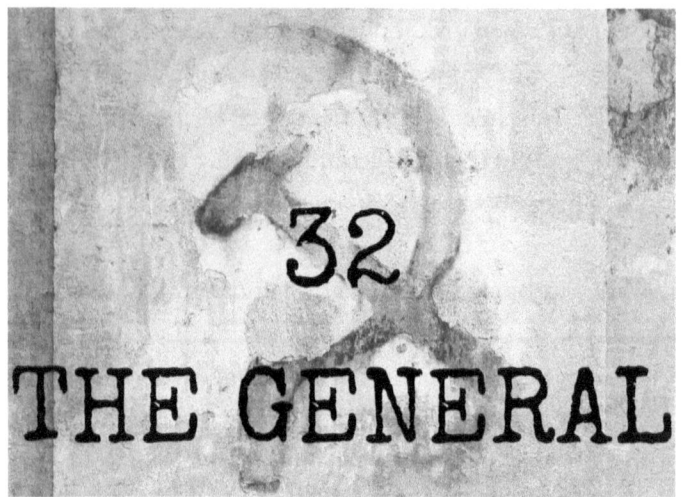

32
THE GENERAL

Laura found it hard to believe what she saw, yet was glad that Mei Li, previously isolated for years, had been a great help, seeing her with Cristal on a bench in the *Palazzo's* inner garden. The girls were engaged in a peaceful chat, with their hands resting together in their laps.

Mei Li appeared serene, but Boss Yang, who exploited her for his own gains in power and matches, actually scarred her, even convincing her through manipulation that she was a monster whose only use was to defeat her rivals. He also viewed her as a vital element in the defunct *Operation Catastrophe*. But when Laura first stepped inside the *Tian Chao* that Spring of 1953, Mei Li knew that her life was about to change because she sensed her.

She was twelve years old. Now, as a young woman, she seemed placid and content with her current life.

"Miss Doncelli?"

Laura looked back at her office, now a computer room, and saw Henri unpacking a box with black phones, placing them on the desk near the keyboard. The writing on the cardboard package was familiar, and she knew it was from Rome. Despite this, the *Poste Italiane* stamps showed the item was mailed nearby. "Is General Yarakov still in Trebisacce?"

"I'm told he's having fun on the beach, drinking vodka," Henri responded, keeping his eyes on the devices, as he also pulled a cable from the box. "Naturally, it's all at the expense of Interpol."

She smiled as she found it amusing, lit her cigarette, and crossed her arms. "These damned Russians always take advantage of Western comforts when they get the opportunity." She moved through the room, accustomed to the computers' mainframe beeping with the sound of rolling tapes, and headed towards the other window to look out at the garden bathed in afternoon sunlight. "Will we be able to contact the Interpol headquarters?"

"*Oui*," he said, checking out the telephones. He paused, then lit a *Gauloises*, gazing at her by the window. "Direct line to Monsieur Durant. And Nico in Rome."

Laura wandered through various ideas and shifted between them, lost in thought. "Was necessary to bring the General here?" She asked with a sigh of disapproval. "Perhaps I'll visit him in person."

Henri rested on the desk, putting the ashes into a crystal ashtray that was already full. "You might find him at *Mare Del Nord*, as he reserved a table for the night, paid for by Interpol of course." He blew out a cloud of smoke. "The bastard doesn't want to share the information we need. Not even the hotel name where he stays."

"I could get it my way." She smiled. While looking around the garden, she noticed James, half-dressed and sweating, doing push-ups in the distance. Even from afar, she discovered his arms were more robust. Though no longer the thin man she had met, he remained tall as she remembered. "Would you book a table for me? I need to walk outside to meet someone."

As James did push-ups, able to do a hundred easily, a shadow fell across him. He stopped to look, using his hands to block the sun from his blue eyes. "Ah, that's you, mate."

"Did you even use the gym?" Laura asked, showing her usual boots and attire, while crossing her hands. "It's too hot this afternoon to exercise."

James sat on the floor and shook his head in disapproval. "Are you asking me as my boss?"

"I am just concerned about you," she replied. "But if you don't want me here, I'll just go." Then she opted to go back to the building.

"Wait!" He stood and grabbed her arm. "I apologize. Seeing the gym looking the same is a real blast from the past, but it's making me feel devo about how much time has flown by."

With a quick nod of understanding, she gently removed his hand but kept staring at him with affectionate eyes. She let out a small laugh, observing that James still spoke with the same Australian slang, even after all this time living in England. "I feel the same way sometimes, and I like to recall the good memories of Hong Kong. That's why I've left certain areas of the *Palazzo* untouched."

He was silent for a moment but gave the same tender look. "Us?"

Laura looked back at the structure because something had touched within her and wanted to avoid his eyes. "The girl you knew is still out there, but she's not who she used to be." Her voice shook as she spoke. "She continues to question after all these years why she sacrificed her first and only love."

Surprised, he remained speechless. Although her back was to him, he saw her wipe away tears.

She crossed her arms and finally showed her face to him with a sad expression. "I'm sorry this happened. It's all my fault. I was too young and reckless then."

"It's all good, mate." His throat tightened as he spoke and scratched his bald head. "I was in a time when I felt less like myself and owned by the Triad, and I yearned to feel the way I used to in my old life before the war and the Hiroshima thingo."

Without warning, Laura turned around and walked back to the *Palazzo*. "I must go!"

"Where are you going?!" he shouted, confused.

As she headed for the steps, she said, "I have a date with a damn general!"

"*Benvenuta, signorina!*" The restaurant manager welcomed Laura from his podium. "*Come posso aiutarla?*"

"I have a reservation for Lillian Dover," she replied in British English. She studied subtly around the restaurant, which had few tables, and nodded when she saw someone. Then, she pulled some ten thousand Italian lira bills from her purse and put them under the reservation book. "I want that table." She pointed.

She wore a stylish black dress, a dark, short-haired wig, elegant sneakers, and a pearl necklace. She made herself unrecognizable on purpose.

The manager's eyes grew wide as he slipped the money into his pocket and looked towards the place she wanted. "Of course!"

She went after him, sat at the table she had chosen, and a waiter quickly brought her a glass of water. After that, she pretended to read the menu, but in reality, she was looking at the general in the corner.

Laura was no stranger to the restaurant, as she'd been there with any suitor. The space was a reasonable size, not large or small, but it had a stylish atmosphere, primarily adorned with framed vintage photographs depicting 19th-century Italian sea life. The Rizzotto was its specialty, alongside other seafood dishes. Patrons could wear whatever they liked.

Laura could see the booth steps from her table. From the photographs, she recognized General Aleksandr Yarakov in his fifties, the head of the Red Army in Yakutsk. His unconcerned attitude was once again clear as he consumed a large portion of seafood, primarily peeling the shrimp with his hands. He had a *Stolichnaya* bottle and a glass, which he drank from as if it were water. A short-sleeved blue shirt was beneath the napkin that encircled his neck.

She studied him and took a sip of water. As he finished his plate, she saw his messy attitude, but another plate was put on the table by a waiter. Laura nodded with a smile, as if she'd just had an idea.

The waiter came to her to take her order.

She gestured, saying, "Just a moment, I'll join that man in the booth."

After the waiter acknowledged with a nod, he walked away, and Laura got up with her glass of water.

When he saw Laura standing right there, the general stopped eating, stunned.

"Would you mind if I joined you?" she asked with a smile and with a perfect Russian accent.

The general removed his cloth napkin from his neck and wiped his hands carefully. He saw her, a small and charming woman wearing a black dress, but his astonishment stemmed from what he heard in his own language. "Who are you?" he asked rudely.

"I'm Lillian Dover, and I've been watching you." She sat next to him and used a wet napkin from her glass to remove the seafood stains from his face. "And I am captivated by such good looks!"

He looked pleased, yet he continued to have some doubts. "Do you understand Russian?"

"Of course, sir." She took a clean glass, poured vodka from his bottle, and then took a sip. "My dad was a dealer, and we once lived in Kamchatka."

"Where are you from?" he gave her an odd glance.

"I was born in Hong Kong." She replied after taking another sip. "And what's your name?"

"Just call me Sasha!"

The waiter came over to the booth and asked her what she'd like.

"Another bottle of vodka."

As the server left, the general observed her confused, yet remarked bluntly. "What do you want?"

"No dinner is complete without company," her lips, in vibrant red, curved into a smile. "I'd like an entire night with you."

His eyes widened, and he swallowed.

"What's the matter, Sasha? Don't you want me?"

"*Da!*" he said it while finishing his glass of vodka.

"How about we meet in thirty minutes?" She observed the clock near the entrance. "Where should we meet?"

"*Hotel Stella*, room 456."

"I will see you there."

She made her way to the exit in haste, ignoring the general's surprised expression, bribing the manager with more liras as she left the restaurant.

After stepping outside, Laura moved to the nearby corner with speed, got into a red telephone booth, put in a coin, dialed some numbers, and waited for a man to respond. "It's *Hotel Stella*, Ming. Room 456. You have thirty minutes."

After the call, her head rang loudly, alerting her to an approaching danger.

33
WHISTLE

H e climbed through the wall unseen, like a shadow.

Hanzo dressed entirely in black to blend in with the night's darkness. He walked across the roof with silent steps, from the building's rear to its front, where he gazed down, and again, found out the building was only five floors tall. His task was actually easy.

He spotted a streetlight. To make himself invisible prior to his descent, he retrieved a shuriken star from his belt and hurled it with remarkable accuracy to eliminate the light, thus obscuring the area in night. He placed a thin rope, fastened it to a vent pipe, threw it into the emptiness, and then descended, making sure he was alone.

He moved down from one floor to the next, arriving on the fourth-floor balcony, where he detached the cable, caught it, and secured it within his belt pockets.

Hanzo unlocked the glass door, slid it open, and pushed aside the curtain to enter a modest room with two twin beds. He removed his black headgear for a careful search and examination. He immediately noticed the light was on in an empty room, save for some Russian documents on a desk.

He realized, then went to the nightstand between the beds, dialed the phone, and waited for someone to pick up. "Ming, something doesn't add up."

"I am on my way, so continue searching, please." Ming hung the phone in the booth and walked across the lobby in a swift. Feeling the marble floor, he looked up to observe some employees behind the counter, engaged in an ordinary activity as they worked on paperwork in the absence of customers.

The *Hotel Stella* that General Yarakov had mentioned was not opulent, but a basic one, suited for tourists from cities such as Taranto, Bari or even Naples, wanting a cheap weekend on a peaceful and a nice beach away from the busy places. Ming found it unusual because Soviet officials preferred staying in lavish hotels during visits to countries in the West, even those within the Warsaw Pact.

When Ming got on the elevator, someone joined. He looked at his temporary companion with discretion, a dark-skinned man in a black raincoat, who was concealing something as he glanced at the numbers. "What floor?"

"Four," he replied in a deep voice.

The oddities appeared to be endless. It was a clear night with a warm temperature, so there was no need to wear a raincoat. Ming saw this and pushed the button to head to the same place.

Through his Triad experience, Ming knew the man beside was hiding a large weapon. He subtly put his hand inside his suit and touched his own gun, though he didn't take it out.

Once they arrived on the right floor, both of them got out. Ming, ever cautious, proceeded to the room through a carpeted hallway, but in a flash, he observed the man positioned beside the elevator, guarding it.

Hanzo opened the door after a double knock. His eyes widened as he saw Ming, and he gestured toward the open armoire in the room.

As they approached the furniture, Ming looked inside with a surprised expression. Hanging there were two flowered cheongsams, red and green, in place of typical menswear.

"It can't be . . ." Ming murmured. "I shot her with my gun!"

"She seems very well alive!" Hanzo exclaimed.

The door to the adjacent room, by the desk, swung open, and a familiar face appeared.

With both her arms crossed, Yanmu showed up in a blue cheongsam, looking identical to how she did thirteen years ago. "I knew we'd cross paths again, you bastards!"

Hanzo heard Ming's hushed words as he remained still. "Call her."

As the Japanese tried to reach for the phone, Yanmu quickly threw a dagger with great strength, which destroyed the device and ended up lodging the blade completely within the wall. The men were still and astonished when she put a silver whistle in her mouth and blew it with a silent sound. "He acts just like a dog, always doing what I say, and Boss Yang made this to control him."

"Who are you calling?" Ming asked.

"Are you stupid or what?" She said with a grin. "The *Merzost!*"

Ming drew his weapon and shot at Yanmu several times, but she was still unharmed and standing when his magazine was empty.

"I am fucking invincible now!" she yelled with a laugh.

"Run!" Hanzo spoke in a muted, worried tone. "I'll handle this."

Ming nodded and left the room, hoping to escape, but Yanmu began chasing him, forcing his way past Hanzo with impressive strength towards the elevator.

The man with dark skin saw the pursuit, pulled out an M14 automatic rifle from beneath his raincoat, and aimed it, but he didn't fire. He watched Ming and Yanmu push their way into the elevator and then moved as the doors closed.

After seeing the pursuit, he went into the room after he heard glass breaking and a blast.

As the man came into the room, he found the open aperture where the *Merzost* stood without the sliding doors, with only a hole and remains of a balcony, and bloodied Hanzo lying on the floor, expecting a response from the creature. He aimed his rifle and fired at the shadowy, faceless monster, shooting it repeatedly.

However, the *Merzost* leaped away and vanished.

In the cramped elevator, Ming and Yanmu's struggle, marked by repeated blows and shoves, caused the elevator to bump against the walls on its way down. He hit the emergency button before she could throw him to the floor.

With no apparent explanation, Yanmu's strength had increased, and, somewhat, the arm she had lost in the *Tian Chao* attack by the *Merzost* over a decade prior was back.

When she realized the elevator wasn't moving, she pushed her foot onto his neck and easily opened the doors inside and out to the second floor using her bare hands. After that, she grabbed Ming's clothes, brought his head to the edge, and then disabled the emergency button, changing it to an upward direction.

Ming couldn't find any reprieve from her extraordinary strength, as she seized him by the neck while he watched the elevator ascend, anticipating his death. His head was outside, and his body was inside.

A thump came from the ceiling, and an opening appeared immediately. Laura jumped on Yanmu quickly, hitting the emergency button with Ming's head almost severed by millimeters. He could retreat inside to join Laura in their fight against Yanmu.

Fatigued after a lengthy battle against two opponents, she leaped and escaped through the ceiling. She smirked and said, "Try to catch us!" And left.

Exhausted, Laura sat with Ming and, surprised, asked him. "Was that Yanmu?!"

34
KENDI MONGO

La Polizia Italiana were called to the hotel because of severe room disturbance and reports from guests about both the damage and disturbing noises. A dozen patrol vehicles pulled up and stationed themselves on *Viale Magna Grecia*, and they first saw a hole in the fourth floor and the remains of a balcony.

If Henri Garnier had not intervened upon hearing the news and arriving at the scene, authorities would have arrested all those involved.

Interpol's authority surpassed that of the local police force.

James came with him in the same car.

After that Henri briefed him, Nico was also en route from Naples, where he was temporarily living to maintain close contact with both the *Palazzo* and Rome, in his capacity as the director of Interpol Italy.

"This is a mad thingo!" James exclaimed when he noticed the damage illuminated by a large searchlight that the authorities had installed.

Henri simply nodded, then requested him to come into the hotel, where he presented his Interpol credentials to the police officers installed around the building, while observing the curious onlookers gathered outside in a silent stance despite the night. They let them pass inside.

When they entered the reception, they noticed the forensic team inspecting and collecting evidence from an elevator that had suffered significant damage. Laura spoke briefly about the incident involving Ming and the presumed dead Yanmu, in a call.

"The *Carabinieri* are on the way here, Signore Garnier," a senior police officer said as he observed them examining the elevator. "Trebisacce has seen nothing like this happen before, not since the war."

"Believe me, *Capitano*. We were working on the case, but we didn't expect it to happen in this exact place."

The officer replied, "Handle that shit before it's too late."

Henri nodded and poked James, intending to go upstairs via the stairs.

"What's your fucking name, and where do you come from?!" Seated in a chair with the balcony in ruins behind her, as the breeze accompanied the wind inside, Laura screamed at the man with dark skin.

"My name is Kendi Mongo, from Kaluba, Congo," he replied, yet distrustful of her.

Ming, battered from the recent struggle, was present during the questioning, gripping the M14 rifle on the ground.

"What were you doing here?!"

Ming, placing his hand on her shoulder, had to soothe her because she was so angry and frustrated. "How did you know he was here?" With a calm tone, he asked. As he was perceptive, he realized Kendi, who appeared young, posed no danger.

"I've been after the general these years to keep my family promise," answered Kendi. "I was present during every attack the bloody beast made, hoping to execute it."

Laura, now calmer, lit a *Fatima* and scrutinized him. "So, you're saying you even went to the Soviet Union?"

"That's right," Kendi said with a nod. "Since Yakutsk, I've tracked the beast and the general with his whore to this location."

Laura exchanged stares with Ming and asked, "Why are you following the *Merzost*?"

"It was during the Congolese Civil War. Soviet officers and that damned general visited my town, but when the people fought back, they called in the fucking beast, and it slaughtered everyone." He spoke with a slight tremor. "He also murdered women and children. Among them were my parents and sisters."

"How old are you?" Ming asked.

"Twenty-two."

Laura stood, faced away, and walked towards the aperture with the shattered glass door on the floor, exhaling smoke pensively. "Tracking the untraceable while traveling half the world is impressive. You would be a great help."

Kendi asked, unsure, "What do you mean, Miss?"

"Join the *Forza Catastrofe*." She turned around, holding her cigarette. "We're going to help you execute that beast."

On the fourth floor, Henri and James noticed the police, expectant forensic technicians, and a pair of paramedics that filled the simple hallway. They also found Hanzo on the floor, leaning against the wall, and being treated for his cuts and bruises.

Once he saw them, the Japanese spoke. "That African man shot at him, and the *Merzost* fled."

"I was told a fight happened in the elevator," Henri said as he lit his *Gauloises* cigarette. "Do you know anything about it?"

"That was Yanmu."

"Crickey!" James' blue eyes widened. "Are you sure it was she?!"

"She's still alive, and her severed arm is back. Worse still, Ming's shots had no effect. She appeared invincible."

"Yanmu, who's that?" Henri was oblivious as he searched his memories.

"I'll tell you about her at a later time." Laura emerged from the room and replied. "Right now, let's track the *Merzost* and the fucking general who tricked me."

Kendi and Ming, holding the automatic rifle, showed up behind her.

Henri frowned when he saw the Congolese. "He needs to be arrested immediately for illegally having a weapon and using it on private property."

"Cut the Interpol crap!" Laura replied with a firm voice. "He's going to be a great help in catching the *Merzost*, and he's coming along!"

Henri sighed and nodded, though he seemed uncertain as he shrugged.

After inviting Kendi and Ming to go ahead, Laura went after them, under the intrigued gaze of those in the hallway. However, James surprised her by stopping her when he grasped her arm.

She looked at him, annoyed.

"You shouldn't be in situations like this, mate!"

"Unlike you, I've dealt with this many times, and not in a circus!" She pulled her arm out of his hand roughly. "Mind your damn business, James!"

As the forensics team and police finally could enter the wrecked room, James observed her departure from the hallway. He felt a hand on his shoulder, and when he turned, saw a familiar face.

"James, you wouldn't recognize her. She's changed so much," Hanzo shook his head.

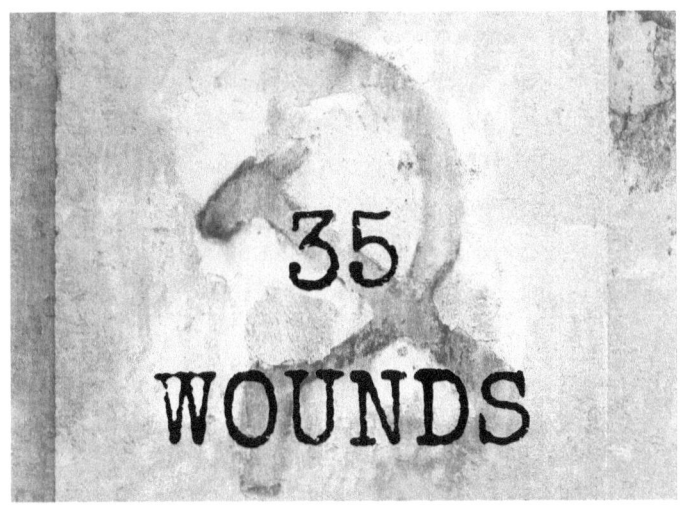

35
WOUNDS

The computer room's corner held Laura's aged desk. From this spot, she reviewed many dossiers that Henri had earlier supplied at her request.

With crossed arms, Nico, in his sleeping robes, watched her and saw her despair and apprehension. He shook her head and spoke while a somnolent Henri watched from his desk with a cigarette. "You won't find the answers there."

As she lit her *Fatima*, she gazed at him, leaning on her chair. "I'm still in disbelief about what happened last night."

"Not your fault, Miss Doncelli. General Yarakov was unscrupulous with everyone when we asked for his help."

She drank her tenth cup of coffee, having stayed up all night looking through files and keeping Henri awake. "I simply don't understand how I missed it!" With a sigh, she turned her gaze to the window, understanding that the morning had begun with the appearance of the sun. "I knew something was about to happen when my head started ringing, but it was already too late."

Nico was yawning, having failed to get a good night's rest because of his journey from Naples and his conversations with the local authorities. "Is it possible that the person you saw is Yanmu's child, an exact copy?"

Henri was close to laughing, yet he suppressed it.

"*Cosa c'è che non va*?" Nico inquired, clueless.

"You did little research on those altered individuals." Henri turned to Laura afterward. "No offense, Miss Doncelli."

"None taken," she replied with a faint smile and a wisp of her smoke.

"They have unique peculiarities that set apart from average people," he explained to Nico. "And one of them is that they can't bear children."

"We've figured out that Yanmu was the one behind everything in Hong Kong thirteen years ago, especially where the *Merzost* was involved." Laura got up from her chair, walked to the window, and looked at the inner garden while pointing out. "But we must discover why Yanmu hid her skills, and her connection to General Yarakov, along with the *Merzost*."

Nico waved his hand in annoyance, then tied his robe covering the pajamas. "*Qualunque cosa!* You do your homework!" He went to the door while Henri saw him leave. "I'm really craving my breakfast!"

From the computer room through the window, Laura recognized Cristal sitting quietly, appearing to be in a meditative state, on a bench surrounded by bushes and statues of Chinese dragons, while Kendi stood nearby, taking in the sights of the *Palazzo* from the inner garden. "Henri, could you and Ming travel to Taranto to purchase a radio capable of receiving police communications?"

Not long after Henri and Ming left for Taranto, Mei Li entered the computer room and saw it for the first time, noticing its transformation from an office, although she had been there twice since the Palazzo's modification. In a state of amazement, she slowly advanced toward Laura, engrossed in the dossiers, trying to find answers. Her tired, uncovered feet rested on the desk, and her boots were underneath it.

Laura started talking, uncertain if she was talking to herself or the visitor. "Boss Yang didn't mention a whistle, but Yanmu used one to call the *Merzost*. However, despite my vague memories, I seem to remember her having one during the fighting event that night of the attack." Setting her cigarette down, she saw Mei Li in a simple blue dress from France, and understood how feminine she was, despite her frightening abilities.

"Laura, you shouldn't be so hard on yourself," Mei Li said as she pulled a chair and sat gazing at the piles of dossiers on the desk. "Do not allow anger to take control of you!"

"You're acting like Doctor Freud now!" she responded with sarcasm. With a smile, she kept smoking while looking at her. "You wouldn't be here if you didn't have something to tell me."

"Your anger and frustration stemmed from revisiting the night you met Boss Yang and the *Merzost*, prior to the fire." Mei Li stated with absolute calm and certainty.

Laura was speechless. She stared, but tears formed, which she quickly wiped away, afraid of being seen.

"Don't be ashamed to let it out. Allow your soul to cry."

Laura nodded, went up to Mei Li, and knelt down, burying her face in her legs, weeping silently with only the faint sounds of her sobs.

The young woman waited until she stopped crying and stroked her hair.

"I spent all those years wondering if I had made the correct choice that night." Laura looked at her. "Was the confrontation with Boss Yang and the sacrifices justified?"

Mei Li smiled and wiped her damp face with her dress, behaving like a younger sister tending to her older sibling. "We'd discussed it many times," she said with a nod. "I have to say, if that night hadn't happened, *Forza Catastrofe* wouldn't be around."

Laura got up and used her arm to wipe her nose. "What makes you think *Forza Catastrofe* is the most important thing in the world, and why are you so persistent about it?"

"For several reasons," She then turned her gaze towards the window, which offered a view of the inner garden. "These two are one of them."

"Who?"

"Cristal and Kendi. They are connected, but they haven't spoken yet, though they're about to. Their backgrounds are similar, even though they come from different places. One lived with the guerrillas, and the other bore civil war scars." Mei Li concluded.

Kendi was in front, and Cristal looked up from her fashion magazine. "Is something wrong, señor?"

The young African, feeling anxious, let out a sigh and briefly checked the garden, taking in the sight of the golden Chinese statues nestled amongst the plants. He then returned to see the girl sitting on the bench. "I am told you are from Colombia."

She gave him a look of some strangeness. "Is there anything I can do for you?"

"Can I sit here, miss?"

Speechless and surprised, Cristal repositioned her magazines and motioned for him to sit down. "I'd rather leave if you're going to ask about my country, as I have unpleasant memories."

Kendi smiled and nodded. "I will not miss. What would you like to talk about?"

"Why don't we stay here and enjoy the garden around us?"

"Sounds good, miss!" he nodded again.

They both looked at the plants, flowers, and statues around them.

"Call me Cristal!" the girl demanded. "When you call me a *miss*, I feel old."

"My name is Kendi. You can call me that."

"Look!" she pointed in a certain direction. "Isn't it an Asian orchid?"

"I wouldn't have any knowledge of it, apart from the flowers in my homeland."

Cristal observed him with a touch of amusement, appreciating his appealing dark features and striking figure. "Tell me about flowers where you live."

Just as Kendi was about to reply, they both turned their heads at the sound of footsteps.

"Kendi, we need you in the computer room," Ming said, folding his arms. "We've set up a radio so you can begin tracking."

James and Bubba loaded their luggage into the Triumph Herald's trunk, which was parked near the beach, next to the *Palazzo's* multi-car garage. James had advised him to depart for Liverpool, considering his sour encounter with Laura the night before at the hotel.

Bubba disagreed with his decision, though still supported him always. "Mate, think twice before you mess up!"

"I don't think she needs me anymore after she racked me off," James responded as he closed the trunk. "There's nothing left here."

With his exceptional strength, Bubba kept him from getting into the vehicle and then, by lifting him by the shoulders, moved him, placing the feet on the ground. "Listen! Think with the head! Not with the heart!"

"James, you should listen to him." Laura's unexpected arrival caused both of them to turn.

"I believe I left something in there," Bubba said anxiously as he went back into the *Palazzo*.

James and Laura exchanged glances, speechless, unable to utter a word.

She went up to him, seized his white shirt's collar, and, because of their height difference, forced him to lower himself. Her eyes moistened as she gave him a brief, meaningful kiss.

James stood still, astonished, and didn't know how to react.

"Thirteen years after I gave up our relationship, I've been with many, but here is the eighteen-year-old girl who still loves you, whether you believe it." She spoke with her voice catching in her throat. "I've always needed you, and still do!"

His blue eyes widened as he struggled to find a response to her.

"I've been longing to give you this last kiss since before you left Hong Kong," she said with a nod and a slight smile. "Don't let my outbursts carry you away."

"Are you trying to return to me, mate?" he asked, unsure.

"I wanted you to know my feelings despite all that time, James," she replied. "Don't take it for granted!"

"Is this? A goodbye kiss?"

"If you want it that way," she turned and walked back inside. "Join us in the computer room if you wish, as Kendi already began on the radio."

James found everyone already in the computer room. The space was broad, but it seemed too crowded.

Kendi sat at a table brought from another room, listening to the radio transmissions, mainly in Italian, while Ming whispered the translations beside him.

Laura watched with Henri and Mei Li.

Bubba and Nico were there too, with Hanzo behind.

Cristal stood near the window to the outside.

Even Juliette, with her metal gloves, remained alone in a corner.

Kendi used a pencil to write what Ming whispered at every radio message. By adjusting the tuner, he altered frequencies, picking up various police, Carabinieri, and military communications. "Do you have a map?" He urged.

Henri promptly found a map of Italy in his desk's drawers and gave it to him.

Kendi unfolded the map and put it on the table, then reviewed his earlier written notes. "The police received a report of a stolen vehicle on E90 near San Basilio last night, with witnesses describing the perpetrators as an Asian female, an adult male, and an unidentified black individual," he stated as he drew a circle on the map. "This morning, they found the same car near Taranto, close to Montemesola. They abandoned it." He marked the map again.

"What's the point of all that?" Nico spoke, unconvinced.

Bubba hushed him by putting his finger on his lips. "Let him work!"

Kendi continued, "They saw them again without the dark one, arriving at a train station in Gorgofreddo with a destination to Monopoli."

"Monopoli!" Laura exclaimed in surprise. "They are going to Bari intending to take a ferry."

"Why?" Nico asked, still incredulous. "Where?"

"I recall that bitch of Yanmu challenging us to pursue them after the fight in the elevator," she replied. "They want us to go to Eastern Europe."

"Dubrovnik," Ming said, with a stiff nod.

"Who is going with you, Miss Doncelli?" Henri asked. "The Yugoslavian authorities are difficult to handle. Also, it will get tougher once you cross the Iron Curtain."

"I am going," James said determined.

Each person volunteered to join, one at a time. Even Cristal demanded to go despite Kendi's quiet objection.

"I will go too!" Juliette shouted to everyone. "Nothing can stop me! Not after all the years locked in a cell!"

"A *Volkswagen Kombi* is at the garage." Laura spoke, and then everybody rushed to leave the computer room.

The only people remaining in the room, Henri and Nico, exchanged glances.

"I suppose I must look after the *Palazzo*." Henri lifted his shoulders in a shrug.

"I am going to the kitchen to make myself a panino!" Nico exited, upset.

36
DUBROVNIK

As a member of Interpol, Yugoslavia was unusual because it was a communist nation, yet its president, Tito, the *Benevolent Dictator*, frequently opposed the Soviet Union's efforts to enforce its policies. He aimed to remain neutral in a world dominated by two superpowers.

But following a recent event in Dubrovnik, Tito connected with the Soviet Union.

A bizarre massacre had taken place in the Old Town.

Yugoslavian General Nikola Ilić and Soviet Colonel Sergey Andreeva received Laura Doncelli after the local police brought her from the Port of Gruz. She was not alone. The Australian Scorpion James Trask, Mei Li and Ming were with her.

Hanzo, hidden from everyone, roamed on the rooftops wearing black as he followed them without suspicion.

Past the summer midnight.

The police were the only ones there as they walked towards the arches, with the cathedral behind them. As they got closer to the area with the medieval paved floor, they stopped.

"I can't go there!" Mei Li pulled Laura's arm, whose face showed distress. "I feel a harrowing presence!"

Laura knew her fears could trigger her abilities, so she conceded and let her wait at a distance, outside of the restricted zone.

James and Ming, along with the two officers, were the only ones who went with her.

"The victims were tourists." General Ilić spoke in Serbo-Croatian language while holding a flashlight. "Swiss tourists, all elders."

Laura listened, nodded, and then talked to the Soviet officer. "I sincerely hope you are the actual person from the Red Army, not a fraud like Yarakov."

James walked in farther, and his feet were making a splashing sound as they hit something on the floor. "I believe there's a damn leak!" He noticed an odd, potent metallic stench.

Although he only knew basic English, the Yugoslavian general understood, and he answered in the same way, interrupting the Colonel's words. "You've just walked into a huge puddle of blood." He directed the light toward it.

The presence of red liquid staining his boots filled James with horror.

The Soviet Colonel, who also understood some English, switched on his flashlight and directed it upwards, toward the ceiling between the building and its inner arches.

Blood was still dripping from the gruesome tapestry that hung between the two columns, a drapery that was crafted from fresh human remains such as bones, skin and various body parts.

Ming shifted his gaze to another scene, impressed.

James quickly ran away to a corner to throw up.

Laura studied the horrid craft as thoroughly as she could, then looked down and examined the blood-soaked clothes and jewelry beside her. "The Yakutsk report's description of the *Merzost* as an uncontrollable creature was correct." She walked away, lit a cigarette, and spoke in Russian. "If a whistle controls him. Why is he going too far?"

"It wasn't like *Merzost* was thirteen years ago." Ming stated. Over time, he understood almost all the languages Laura knew, like Russian, even if he couldn't speak them.

James, looking pale and slightly faint, rejoined them, eager to leave.

Laura glanced up at the roofs and secretly saw Hanzo's silhouette in hiding, watching. "I'm sure Yanmu and the phony general have something to do with it."

"We don't have an Aleksandr Yarakov listed in our organization, Miss Doncelli," the colonel clarified. "He was a criminal who had rebelled against the Politburo and the Communist Party."

"A dissident who joined forces with Yanmu," Laura stated as she and her group made their way towards the police officers covering the area. After letting out a cloud of smoke, she kept talking. "Now that *Operation Catastrophe* is over, what is Yanmu's purpose? What is their reason for wanting the *Forza Catastrofe* to track them?"

"I don't fucking care what they wish!" the general said harshly. "The president wants them out of Yugoslavia!"

"And prevent them from entering the homeland!" the Soviet colonel added.

"We'll give them a damn chase if that's what they want!" Laura nodded, then thoughtfully gazed at Mei Li, who was standing nearby in one of her feminine dresses and leather sandals, illuminated by a street lamp. "Kendi could track them, although Mei Li's help would be faster, and she would know their next destination."

"I'm not doing it!" Mei Li screamed.

Laura noticed her terrified, with her arms folded and a cigarette kept in one of her hands. "The *Merzost* killings put us against the clock."

"He's deliberately using lives to track them," Ming said, trying to persuade her. "We have to stop new massacres."

Mei Li, with a wet, shuddering face, looked at Laura and Ming. She saw the military officers and police awaiting a long way away. With tears in her eyes, she turned to James, who was behind, and addressed him. "I need one of your boots."

James's blue eyes grew wider in surprise, but he then showed his agreement with a nod. He removed his right cowboy boot, which had a nearly dry bloodstain on it, and handed it to her.

Mei Li, holding the boot, looked at everyone and spoke in a shaky voice. "Leave me alone while I do this. I don't want to hurt anyone."

Laura nodded in agreement and asked everyone to let her concentrate, while also causing James to limp because only a white sock covered his right foot.

Mei Li took off her sandals, put her bare feet on the ground, squatted down, and held the boot. A trance seized her, and her disturbing actions frightened the observers, the authorities, who were retreating even being far enough.

The men aimed their weapons at her.

"Hold your weapons!" General Ilić gave a warning to the police and military forces. "Or there will be consequences if anyone fires a shot!"

Despite the warning, terror seized some because of Mei Li's powers, and men were about to shoot. James used his power by putting his hands together on the ground, forming a radiant energy barrier to encircle them and prevent any harm from discharged bullets. Laura and Ming were astonished because they had never seen his full potential.

The *Scorpion*, in all his splendor.

As Mei Li dropped the bloody boot, the luminous barrier vanished, and Laura rushed to her side, seeing her weakened state after collapsing from a trance.

"Are you alright?" Laura asked as she held her in her arms.

Mei Li's eyes regained the normalcy, and color returned to her pale face as she responded weakly. "They're heading north, but he continued his killing rampage and left a message for us at *Vila Planina* near Pobrezje."

37
SARAJEVO

Nestled in the mountains, *Vila Planina* was a tiny collection of chalets that offered a stunning view of the Port of Dubrovnik. It was essentially a resort, offering stays for those wishing to hike and enjoy other outdoor activities.

Since it had been closed for long, no tourists came, making it suspicious when armed Yugoslavian soldiers arrived at dawn. With the iron gates open and a broken chain, the *Merzost* clearly was responsible.

General Ilić had prohibited motorized vehicles, so the men entered the property on foot, carrying rifles. Laura led the way as she held her Beretta while being followed by some *Forza Catastrofe* members. Kendi also walked with his automatic rifle.

Cristal insisted on accompanying them because she believed Kendi's presence would make her feel safe. However, James, Ming, and Bubba were all around protecting her.

Hanzo was aware of the surroundings while hiding in the woods.

The soldiers reached the reception office, which was the first chalet, after passing over the narrow walkway for some time. The young officer signaled with his hand, instructing two soldiers to follow him into the building while the others were told to remain outside.

No one spoke. All held their breath, fearing a dreadful outcome, particularly after the incident in Old Town.

Eventually, the soldiers got out, repulsed, and hurried off to vomit close by.

Laura closed her eyes, envisioning something similar to what she'd seen the night before. "Shit!"

The young officer emerged unaffected and searched until he spotted someone. "Miss Doncelli, please come here!" He requested in Serbo-Croatian.

"Ming, you come with me, and the rest of you stay here." Laura instructed her group as she went in with him.

After entering, the officer provided some comment. "We had touched nothing, but I assumed it was best you could inspect it before the General Ilić arrives along with that Soviet bastard." He pointed in a direction. "It's in the kitchen over there. Not as gruesome as Old Town, but still unpleasant to look at. The owner of this place is dead."

Laura appreciated it and rapidly looked around. On one side, she saw a counter with some papers and a window framing the mountains, while on the other side, a small cafeteria had tables and chairs stacked against the wall, and it was currently closed. "Look, Ming, the kitchen is right there."

He went after her, and they pushed the swinging door to go in.

The warning proved accurate, and they discovered a man's body, which was in fragments and spread all over the floor.

"As you said, the *Merzost* crossed the line this time," Ming said with his regular stiffness as he scanned everywhere.

Laura looked over the counters and saw drug paraphernalia, such as two empty crystal syringes, some heroin powder, tubes with blood, ties, and a spoon that was clearly used for heating on a stove. The discovery brought back memories of her gruelling experience with Boss Yang, who used drugs to enhance the abilities of the altered. "No doubt the fucking bitch of Yanmu used it!"

Ming said, "It explains her unexpected abilities."

"The *Merzost*, or whoever is with him, gave us a message similar to the one in the *Tian Chao*." Laura pointed to the wall beyond the kitchen appliances, where he had painted the Soviet hammer and sickle emblem in blood. Yet, written words underneath read—*Maršala Tita 25*.

Laura stood on the third-floor balcony of *Hotel Centar*, watching the building's facade while lighting a cigarette. Allegedly, the *Merzost* selected the *State Investment Bank of Yugoslavia*, though the reason was unknown.

Adding to the enigma, she received a note written in Cantonese, penned in Yanmu's distinct handwriting, upon arriving at the hotel the Interpol had selected. She became aware at that moment that she and Forza Catastrofe were under watch. The instructions clearly showed that she would call to set up a meeting at the bank.

General Ilić instructed the Yugoslavian forces to encircle the building and set up security checkpoints throughout Sarajevo, while Colonel Andreeva contacted the Soviet Supreme, which immediately began gathering information from the KGB concerning *Merzost* and Boss Yang.

Lost in thought and exhaling smoke, she was bathing in the midday sun when a knock at the door startled her. She took out her compact Beretta, warily moved towards the door, felt the surface, and then spoke. "Who is there?"

"It's me, Nico, Miss Doncelli!"

Surprised, she nodded slightly as she recognized his Italian accent, then opened the door. She saw him smiling, and it seemed like he was visiting a relative. "This is a bad time for a vacation!"

"I'm here to deliver something to you—a gift from Interpol." He revealed his thick leather briefcase with a double tap on the surface. "*Lasciami mostrare!*"

Nico, excited and in his summer clothes, entered without being asked and put the briefcase on the bed. Laura watched him with a sigh and rolled her eyes as she closed the door behind her.

He opened the case, and it revealed a new type of pistol. "This is the M1966D, a unique model, specially manufactured for you directly from the Brescia factory." His excitement seemed more like a salesman's. "It's more precise and lighter than yours, and even though it's larger, it's easy to handle, which will help with your accuracy."

Laura's new weapon surprised her. Initially, she was hesitant even to take it. She took hold of it, assessed its lightness, and pointed it toward the balcony. "I like it, but I'll have trouble getting rid of my small, fifteen-year-old gun."

"It's time to put down that relic and embrace the innovations!"

As she was about to speak, the black phone on the bedside table rang, surprising both of them.

Nico saw Laura answer the phone in Cantonese, leave her new weapon on the bed, and then end the call after a few minutes.

"Yanmu demands to meet me at the bank over there." She pointed outside and spoke with utmost seriousness. "She wants me to bring five of my team, warning me that the *Merzost* would kill soldiers if I don't comply."

The bank's interior captivated Laura, an early 20th-century classic and a testament to the Austro-Hungarian

Empire, having endured both World Wars. Her presence wasn't for tourism. She was there to satisfy Yanmu's requirements. She swiftly surveyed the two-story structure from the marble square, and she gazed upward to see a large chandelier, which illuminated the space and had been added in recent years, hanging from a glass ceiling.

She brought along five members of the *Forza Catastrofe*. Her choices were Bubba, Cristal, Juliette, Kendi, and Ming. She decided not to bring Mei Li, as she was still unwell after what happened in the Old Town, and James was also absent despite his disagreement. She wanted to prevent his strengthened powers from accidentally flaring up, so both stayed at the hotel with Nico.

Laura and her team stood in the evacuated bank's center, waiting for the clock on a column to strike two, with only a few minutes remaining.

Alert, dozens of Yugoslavian soldiers surrounded the building with a perimeter, ready to respond to any threat. There was even a unique cage built to capture and transport the *Merzost* back to the Soviet Union.

"Where's that bitch, Miss Doncelli?" Kendi approached and whispered. Cristal followed him in silence, seeking a sense of security.

"In a couple of minutes." Laura couldn't take her eyes off the clock, and although its hands kept moving and time was flying by, it felt like ages.

"What's the fucking point of keeping me around when that idiot made all these demands?" Juliette could not hide her dissatisfaction standing with her heavy metallic gloves.

Bubba hushed her by putting his fat finger on her mouth. "Shhh!"

Laura's hands shook, and her head rang loudly, warning her of the imminent danger as the last minute ticked away. Then, she signaled Ming, who was right beside her, understood and quickly used the walkie-talkie to send a warning to General Ilić.

Footsteps resonated in the nearly deserted bank, and Yanmu emerged from a corner, dressed in a red floral cheongsam, with noticeably heavy makeup, especially her red lipstick. "Mui Mui, we meet again." She halted several meters away from the group.

Laura couldn't get a good look at her in the elevator struggle, but the bright light from the glass ceiling gave her a better view. She nodded, staring at her, still finding it hard to believe that her arm had regrown, well alive after Ming shot her that night. "I saw you die in Hong Kong. How?"

A slight chuckle accompanied Yanmu's response and smile. "Boss Yang had just used his formula to inject me with the *Merzost* blood, which permitted me to live."

"It explains why he was in that room after the laboratory," Ming whispered from behind.

"Can you tell me how the *Merzost* survived?" Laura asked her. "Everybody watched him die with the Fireman."

"One of his many abilities is resurrection," she replied with a smile. "He will always come back, no matter how much you damage him."

"Tell me, what do you fucking want from us?"

"Your team, Mui Mui. The *Forza Catastrofe* belongs to us. It was a creation to serve the Soviets."

Laura acknowledged something with a nod. "You and the *Merzost* caused that massacre in Yakutsk, so you could find us. Isn't that right?"

"You are not in the wrong, Miss Doncelli. Or shall I call you Lillian?" General Yarakov showed up, with his hands shoved into his pockets. "We learned about you from the news, about the casinos and your wealth, your travels to Monaco, and we knew you lived in Italy."

"However, only a massacre caused by an overpowered individual could grab attention and unite the *Forza Catastrofe,*" Yanmu kept explaining. "This team you have was born from Project Catastrophe, only that Hong Kong is no longer the goal."

"It's my homeland, Miss Doncelli," Yarakov said with his thick Russian accent. "To overthrow all those damn leaders and every member of the Communist Party. They have to pay for everything they had done."

"So, Mui Mui. Give us that team, and we will spare the lives of the soldiers outside."

Laura looked down at the marble floor, deep in thought, yet the ringing wouldn't stop. "*Preparato,*" said to Ming, then glanced at Yanmu. "No."

"Just as I thought," she said, then took out a metal whistle from her pocket and blew it, creating a sequence of silent notes.

Yanmu and Yarakov quickly escaped to safety as the glass ceiling shattered. Amidst the shattering glass, Bubba used his size to protect three people, Ming sought refuge under a desk, and Laura, while fleeing, drew her Beretta, which she'd got in Turkey, and successfully somersaulted to avoid the dangerous shards.

Two figures in black plummeted onto the marble floor from the third story. Hanzo, in his ninja gear, had driven his samurai Katana into the *Merzost's* stomach, and he came to rest on the creature without injury. But soon after, the *Merzost* slammed him into a hard column, and he lost consciousness.

He rose to his feet, revealing his true form as the others watched, then flung the blade away after taking it from himself.

The *Merzost* allowed his true appearance to be seen. Disturbing, round, white eyes defined his face with small black pupils. His mouth, lacking lips, was always open, exposing sharp, pale teeth, and excessive saliva dripped from it. With a twisted, dark physique, he possessed powerful arms and hands showing extended, sharpened nails.

Laura nodded, recalling the notes from Boss Yang after observing him. Since he discovered his ability in his infancy, he underwent various experiments and alterations, which ultimately shaped him into the monstrous being he became.

Once again, Yanmu appeared and whistled.

The *Merzost* darted across the window, shattering it, before rushing toward the soldiers outside, who subsequently shot him with automatic weapons fire. He vanished once more.

General Yarakov, armed with an RPK, fired multiple shots at Laura's team while approaching them.

From their spots, Laura, Ming, and Kendi returned fire at him while Bubba shielded Cristal and Juliette, taking two bullets in the back.

Yanmu remained unharmed even though they shot her many times. She seemed to enjoy it.

Cristal, in a moment of terror, screamed at the top of her lungs with her eyes wide open. An invisible shield-like force abruptly pushed Yarakov away, like a thrown doll, and he lost consciousness after hitting a solid column.

The fire exchange stopped. Yanmu fled, and then, as Cristal fell silent, Laura looked back to find Bubba on the floor. Juliette and Kendi were already checking him, and there was some blood on his back.

Ming rushed to see how Hanzo was doing, finding him still knocked out.

The *Merzost's* fury and atrocity toward the soldiers was boundless and cruel. He gruesomely took the lives of the soldiers and, with his incredible strength, ripped apart even the toughest cars to access his victims inside.

Nothing could harm him, not bullets, not weapons, nor even a cannon shot from close range.

Seeing the military's disadvantage against the creature, the Australian Scorpion, filled with urgency, ran from the hotel where he and Nico were witnessing. Then, after turning the corner, he leaped in just as the *Merzost* was about to claim the next victim.

With energy flowing from his hands, James penetrated inside the dark monster, which responded with an anguished screech. They fought for a few moments, but the *Merzost* hurled James to the ground, then leaped away, disappearing over the roofs.

Laura emerged from the bank to find a terrible sight. A dozen soldiers lay dead or wounded in the street, while the survivors were tending to their injured comrades.

A look of sorrow and disappointment caused her to shake her head. She dropped to her knees, feeling helpless as she wondered whether she and her team could ever defeat the *Merzost*.

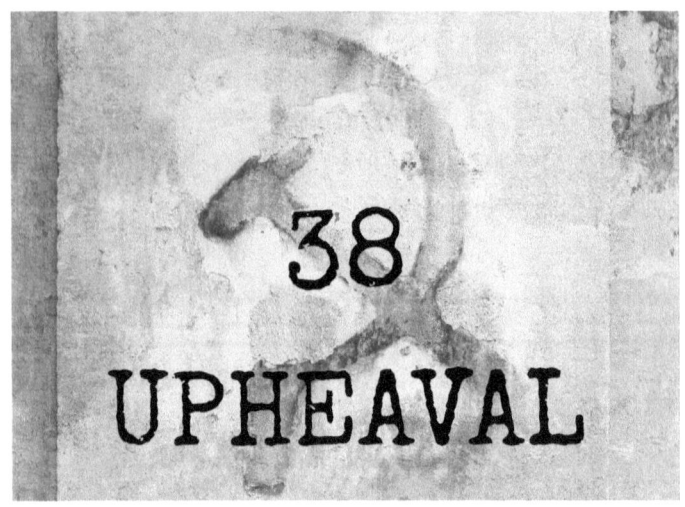

38
UPHEAVAL

James Trask sat on a small stool while he looked around. He was in the infirmary at the Novi Sad military base and could see the trees, along with a view of the nearby Danube, and he also saw a framed portrait of Marshal Tito hanging on the wall between the windows.

He saw the six Yugoslavian soldiers wounded by the *Merzost* lying on beds, and he saw that some were badly hurt. Given the gruesome wounds and mutilations, one might have believed a brutal war had occurred, but in reality, they were the creation of a single creature.

A nurse came over and gave a shot of morphine with a glass syringe to a naked patient, who had bandages on his stomach and was in agony, fighting for his life. Then, she put the syringe down on the nightstand tray, glanced at James, and gestured a negative response.

"Won't he survive, miss?" he asked with a serious expression.

The nurse stated, "He tore out some of his organs, and he's just waiting to die."

"Your English is good, miss. Where did you learn it?"

"I was in England during the war," she said while checking on the patient. Then she left without delay.

"Is it you, mate?"

When James saw Bubba had regained consciousness after his surgery to remove two bullets from his back, he felt dazed. He found it amusing to see his large friend's feet extending beyond the too-small bed. "Yes, partner. We had to bring you here."

"As long as the others are safe, I don't mind." After, he glanced around. "Are we still in Sarajevo?"

"The military moved us to Novi Sad to keep us safe because we don't know where that *Merzost* or the bitch of Yanmu are."

"It seems like we're having an unforgettable holiday!" Bubba exclaimed with a smile. "I like Yugo. We might bring our circus here."

James knew Bubba was under the effects of the morphine that was given to him, so he couldn't be serious. He got up and patted his exposed muscular shoulder. "We will see about it, partner."

After leaving his friend, he again observed the dire condition of the injured in bed, with the most critical cases receiving care from various nurses and a couple of doctors.

He walked out into the hallway and found Laura, who was leaning against a wall, smoking her usual cigarette.

"Is he alright?" She just asked.

"He's drongo because of the morphine, mate." His reply came with a nod. "He'll have scars on his back to show off at the circus. Otherwise, he'll be okay."

Laura gazed at him with admiration and confidence as she held the cigarette between her fingers. "I was unaware of how much your abilities had improved."

"I'm indebted to Bubba for his help, especially after I left Hong Kong." A shy tone colored his reply. "What happened to the rest of the team? Are they all right?"

"Mei Li appears to have recovered, Juliette is resting from what I can tell, and Cristal and Kendi are apparently getting close while on the radio."

"Ming?"

"He is with Hanzo, watched by General Ilić and Colonel Andreeva, while interrogating Yarakov." A cloud of smoke left her lips with her breath. "Nico is at the airport waiting for Durant."

After a brief scratch of his bald head, James shook his head and folded his arms. "Will we ever be able to stop that bastard?"

"I want to show you something, James." Laura finished her cigarette, crushing it in the standing ashtray. "It's in my chamber."

James entered the chamber, a room primarily used for visiting officers from other bases, and saw that it was small and plain, containing only a bed with a nightstand, an armoire, a desk by the window, and no decorations except another portrait of Tito.

He then heard the door lock, and when he turned around, he saw Laura approaching, taking off her jacket, and throwing her little Beretta onto the bed. "What do you want to show me, mate?"

"Silence!" she shushed. She took off her boots and lowered her pants while unbuttoning her blouse. She tugged on his shirt, drawing his face close to hers, and gave him a deep kiss.

Then, she forced him onto the bed, removed his clothes, and made love to him, longing for something she'd lost, recalling the first time they'd been at that hotel in Hong Kong, and the subsequent many nights at the *Tian Chao*.

He couldn't help but embrace her, and in doing so, he lifted the heavy burden he had while experiencing the relief of being with her again after thirteen years.

They restored the sacrificed love.

Laura lit her cigarette as she relaxed on the bed with James next to her. Lost in thought, she gazed at the plain white ceiling and a modest lamp.

He looked at her. Even after all those years, he realized she was still the same in certain ways. He could still feel the eighteen-year-old girl within the thirty-year-old woman. "What are you thinking, mate?"

"If you'd like to, you could move in with me at the *Palazzo*, and Bubba can come too." She said without looking at him. "You wouldn't stress over money, and your support would be valuable if *Forza Catastrofe* continues."

"Is that what you want? Both of us together again?" James asked with certain hesitation. "And what about all the casinos and the patrons you have to look after?"

"In a couple of years, Francesco will be old enough to handle everything," she responded, nodding.

"Is Francesco the orphan boy from the fire?"

"Correct," she replied, still looking up at the ceiling. "I brought him to the *Tian Chao*, and when he arrived in Italy, I legally recognized him as my own, and he took my last name."

Contemplative, James gazed at the ceiling too as they shared the pillow. "I don't think we could leave the circus. We're too attached to it, especially Bubba."

"I could even fund your circus and persuade influential people to get your shows in Monte Carlo." She suggested with a quick glance. "Everyone there knows me, after all."

"Could be. But I doubt Bubba would agree, as he prefers to bring his shows to modest towns," James stated with a sigh. "The common folk of the UK and France, especially children, are his weakness, mate. They are all his toxins."

"Shit!" Laura's eyes grew wide as she put down her cigarette, realizing something. "Weaknesses and toxins!" She quickly stood and put her clothes on. "Hurry James! Get dressed!"

Laura and James stepped into the dark room, where the only source of light was a hanging lamp illuminating naked Yarakov tied to a wooden chair with his feet inside a metal basin filled with water.

Yarakov appeared exhausted and frail, nearing collapse, as Ming, Hanzo, and General Ilić stood around him, while Colonel Andreeva, with his shirt sleeves rolled up, was placing aside the clamps attached to an altered outlet.

Laura saw blood coming from his mouth. She knew Ming had caused it from his slaps. She could agree with it, but she couldn't accept the Soviet practice of electric torture. "We might not like the bastard, but I don't think he needs this fucking torture!"

"He deserves torture and death!" the colonel replied with harsh words. "He has committed treason against his homeland!"

"He doesn't cooperate, Miss Laura," Ming clarified. "He's been that way the whole time."

Laura approached Ming and whispered in his ear after nodding. "*Toksinleri hatırladın mı? Bunları o Beretta için yapabilir misin?*" She spoke in Turkish, a language they were both acquainted with. "*Bana Isaak'ın mektuplarını da getir.*"

"*Evet.*" He nodded and quickly left the room.

She turned her eyes towards Hanzo. "Get the towel and wrap it around him. I don't want Mei Li to see him fucking naked."

"What are you doing?!" Colonel Andreeva asked, displeased, as he watched the Japanese cover Yarakov's body.

Laura, in a harsh tone, addressed the Soviet officer directly. "Shut the fuck up!"

"Stop pestering and let them do their work, or I'll get you kicked out of my country!" General Ilić approached, imposing. "My soldiers perished because of your damn secret experiments and projects!"

With a nod of thanks to the Yugoslavian officer, Laura opened the door, and a hesitant Mei Li stepped inside, now face-to-face with the man.

In contrast with her feminine and vibrant dresses, she donned Yugoslavian military garb, which was provided to her so she could dress appropriately for her tasks. She saw the nearly naked man wrapped in a towel and observed his semiconscious state. "Is he the one?"

"That's correct, Mei Li." In silence, everyone watched the small woman as Laura answered.

"I feel his pain, anguish, suffering, and a strong desire for revenge." With a trembling voice and tear-filled eyes, Mei Li spoke. "Held captive in the gulag, he endured failed experiments arranged by Boss Yang under Stalin's orders. Yanmu, while promising freedom, manipulated him."

"So it was all on that bitch, then," James stated.

Laura hushed him so she could continue working. "Can you tell me the location of Yanmu and the *Merzost*?"

Mei Li, though still unsure of what she could see, afraid of more harrowing things, nodded and looked at him. Her eyes went vacant in a trance, which triggered the room's only light to blink, frightening General Ilić, who did not react, and she then spoke a series of Russian phrases originating from Yarakov. James quickly caught her in his arms after she almost passed out.

Laura knelt down and gently touched her face with empathy. "Did you get something?" She whispered.

"*Zorka Chimico* in Dobanovci, northwest of Belgrade," Mei Li replied faintly.

"He's gone," Hanzo stated, touching Yarakov's neck with his fingers. "His heart stopped."

"I am arresting you in the name of the Socialist Federal Republic of Yugoslavia for murdering a man within our borders!" General Ilić immediately apprehended Colonel Andreeva despite his protests.

39
BELGRADE

Mei Li pointed to the abandoned location that the deceased Yarakov had revealed through her mind, and it was a vast building from World War II. The Americans and the British, along with other targets, bombed it.

Even though it was remote, in the countryside, it was part of Dobanovci, a suburb of Belgrade. The morning was humid and fresh, even though it was summer.

"The damn Nazis constructed that factory for the production of nerve agent chemicals," General Ilić spoke with a resentful tone. "While I was with the Partisans, we battled the enemy and sent radio signals to the Allies to have them bomb the location."

As Laura and Ming listened, James observed it with his hands resting on his waist.

Alone and distant from others, Juliette took off the hefty metal gloves, and she felt a sense of ease as her hands, now exposed, made fists.

Cristal and Kendi were holding hands, revealing their new relationship, which they had started recently after knowing each other for a short time, though they tried to keep it concealed. Both looked at the factory as if they were on a trip.

"It explains everything," Laura stated with a nod while looking at the bombed factory. "Yanmu always searches for abandoned places, especially the ones with chemical labs."

Henri lit a cigarette and, with his briefcase tucked under his arm, nodded. It had dossiers he had taken from the computer room at the *Palazzo. A*nd accompanied Ming on his return from Italy a couple of days ago.

"So, is the same plan, mate?" James wondered, eyeing the place.

"Like we planned back in Novi Sad, we shall be precise, and not repeat our damn mistakes like we did in Sarajevo." As Laura turned, she saw that hundreds of soldiers were waiting at a long distance from the factory, as she had told them to. She could see a luxury car, inside of which the same Marshal Tito was present, along with Durant from Interpol, observing the moment. The vehicle was under protection of special forces.

"Is everyone going inside?" Mei Li asked hesitantly, as her Yugoslavian military uniform's sleeves extended past her hands.

"Hanzo has already entered and is using walkie-talkies to update Ming and General Ilić," Laura replied. "The army will wait for my signal, as *Forza Catastrofe* begins the operation. So yes, all of us, and let's finish the fucking *Merzost* for once!"

"What are we waiting for?" Kendi readied his M14 rifle he had with him.

"Let's get that bitch and the bastard!" Laura said.

Forza Catastrofe went into the factory through its open gates, and the interior became shadowy as dust and dumped components took on an eerie appearance. A profound and palpable cold permeated the building's interior.

The loud ringings in Laura's mind hinting at an imminent danger emerged, confirmed by Mei Li's sensing of the presence of the objectives inside. Ming and Kendi backed both women and Cristal, with their weapons prepared, and James had his hands ready with the energy emanating.

Juliette followed them in, being the last to enter, with her hands uncovered.

Laura, like the others, walked with caution, clutching her Beretta, which was not the smaller model but the one Interpol had given her as a present. As they proceeded, they discovered another open gate.

The scratched banners decorated with Nazi symbols remained on the walls after the war. The abandoned factory had a terrible reputation, and the local children wouldn't go in, or even nearby, to play.

The next room was even darker, but holes in the decaying roof let in morning light, allowing them to see despite the darkness. They then found an intricate network of decaying machinery and pipes, with clear bomb damage on some segments.

The sight of a shadowy figure on the machinery startled someone, though Laura soothed their fears by explaining it was Hanzo, who was hiding in the dark.

While walking through the eerie, dusty complex of machinery created by the Nazis, a few of them were afraid.

Mei Li could see the Nazis constraining the workers to manufacture chemical weapons, and it caused her pain as her eyes examined the city of pipes.

To feel safe, Cristal trailed behind Kendi, tugging at his shirt.

"This looks so haunted, mate!" James whispered while trailing Laura, as he took in the eerie scene around them.

"Many suffered here, James," with her weapon held high, she said, advancing forward and verifying all in the group.

"Bubba will be upset that he's not here."

"I believe is the best for him . . ."

"Halt!" Mei Li demanded, and everyone listened to her. "She's there."

"Who is she?" Kendi asked as he gripped his weapon.

"Yanmu, for sure," Laura clarified.

"She is in the next room, waiting." Mei Li announced.

"Give that bitch to me!" Juliette exclaimed with resentment.

It was then that Mei Li could peer into the French woman's mind, which exposed a solid link to Yanmu.

As the loud ringing echoed once more within Laura's head, she realized that a perilous situation was imminent. She felt obliged to inform her team about it.

Yanmu was waiting with a Soviet RPK automatic weapon, which surprised *Forza Catastrofe* when they entered the next chamber. A smile was on her face, yet she wore a Soviet military uniform rather than her usual cheongsam.

Laura promptly nodded, noticing her outfit. "For thirteen years I've been wrong. You were a Soviet agent, acting on Stalin's orders." She shook her head. "Boss Yang wasn't your superior, but you had custody of him for decades."

"And I recognized you, bitch!" Juliette came to the front, involving herself in the talk. "You, along with that man with you, injected me, saying it was a vaccine! But you gave me these fucking hands that ruined my life!"

"You and Boss Yang traveled the world searching for the altered. That's how you found me." As Laura spoke, she was still clutching her new Beretta. "However, the war forced you to pause. And you had to move with Boss Yang to Hong Kong."

"How do you know about me? You've got no evidence!" Yanmu continued to grin.

"You're not Yanmu, bitch!" Juliette spoke with anger and resentment.

"That's right," Laura pulled a small stack of papers from her jacket. "When James mentioned toxins, Isaak Kovalev's letters came to mind. Do you remember him, Yanmu? Or shall I call you *Anna Beldlev* from *Khabarovsk*?"

Yanmu's smile faded, and her eyes opened wider.

"The *Merzost* was once human, but your fucking experiments and Boss Yang's changed him into a beast." Laura shook her head. "Vasily was just a baby, and you tortured him!"

Yanmu said with pride, "He was Stalin's greatest achievement ever!"

"Stalin was a monster, just like you or Boss Yang." Laura nodded. "He responds to your whistle much like a dog. You always went with him, and you instructed him to violate my friend Ayla, aware that she would take her own life, as well as execute Issak, because they possessed sensitive information regarding you and your activities."

"On that night in the *Tian Chao*, you told him to sever your arm, knowing it would grow back." Ming added, staring with an intense gaze.

"Since the *Merzost* is like an animal, it couldn't have possibly drawn that Soviet emblem on the wall, not even once," Laura stated. "It was you, Yanmu. You did everything. Why?"

"*Forza Catastrofe* belongs to me, Mui Mui," she grinned once more. "Come with me, and together we can govern the world's biggest nation. We should unite and strip the communists of their power to claim the Soviet Union for ourselves!"

Laura shook her head. "You are fucking crazy!"

Yanmu lowered her weapon, chuckling while looking down. "Right behind me there's a large pit where the Nazis discarded their failed nerve agent tests and those who stood against them." She glanced up to see the *Forza Catastrofe*. "If you don't join me, this hell is where you'll go."

"No, that is where you'll go," Laura fired her new Beretta without a second thought.

Yanmu winced in pain as she realized the bullet had pierced her stomach. She dropped her weapon, reaching for the wound to staunch the flow of blood. A look of fear washed over her as she stared at Laura, and a sudden realization dawned. "How?"

"This was no ordinary bullet," Laura said. "Boss Yang's notes included a chemical formula for creating toxins, intended to weaken the altered and render them defenseless. He developed it as a precaution. I had Ming duplicate the toxin and load it into bullets. Upon entering your system, it would spread, causing you to weaken."

Yanmu's bloody hand moved fast to retrieve her whistle and play it.

"Don't you dare, bitch!"

Juliette, disregarding attempts to stop her, sprinted forward and seized Yanmu by the neck, using a searing touch that caused a pained scream. They struggled momentarily before both plunged into the pit. Their echoing shrieks ceased abruptly as their bodies struck the bottom, resulting in instant death.

"I . . . can't sense them anymore!" a shaken Mei Li confirmed their demise.

Laura turned around, finding most of the team impressed, and spoke to them. "There will be time to mourn Juliette. For now, we must be prepared to confront the *Merzost*!"

Entering the last chamber, they found an extensive area with giant containers. The chemical had spilled and dried on the floor. The 1944 Anglo-American bombing of Belgrade had a devastating effect on the place.

Yet, some tanks remained unopened and contained Sarin, a highly unstable and poisonous chemical.

Laura's eyes followed Hanzo, a shadowy figure, moving among the tanks, as she gripped her Beretta. She listed the group members who were present, noting that only Cristal, James, and Mei Li possessed their abilities, while Ming and Kendi relied solely on their weapons, just like her.

Laura nearly got a headache from the internal ringing, which returned with increased intensity. She realized the *Merzost* was much closer than thought and warned her team, urging extreme caution. Next, she made a sign with her hand so Hanzo, from his hiding spot, could see it.

"Come on, bastard!" James yelled, as his hands crackled with bright energy.

As *Forza Catastrofe* came to a halt, their eyes scanned the darkness, with the only light filtering in from the bomb-damaged roof.

A sudden metallic clang startled them, prompting them to become warier.

Faint light and darkness created nearly invisible streaks of leaps, prompting Kendi to fire his gun repeatedly upwards until Ming signaled him to stop with a headshake. "There is no point in shooting without aiming."

With the internal ringing growing so loud that Laura struggled to focus while directing her Beretta, a wave of fear spread through the group, and Mei Li sensed the *Merzost* was close. Too close. "He's here."

They looked up and saw the dark creature leap down, ready to strike.

Hanzo's rapid defense thwarted the attack as he expelled the *Merzost*, stepping out of the dark, and, similar to the incident in Sarajevo, the ninja-samurai pierced his Katana sword through the creature. However, the struggle continued as Hanzo plunged his Wakizashi knife into the neck.

The *Merzost* battled fiercely with his exceptional strength, and after the fight, Hanzo lay on the floor, heavily injured.

The creature eyed the *Forza Catastrofe*, consumed by a craving for bloodshed and destruction. The blades lodged in his body as he stood there.

Laura rapidly emptied her Beretta, shooting multiple times with toxin-filled bullets to weaken him. Kendi fired his weapon after her, and Ming also shot using his small gun.

Yet, even after enduring all the shots, the *Merzost* appeared to be uninjured.

"Stop, everyone!" Mei Li screamed. "He is in a lot of pain!"

"How?" Laura responded. "He still looks fucking damn invincible!"

After the constant shots ceased, the creature examined himself, then glanced at them, and approached them.

Even though Laura attempted to stop her, Mei Li raced forward and, neglecting the potential threat to herself, froze the *Merzost* by touching his head with both hands. She glanced into his disturbing eyes and nodded. "I feel your suffering, Vasily."

"Can you see him?"

"I do, and Boss Yang and Yanmu were truly disgusting to him."

This is what Mei Li saw.

Vasily appeared to be a normal baby at birth. However, Boss Yang learned of him after reviewing a health examination revealing strange levels, as reported by a medic from a remote Siberian town.

Once Stalin gave his consent, they took the infant away. His parents were sent and executed in a gulag. Boss Yang and Yanmu promptly took the child to a Leningrad lab, where they began their experiments and alterations. Throughout his life, he would only know suffering.

A sequence of shots, injections, and medications caused the baby a lot of pain to trigger his inner ability, but Boss Yang later found out the catalyst was plutonium. And from that time forward, they could do anything they wanted to him.

They deprived him of his right to think. Instead, they instilled in him a killer instinct.

They removed his free will. Total and blind obedience was a must.

They corrupted his body. They injected Vasily countless times, gave him various drugs, including heroin, and frequently mutilated his limbs to test his regenerative abilities since he was only ten.

By the time he reached adulthood, his physique had already changed. His complexion darkened because of the many drugs he'd taken.

He could only obey at the sound of a whistle.

His prizes were more people to kill, and the freedom to eat and have sex with whomever he chose.

Blood was his precious drink.

He had become in the *Merzost*.

An abomination, feared and hated by many.

"He wants his life to end!" Tears streamed down Mei Li's cheeks as she screamed, gripping the still-paralyzed creature's head. "He kills because he wants relief!"

Laura and her team understood that Mei Li couldn't stop touching the *Merzost*, or else his rampage would continue. Even the bullets with toxin couldn't hurt him.

"There should be a fucking way to kill him!" Laura said in despair.

"There's a way, mate," James said, nodding and gazing into her. "*The Sting*."

She saw his sorrow and resignation, and her eyes grew wider. "No!"

He came closer and cradled her shoulders before kissing her. "I've always loved you." Then, he turned his head and saw Mei Li holding the *Merzost's* head. "You know what's gonna happen?"

"I do," Mei Li replied with understanding and acceptance. "But hurry, before it's too late, or I won't be able to hold him anymore!"

Laura held James' arms and, with wet eyes, shook her head while he silently mouthed, "I am sorry."

Ming, realizing the gravity of the circumstances, struggled to carry the injured, unconscious Hanzo away. "We must go, Miss Laura!"

She refused to go, but Kendi and Cristal persuaded her to leave quickly. Laura's last sight was of her friend and confidant, still holding the *Merzost's* head during a tense moment, as James gave a quick, encouraging smile while rubbing his hands together to create more energy.

The remaining members of the *Forza Catastrofe*, with Ming bringing the badly hurt Hanzo, Cristal, Kendi, and a heartbroken Laura, raced back through the deserted factory to escape.

Laura grabbed the walkie-talkie from Ming and urgently instructed General Ilić to evacuate the area immediately. She also cautioned about the existence of the Sarin gas.

Cristal stopped Kendi with a look as they were leaving the factory and spoke. "I have to do something!" Afterward, she hugged him dearly and, ignoring the objections, re-entered the factory to join James and Mei Li with the *Merzost*.

James saw Mei Li's weariness increasing with the danger of leaving *Merzost* loose again.

He created a huge energy sphere by clapping his hands together twice, lifted it above his head while in a trance, and waited for Mei Li to look at him.

She turned to him, with a pale face, accepting her fate.

His energy cast a full light across the chamber, exposing all the machinery and piping of the factory, and invoking an unsettling sense of a grim history.

The *Merzost*, with horrid eyes, glanced at James with an air of anticipation and comfort.

"Ladies and gentlemen!" James, already having created an immense ball of fire, screamed, pretending to be at his circus, with tears. "Here's the *Scorpion Sting*!"

His last memory was of young Laura leaning against the balcony of the Hong Kong hotel in Wanchai.

Once again, he clapped over his head.

A massive explosion devastated the factory and the region surrounding it, generating a mushroom cloud that was both visible and capable of causing a tremor in Belgrade.

40
GRAVESTONE

T he sound of the black cat's meow woke Laura that morning. She wiped her tear-filled eyes to see the familiar scenery outside her room's window, which gave a view of the Ionian Sea. She lay on her disarranged bed.

She stroked her cat before it went away.

With the sound of footsteps growing closer, she swiftly pulled her sleeping robe around herself to wrap her nudity, anticipating Ming's knock and the door's opening. "Durant is down with Henri, Miss Laura."

She exhaled and lit a *Fatima* cigarette as she placed her ashtray on the bed. "What the hell does he want?" She sat and wore her black slippers. "He can have that fucking expensive computer back!"

"He told me he wants to meet you, or so I believe."

She sighed again and nodded. "Please allow me a moment to refresh."

Ming closed the door after nodding.

After she was alone, she couldn't stop the tears from flowing. It has been three months since the explosion at the Nazi factory near Belgrade.

As Laura walked out of the room, wearing only a robe and slippers, she saw that the door to the next room was slightly open. She could look at Kendi sitting on the bed, looking worried.

The room was no longer Hanzo's, but she had to talk to Durant before finding out what troubled him.

Rather than taking her usual route, she opted for the Chinese-themed hall, which had remained unchanged since the *Tian Chao*, because she wanted to check on someone's well-being.

When she walked past the room, Mei Li was sitting on pillows on the floor, with a book nearby, but holding Cristal's hands as they listened to a Beatles song. They appeared to be engaged in a deep discussion, as they had developed a close friendship and trusted each other.

Laura smiled faintly and continued going down the stairs to the inner garden. She moved through it, enjoying the cool morning air and the gentle breeze from the sea, even though the walls enclosed the garden. She proceeded to the other end and eventually arrived at the computer room, which had once been her office.

Henri was leaning on his desk, smoking a *Gauloises*, and chatting with Durant, who was sitting and holding his briefcase. Nico was checking out the gardens from the window.

Laura walked in, grabbed a cigarette from Henri, lit it, crossed her arms, and glared at the three Interpol men, not caring about being seen in her robe. "I thought we were done with it!"

"We are done, Miss Doncelli," Durant replied with a smile. "However, your excellent work impressed our members, and they asked me to keep you in the organization."

Henri and Nico exchanged worried glances, anticipating a refusal.

She fell silent, gazed at them, and after two puffs of smoke, she answered. "Will you try to blackmail me again?"

Durant took his cigar from his suit, lit it, and after a long puff that filled the room, he spoke. "We worked with MI6 to make your records disappear. Now, it's your choice. You are free."

"*Certo, perché no?*" she studied Durant, suspecting something. "You have a case for us. Am I right?"

He chuckled, then smoked his cigar before answering through the smoke. "Miss Doncelli, the Shah of Iran has asked for our cooperation, and he requires you. Something is happening in Tehran."

"Durant, please have Henri give me all the details," she requested, grinding her cigarette out in the ashtray. "If you'll excuse me, I wish to return to my room and spend the day there."

"Before you leave, Miss Doncelli," Durant opened the briefcase and took out some items. He handed her a newspaper, folded. "Considering it was published in Paris, I think you can grasp the importance of the *Forza Catastrofe*."

Though tears welled up, she suppressed her emotions and spoke with a voice that trembled. "Following the explosion at the factory, which released Sarin gas and forced our evacuation for several days, I believed there were no survivors. However, a miracle occurred as Cristal used her invisible shield to protect both Mei Li and herself. So yes, my children, my *catastrophe's children*, have a reason to be alive, and I will make sure of it."

Noticing her emotional state, no one dared to reply to her declaration.

She then received two small black cases from Durant. Inside the initial box, Laura found a *Hero of the Soviet Union* award—a gold star attached to a red ribbon. "After all the fucking harm they've caused over the years, I want nothing to do with this shit!" She tossed it into the trash can, clearly disgusted. She then opened the second case.

"Marshal Tito asked me personally to give it to you, Miss Doncelli." Durant said, pointing to it while keeping his cigar in the other hand.

She discovered inside a medal of the *Order of the Yugoslav Great Star*. "I'm giving it to him directly. He deserves it."

The three men watched as she exited the room.

Laura left the Palazzo, went through the garden, followed a path, and then stepped onto the grass to reach a spot with a gravestone among bushes and cypresses. It had two engraved names—*James Trask*.

Her face remained emotionless until she faced the gravestone. Then tears flowed as she knelt. Since James's body completely disappeared during the *Sting*, she erected a memorial instead of burying any nonexistent remains of him.

Laura tossed the newspaper, with its cover exposed, onto the stone. A photograph of the Belgrade funerals, where the coffins had the flags of Australia, France, and Japan draped on them, was on the Parisian newspaper.

Officials and Interpol mourned James, Juliette, and Hanzo, who succumbed to severe injuries from the struggle against the *Merzost*.

She placed the Yugoslavian medal on the ground close to the gravestone. "You've earned this," as she wiped away her tears, she whispered. "I might have been with different men, but our fucking love was special, and we sacrificed it. Twice."

The wind then tousled her hair, perhaps as a calm sign from him.

A shadow crept up on Laura, startling her, but it was just Mei Li, who looked very serious, causing her to look up and shade her eyes. "What's wrong?"

"Did you not mention that we, the altered, can't have children?"

Laura moved her gaze while thinking, then gave a nod. "Yes, why?"

"Cristal just found out she's pregnant."

THE END

Laura Doncelli and *Forza Catastrofe* return for a New York case in *THE CITY OF OZ*.

This book is especially significant, as it was written during
a time of loss.
A loss for all of us.
Dave.
Our own catastrophe.
You have departed, yet you remain in our memories.
We are thankful for your presence in this world.

I am very grateful for the patience and support provided
during the writing of this book.
And I appreciate all my readers' encouragement to continue writing.

A versatile author, **Joseph Kopel** has explored diverse genres, currently focusing on fantasy. Yet, he is a multifaceted author.

Raised in Mexico City by a US Marine and an English teacher, he gained bilingual fluency. His education comprised a focus on Hispanic literature, where he gained familiarity with Magic Realism, which was broadened by further study in English literature at the American Institute as an addition.

From a young age, he's written across many genres for over 35 years, hoarding unpublished drafts in the closet.

He started with Sci-Fi inspired by Ray Bradbury.

After publishing two fantasy novels, "*The Empress' Journey*" and its sequel "*The Empress' Palace,*" as well as "*Catastrophe's Children*", he is working on the third installment of *The Nehel Series* and preparing the second standalone book of the *Forza Catastrofe*.

He enjoys time with his wife, three children, and pets in his small town in Northwest Missouri.

B ooks from *Joseph Kopel*.

The Nehel Series
The Empress' Journey (2023)
The Empress' Palace (2024)
The Empress' Reclamation (2026)

The Forza Catastrofe Series (Standalone)
Catastrophe's Children (2025)
The City of Oz (2027).

Please provide honest reviews on various platforms, regardless of your opinion of my books. I would appreciate that.